P9-DWF-661

"Let Cates cast her spell over you with this charming debut series entry that brings in the paranormal but never forgets the warmth that cozy readers often request." —*Library Journal*

"Ms. Cates has most assuredly found the right ingredients . . . a series that is a finely sifted blend of drama, suspense, romance, and otherworldly elements." —Once Upon a Romance

"A very comfortable world with interesting characters and a well-paced plot that will leave readers anxious to return to Savannah and the Honeybee Bakery." —The Mystery Reader

"Filled with red herrings and a delightful tour of the Downtown District, fans will enjoy this whodunit, which is a very special reading experience." —Genre Go Round Reviews

ALSO AVAILABLE BY BAILEY CATES

THE MAGICAL BAKERY MYSTERIES

Brownies and Broomsticks
Bewitched, Bothered, and Biscotti
Charms and Chocolate Chips

PRAISE FOR THE
MAGICAL BAKERY MYSTE

Bewitched, Bothered, and Biscotti

"Cates is a smooth, accomplished writer who combines a compelling plot with a cast of interesting characters that are diverse and engaging without falling into simplistic stereotypes . . . a charming addition to the food-based cozy mystery repertoire, while the story's magical elements bring a fun, intriguing dimension to the genre."

—*Kirkus Reviews*

"[A] promising series."   —*Library Journal*

"Cates delivers a tale of magic and mayhem. . . . The mystery plot will have readers guessing 'whodunit' all the way to the very end . . . a great read."   —*RT Book Reviews*

"With a top-notch whodunit, a dark magic investigator working undercover, and a simmering romance in the early stages, fans will relish this tale."   —*Gumshoe*

"Brimming with positive magic, delicious characters, and a tasty batch of clues, this book should satisfy the appetite of the most voracious mystery reader. If you enjoy books like Ellery Adams's Charmed Pie Shoppe Mystery series and Heather Blake's Wishcraft Mystery series, you are destined to enjoy the Magical Bakery Mystery series."

—*Myshelf.com*

continued . . .

"Complex and intriguing. If you like a little magic, you will want to read this series." —Fresh Fiction

"I see so much more coming from Bailey Cates. She pens a bit of magic for the reader."

—Once Upon a Romance

"*Bewitched, Bothered, and Biscotti* continues to showcase the charming characters, humor, and fun . . . displayed in the promising debut of this series . . . engaging, compelling, and quite tasty."
—Kings River Life Magazine

Brownies and Broomsticks

"Katie is a charming amateur sleuth, baking her way through murder and magic set against the enchanting backdrop of Savannah, Georgia. With an intriguing plot and an amusing cast of characters, *Brownies and Broomsticks* is an attention-grabbing read that I couldn't put down."
—*New York Times* bestselling author Jenn McKinlay

Some Enchanted Éclair

A Magical Bakery Mystery

Bailey Cates

AN OBSIDIAN MYSTERY

OBSIDIAN
Published by the Penguin Group
Penguin Group (USA) LLC, 375 Hudson Street,
New York, New York 10014

USA | Canada | UK | Ireland | Australia | New Zealand | India | South Africa | China
penguin.com
A Penguin Random House Company

First published by Obsidian, an imprint of New American Library,
a division of Penguin Group (USA) LLC

First Printing, July 2014

Copyright © Penguin Group (USA), LLC, 2014
Penguin supports copyright. Copyright fuels creativity, encourages diverse
voices, promotes free speech, and creates a vibrant culture. Thank you for buy-
ing an authorized edition of this book and for complying with copyright laws
by not reproducing, scanning, or distributing any part of it in any form without
permission. You are supporting writers and allowing Penguin to continue to
publish books for every reader.

OBSIDIAN and logo are trademarks of Penguin Group (USA) LLC.

ISBN 978-0-451-46741-6

Printed in the United States of America
10 9 8 7 6 5 4 3 2 1

PUBLISHER'S NOTE
This is a work of fiction. Names, characters, places, and incidents either are the
product of the author's imagination or are used fictitiously, and any resem-
blance to actual persons, living or dead, business establishments, events, or
locales is entirely coincidental.
    The recipes contained in this book are to be followed exactly as written. The
publisher is not responsible for your specific health or allergy needs that may
require medical supervision. The publisher is not responsible for any adverse
reactions to the recipes contained in this book.

If you purchased this book without a cover you should be aware that this book
is stolen property. It was reported as "unsold and destroyed" to the publisher
and neither the author nor the publisher has received any payment for this
"stripped book."

Acknowledgments

I shudder to think what my stories would be like without the people who skillfully make them into books. The amazing team at Penguin/New American Library includes Jessica Wade, Isabel Farhi, Jesse Feldman, Gleni Bartels, and Danielle Dill. I am forever grateful for their help and hard work on this project. Many thanks go to my agent, Kimberly Lionetti, for her advice and expertise. I am blessed to have amazing writers in my life who critique me, inspire me, and light fires under me, not to mention the wine, food, and laughter: Mark Figlozzi, Janet Freeman, Dana Masden, Laura Pritchett, Laura Resau, Bob Trott, and Carrie Visintainer. I also appreciate all the taste testers, the garden gurus, and the cooks and bakers who inspire the culinary selections in the Honeybee Bakery. And then there's Kevin, who is always on my side, including the occasional push toward the keyboard. Thanks for that, too.

Chapter 1

The friendly chime of the bell over the entrance to the Honeybee Bakery sent a shot of adrenaline through my veins. I looked up from where I was quickly counting out change for a customer and saw two giggling teenaged girls enter. Their similar features suggested they were sisters, and behind them followed a tired-looking couple I pegged as their parents. The family paused to take in the high ceilings, warm amber walls, and fully occupied blue and chrome bistro sets before shuffling to the back of the line, which was already five deep at the register.

Uncle Ben, Aunt Lucy, and I had started the bakery more than a year ago, and we'd worked hard to develop regular clientele as well as to attract Savannah's tourist trade. The sound of that bell meant customers, and customers meant business, and business was a good thing almost without exception.

Never mind that Lucy and I were on our own

these days, juggling the busy morning rush without Ben's help. Usually he ran the register, chatting with people as if they were his best friends as he took orders and rang up purchases. His natural style combined with genuine interest to make each person feel special. I tried to emulate him, but my mind kept darting back to the kitchen.

Aunt Lucy cast a harried glance my way before quieting her features and returning her attention to the espresso machine. Two patrons who had already ordered stood near the counter, patiently waiting for their coffee drinks. They nibbled on confections purchased from the brightly lit glass case that was usually packed with all manner of Honeybee pastries, cookies, scones, muffins, and the like. With dismay, I realized the shelves were half-empty.

Pasting a cheerful smile on my face, I asked the gentleman who was now at the front of the line, "And what can we get for you today, sir?"

The man's gaze remained trained on the chalkboard menu on the wall above and behind where I stood. His thinning hair wisped above light eyes in a pale face. He shuffled his feet and jammed his hands deep into the pockets of his Dockers.

"What do you have that's gluten-free?" His voice was so soft I could hardly hear him.

"How does a peanut butter cookie sound? Or an apricot-almond tart?" I pointed to the clearly listed gluten-free options we'd recently added to the menu. "They're sweetened with clover honey. Or how about a chunk of peanut butter fudge?" I suggested the daily special as an alternative to the items listed behind me.

He glanced at me with wide eyes before his gaze fell to the floor, and he sighed heavily. "Fudge is candy. I don't want candy. What about a corn bread biscuit?"

My cheeks were beginning to hurt from the effort it took to keep smiling. One of the young girls rolled her eyes and said to the other one in a loud voice, "This is going to take *forever*."

"Kelsey," her mother said without much feeling.

"Well, it *is*." The girl spun around and opened the door. She stuck her head out and looked down the street. Sticky May heat rolled into the air-conditioned seating area, and I bit my tongue as I thought of the electric meter working overtime.

"I'm afraid only those baked items listed under the heading 'gluten-free' are, you know, free of gluten," I said to my customer.

The tall woman behind him snorted. It was Mrs. Standish, one of our regulars. Today she wore a crimson turban and a swirling white caftan covered with giant Oriental poppies the same color as the headdress. I was perpetually amazed at the bold fashion statements she managed to pull off.

Lucy moved to my side, the seafoam green of her batik skirt swirling around her slim hips. She'd tamed her long gray-blond mop into a thick braid that fell down her back and wore a simple blue chef's apron from my considerable collection.

"I bet you'd like the apple-fennel muffins," Lucy said to the wispy man standing in front of the register, and then to Mrs. Standish, "Your usual drink, dear?"

"Please, Mrs. Eagel," she said.

The other people waiting in line appeared relieved at Lucy's efficiency. As my aunt turned, she caught my eye and gave the slightest of winks. *Darn it*—I'd been so busy trying to catch up that I'd missed the clues from our gluten-intolerant customer. His lack of eye contact, the weighty sigh, all that looking down at the floor, the pained shyness.

This guy was lonely. Extremely so.

Lucy had suggested the muffin to him because she knew it contained more than savory-sweet goodness. She was still teaching me about the Craft of hedgewitchery, but by now we regularly worked together to add a bit of green magic to our baked goods—a bit of herb there, a sprinkle of spice here, a murmured incantation. Everything that came out of our ovens had a special ingredient no other bakery in town could copy: spells intended to be helpful whenever and wherever they might be needed. My aunt was quite talented at steering people toward exactly the right treat for them on any given day. Our customers might not know why they loved the Honeybee as much as they did, but my pastry school training and our family practice of herbal witchery were a happy combination.

As we'd tinkered with the gluten-free muffin

recipe a few weeks before, Lucy had commented, "We need apples in this one. After all, who couldn't use more love, peace, and happiness?"

"Mmm," I'd said. "Nice tart Granny Smiths. And how about fennel, too? The flavors enhance each other, and it will add a boost of courage."

But now my customer frowned. "That muffin sounds good, but you seem to be out of them."

"Oh!" I held up my finger. "We haven't had a chance to restock the case. Give me a sec, and I'll grab some more."

The teenager's sigh must have been audible clear over on Tybee Island.

I hurried into the open kitchen at the rear of the bakery. Rounding the big stainless-steel refrigerator, I saw little Mungo peeking around the half-open door of the office. Concern shone from his cocoa brown eyes.

"Sorry, buddy." I waved the Cairn terrier back toward the club chair where he lazed most days at the Honeybee. "I know you'd help if you could, but you know the rule—no dogs in the kitchen."

He panted and grinned up at me.

"Or in the reading area, either. At least not while it's still so busy."

My familiar huffed his disgruntlement and backed into the other room. I shut the door, piled a plate high with muffins, and quickstepped to the register.

Mollified, the man paid and left. Mrs. Standish stepped up next. "Today I'll take two of those scrumptious red velvet whoopie pies, Katie my

dear. Red velvet cake was my dear Harry's favorite." Suddenly, she sighed, and I saw another kind
of loneliness in her eyes, the kind that comes from
the lingering loss of a loved one. Her husband had
died a bit over two years before, but she rarely
referred to him. "While you're at it, throw in some
of those pistachio cream éclairs. Is that toffee on
top?" Her deep voice rose and fell over the sylla-
bles as only a native Savannahian's could.

Lucy handed her a tall steaming drink with a
smile and turned to the next customer in line to
get a jump on his order.

"It is indeed." I grabbed a paper bag and slid
open the back of the case.

"How is it you two are working alone today?"
Mrs. Standish asked as I selected one of the ruby-
toned whoopie pies filled with homemade coconut marshmallow cream. "Where on earth is your
uncle?"

"He and Declan are working security on the
movie set over by Reynolds Square." I shook open
the bag with the Honeybee logo printed on the
side. It was a depiction of Lucy's familiar, an elegant orange tabby cat named, you guessed it,
Honeybee.

When A. Dendum Productions had come to Savannah, Georgia, to film a romantic comedy set
during the Revolutionary War, the chief of police
had recommended Uncle Ben to head the small security detail intended to keep fans and paparazzi at
bay. Ever the loving wife, Lucy had assured Ben
that she and I could handle the bakery on our own

for a couple of weeks. Since Ben was Savannah's recently retired fire chief, he was immediately hired. His security crew consisted of off-duty firefighters whom he'd worked with over the years, including his protégé—and my boyfriend—Declan McCarthy.

I filled the bag with the requested pastries and handed it to Mrs. Standish. She moved to the side so I could ring up the next order.

"What about your usual helpers?" Mrs. Standish was referring to the members of the spellbook club who stepped in to assist in the bakery when needed. She knew the six of us were in a book club, but she didn't know we were an informal coven of witches.

"Over at the set," I said. "Except Cookie, who's still in Europe, and Jaida, who I'm pretty sure is in court today." An attorney, Jaida French had a special interest in tarot magic.

Mrs. Standish snorted again. "Bunch of lookyloos. I'd expect more decorum from native Southerners." The teenagers' father glared at her implied insult to tourists, but Mrs. Standish didn't notice. "It's not as if filming in Savannah is anything unusual," she continued. "They've been doing it since 1915, for heaven's sake."

Lucy spoke up from behind the espresso machine. "They're helping out, not standing around gawking. Bianca is even going to be in a couple of scenes." Tall, elegant Bianca Devereaux was a traditionally trained Wiccan and the single mom of seven-year-old Colette.

"Bah." Mrs. Standish waved her mannish hand in the air. "She certainly possesses the beauty and bearing to dominate any movie screen, but those Hollywood types are nothing but trouble. Do you know they've completely closed a section of Abercorn Street?"

I nodded. "I've been using a different route to come to work."

"Julian Street, too," she went on. "There are dirt and straw all over the place, not to mention the disgusting road apples from the horses. My Lord, I'll be happy when they finish up their nonsense and go home, let things settle down to some semblance of normal around here."

But, as usual, her ire didn't last long. Spinning around, she beamed at the family of four who had been not-so-patiently waiting. "Y'all are in for such a treat. Katie here is the best baker in town."

The bell over the door rang again, and my heart sank. Just as we were getting caught up. Then I saw who it was, and relief whooshed through me.

Mrs. Standish exclaimed, "Mimsey Carmichael, as I live and breathe." Winking at me, she said in a loud whisper, "Reinforcements at last." Three long strides later she was at the door, stooping to kiss our friend on the cheek before sailing into the late-spring morning with her whoopie pies.

At seventy-nine, Mimsey was the eldest member of the spellbook club, though she looked more than a decade younger. When Lucy first told me our unofficial leader didn't use magic to maintain her youthful appearance, I didn't know whether to believe her. However, over time I'd come to agree with my aunt's assertion that it was her heartfelt affection for people and a vivid enthusiasm for life that gave Mimsey such vigor. I also admired her continued involvement in the day-to-day business of Vase Value, the flower shop she'd owned for decades. She was a cream puff of a woman, shorter even than Aunt Lucy, though considerably more padded. Her smooth white pageboy sported a bow that mirrored the sherbet orange of her pantsuit, and her blue eyes crinkled at the corners when she saw me.

A man had followed her into the Honeybee, and she reached over to give his arm a quick pat. He directed a distracted smile down at her. Not much taller than my five-nine, he nonetheless towered over Mimsey. His short sandy hair was lightly threaded with gray, though from my vantage point his face appeared unlined.

I hurried to help the family who had finally reached the register. Even the girls seemed happy enough once they had an assortment of cookies in hand and settled at a table by the window.

Mimsey's intelligent gaze raked the room, taking in the situation. "Have a seat, Simon," she cheerfully instructed her companion and bustled into the kitchen. Before I knew it, she was restocking the glass display case with blazing efficiency.

Simon, as she'd called him, slid onto a recently vacated seat near the door. I could sense his skepticism from across the room.

I didn't actually see auras, but after more than

a year of practicing magic, I could sometimes sense the energy around other people as what I could describe only as flavors. It helped to have physical contact, and even then it didn't happen all that often. But once in a while I could tell if a person was inherently sweet or salty or, in some unfortunate cases, bitter. Something about the newcomer, backlit by the window behind him, made me want to know more about him. As soon as I'd counted out change to the last customer in line and found myself with a little space to breathe, I centered myself and threw him a big welcoming smile.

He didn't appear to notice, though. His head was bent over his phone, his thumbs tapping wildly on the screen. When it rang in his hand, he answered as if he'd been expecting a call, gazing out the window at Broughton Street and talking rapidly. A couple at a nearby table shot him irritated looks. Perhaps his intensity felt out of place in their otherwise leisurely morning.

I felt Mimsey behind me and looked around to find her gesturing Lucy over to join us. "That's Simon Knapp," she said sotto voce.

"And who, pray tell, is Simon Knapp?" I matched her secretive tone.

"He's . . . I think his title is production coordinator? He's the one who takes care of the actors—and the director and crew on the movie set."

Simon's ears must have been burning because he stood and strode toward us, slipping his cell phone into the pocket of his tan chinos. His muscular arms were tan against the light blue of his silky T-shirt.

Nice.

Mimsey went on. "If they need a certain prop or one of the actresses insists on having a bouquet of a particular flower delivered to her trailer, Simon is the one who tracks it down." She smiled broadly as he stopped in front of the register. "In fact, that's how we became acquainted. He was looking for passionflowers for Althea Cole, and I just happened to have a fresh shipment at the shop." Mischief twinkled in her eyes.

Gentle amusement flashed across Lucy's face, and I refrained from comment. Mimsey was the best of us at divination, and "just happening" to have a fresh shipment of a relatively unusual flower was likely a result of her skill. Her pink, quartz-crystal shew stone often produced somewhat murky results—except when it came to her attraction to color and flower magic.

Mimsey added, "And Bianca agreed to provide the libations for Ms. Cole's nightly wine and cheese parties from Moon Grapes."

"And thank God she did." Simon's words came out fast and clipped. "Because if Althea's unhappy, *everybody's* unhappy." He held out his hand. "I'm Simon Knapp."

Quickly, I brushed my hands on my yellow polka-dotted apron and shook it. Instantly I felt a *zing!* of spicy energy—sexy and definitely high-voltage. His eyebrow twitched up, though his face remained impassive. Had I reacted somehow?

"Katie Lightfoot," I said, letting go of his grip. "Welcome to the Honeybee Bakery, Mr. Knapp. And to Savannah in general. This is my aunt, Lucy Eagel."

"Call me Simon." No standing on ceremony and all business. His urge to hurry, hurry, hurry rolled off him in waves. He reached across the corner of the coffee counter to grasp my aunt's hand. "And you ladies own this fine establishment, I'm told."

"Along with my husband, Ben, yes," Lucy said.

Simon snapped his fingers. "Ben Eagel. I hired him to head up the security teams on the set."

Lucy looked pleased. "That's right."

Simon leaned forward, first looking deeply into Lucy's eyes and then boring into mine. Flecks of olive green brightened his brown irises. "Well, I need help, desperately need help, and Mimsey here says you are exactly the ones to come to."

Alarm tingled along my neck as I remembered the other times Mimsey had decided I could help someone. "Is . . . is somebody . . . ," I stuttered.

Mimsey put her hand on my arm and spoke quickly. "It's a catering job, Katie."

My knees almost buckled with relief. "Oh!" I laughed. "Oh, that might be doable." Lucy and I exchanged glances. The first—and last—time we'd taken on a catering job, it hadn't ended well. "What kind of event?" I asked Simon. "How many people are we talking about? And when would you need us?"

He grinned widely. "Excellent. Lunch. Twenty to thirty people. Now."

Chapter 2

"Now?" I squeaked. Beside me, Lucy's sudden intake of breath mirrored my surprise.

"Yep," Simon said with what I felt was inappropriate cheerfulness. "The caterer I hired to feed the crew during working hours has shown up late three times now, and frankly, the food was not at all what I'd been led to expect. So I fired him this morning."

"And now everyone will be looking for a nice lunch to get them through the afternoon," Mimsey said.

"Maybe Mr. Knapp should have thought of that before firing his caterer," I muttered.

"Katie," Lucy admonished.

But Simon Knapp laughed. "Believe me, I could simply go to a market and raid the deli. In fact, that was my plan until Mimsey here stepped in and volunteered your services."

"Mimsey!" Lucy and I said at the same time. "We don't serve lunch per se at the Honeybee," I went on. "Only a few breakfast items."

Simon waved at the menu. "Oh, please. Just look at the éclairs. Herbed goat cheese with sun-dried tomatoes? Passion-fruit custard with rasp-berry glaze? That's evidence of serious culinary chops. I bet you two could throw something to-gether for my people in no time."

I distributed a helpless look between Simon and Lucy.

"Please?" Simon smiled at me, and even though I knew perfectly well I was being manipulated, I began to run through possible lunch options for a crowd of thirty. "As they say, money is no object," he said.

That's when I saw Mimsey's happy expression and realized she wasn't doing this for Simon Knapp or the strangers in town filming *Love in Revolution*. She had just drummed up a nice piece of business for the Honeybee.

"Lucy," I said. "We'll raid our stores for the rest of the week, but I think we can come up with some-thing for Simon and his friends that will be far bet-ter than cold cuts and hours-old potato salad."

She nodded slowly. "We have several loaves of freshly baked sourdough. That's a start for some sandwiches. And we can use some of the garden produce you brought this morning, Katie." She referred to the basket of greens and vegetables from my overflowing home garden, all of which I'd harvested that morning for her and Ben.

But I was okay with it if she was. "Sounds good," I said.

She hastened into the kitchen, calling over her shoulder, "Let me see what we have in the fridge."

I looked around the bakery. It was late morning, typically a time when the customers thinned before lunchtime. I'd never been so thankful for a lull in business since the Honeybee opened. "Mimsey, can you handle the register?"

"With great aplomb, sugar."

Half an hour later, Lucy and I had gathered enough food for a small army. We used six of the large sourdough loaves to make thick, pressed, picnic-style sandwiches. Two loaves were made into classic BLTs, one augmented with creamy mashed avocado. We figured on at least a few vegetarians, so we packed two loaves with sprouts, heirloom tomatoes, fragrant basil leaves, shredded red peppers, cucumbers, Greek olives, and a generous crumbling of marinated feta cheese. Another loaf contained smoked salmon and cream cheese with onions, capers, and lemon zest, and the last was a club-style combo of ham, turkey, and slow-roasted tomatoes slathered with herbed mayonnaise and topped with tender butter lettuce.

It did drain our supplies, but a few calls to our local suppliers and a trip to the wholesale market would quickly restock the Honeybee larder.

Lucy had created a superfresh salad from some of items I'd picked from my garden that morning, while I'd tossed a medley of fresh raspberries, strawberries, and blueberries with a sweet balsamic glaze. We gathered it all together and presented lunch à la Honeybee to Simon Knapp.

He'd been talking on his phone a mile a minute the whole time we were working in the kitchen but had also somehow sipped his way through a quadruple latte—as if he needed more caffeine. Still, for all I knew, that was what kept him going at the breakneck pace that appeared to be normal for him. He'd also downed a passion-fruit éclair so fast I wondered if he'd even tasted it.

Eyeing our offerings as we piled them on the table nearby, he ended his call and stood. A slow grin spread over his face as he nodded his approval. "Perfect. And none of the gooey grits or fried stuff that other caterer seemed so fond of. Heart attack waiting to happen."

Also classic Southern fare any caterer in Savannah would have in his or her repertoire, I thought, wondering whether Simon had suggested to his caterer that lighter dishes might be more appropriate for the fancy folk watching their waistlines. He seemed to make lightning-fast decisions. Had he even given the original caterer a chance?

"Do you mind my asking who you hired—and then fired?" I asked as I loaded up a variety of scones, cookies, éclairs, and rhubarb mini-pies for dessert or afternoon snacking. Lucy carried out two gallon jugs of minted sweet tea and set them next to our big drink dispenser.

"Bonner Catering," Simon volunteered easily. "*Not* up to my standards."

I hadn't run across the name before and wondered if it was a new catering company. I hoped the emergency Honeybee luncheon met with general satisfaction since it was evident that getting on Simon's bad side could be bad for business—no matter how much he was about to pay us.

Speaking of which. I told him the total, to which I'd added a significant "rush" fee. Lucy looked at me in surprise, but he handed me a credit card with hardly a glance and began toting the food out to Mimsey's car. She threw an approving smile at me over her shoulder as she opened the door for him.

"Here," I said when he returned for the sweet tea. "Take this and keep it on ice." I handed him a chilled whole watermelon I'd picked up at the market for myself the day before. "It'll be welcome later in the afternoon when it gets hotter."

Simon assured us they had plenty of paper plates, flatware, plastic cups, and the like. Lucy added serving spoons, a pile of napkins, a couple garbage bags, and a knife for the watermelon. "Let us know if you need anything else," she said.

"This is great. I'll have my assistant bring back the drink dispenser and utensils." He hefted the watermelon and gently took a heavy jug of tea away from Mimsey. "My dear, please let me get this."

Apparently, Simon wasn't entirely devoid of manners.

At the door, he paused. "I don't suppose you'd consider serving all our lunches, would you? We'll only be filming in the area for another week."

I looked at my aunt. It would be difficult to add

so much to our workload, but it would also mean a significant chunk of cash.

"We can do it again tomorrow," I said. Lucy's chin dipped in agreement. "But we'll have to talk about doing more than that and get back to you."

"Sounds good," he said. "Stop by the set if you've a mind. I'll make sure you can get in."

I thanked him, and he and Mimsey left to feed the crew.

Books crowded floor-to-ceiling bookshelves at the far end of the bakery we'd designated as an eclectic mini library. Honeybee patrons donated or took reading material at will, so the titles were constantly changing. Each weekend a few members of the spellbook club brought in items they had a feeling someone might want during the coming week. Call it magic or intuition—they were often the same thing, I'd found—but the ladies were usually right.

Standing behind the register, I held the phone to one ear and watched Lucy return a few volumes to the shelf, fluff the cushions on the poufy brocade sofa, and move the jewel-toned chairs back to their original positions beside the low coffee table. I concluded my call with our local pork supplier and hung up. Glancing at the clock, I saw it was a bit after one.

Lucy gave the coffee table a swipe with a damp towel, nodded to a couple of our regulars on her way to the espresso counter, and began wiping that down, too.

"We're set," I said. "At least for the extra delivery of bacon, ham, and sausage."

She nodded, thoughtful. "I guess we should talk about whether we can pull off a week-long catering job without your uncle's help."

"I think we can. We'll have to brainstorm menus, of course, but I ordered extra of everything, just in case."

The bell over the door chimed, and Mimsey entered the bakery for the second time that day.

I came out from behind the counter and gave her a hug. "Thanks for suggesting us to Mr. Knapp."

"You saved the day, darlin'." She grinned. "Between the Honeybee, my flower shop, and Bianca's wineshop, this movie has sure been good for business."

"Except for Bonner Catering," Lucy said. "Are you familiar with them?"

Mimsey waved her hand. "Never heard of them until yesterday, when Simon fired Robin Bonner in front of everybody."

I winced.

"He'd shown up late for the third day in a row. Honey, your food is much better, believe me."

"Do you have time to stick around here for a little while?" I asked.

Mimsey cocked her head at the petite gold watch on her wrist. "I was on my way to the shop to confirm an order of gerbera daisies for a wedding we're doing this weekend, but I could simply call instead. Why?"

"That spread for all those film stars wiped out

our stores, and one of us needs to make a run to restock. It's been busy today, and I don't want to leave Lucy alone to handle all the customers."

"Of course," the older witch said. "I can stay for an hour and a half or so."

Quickly, I untied the strings of my apron. "I'll hurry. Lucy, let's talk later about menus, but in the meantime, what do you think about a kabob lunch for tomorrow? Something along the lines of chicken satay skewers with peanut sauce, shrimp cocktail skewers, rare beef and bleu cheese kabobs marinated in vinaigrette, and then a few others that are more saladlike. I'm imagining Caprese with those little balls of mozzarella—ciliegine, right?—and yellow pear tomatoes and basil from my garden. Another simple option would be three kinds of melon balls, and finally a vinegary potato salad with and without chunks of ham. All would be fine at room temperature. We could even string pieces of firm tofu soaked in chili sauce on skewers."

Lucy clapped her hands. "Lunch on a stick! Easy and fun and delicious. Yes. Perfect. Throw in some salted edamame and we're golden."

Mimsey shook her head. "You know you could make the Honeybee into a full-fledged restaurant, don't you?"

"Nuh-uh, no way. I love baking too much," I said. "This is just exception."

She shrugged. "Suit yourself."

"Man, am I ever tired," I murmured to Mungo later that afternoon. I was in the office after restocking the kitchen and whirling through the prep work for the next day's baking and the additional catering on top of that. "I could really use a run."

"You and Declan are still coming over for supper, aren't you?" Lucy asked from the doorway.

I stifled a yawn. "Yep, that's the plan. He'll come home with Ben after they're done with their shift."

She examined my face. "Do you have your running clothes with you?"

I nodded. "In my car." I'd been taking Mungo for runs at the Savannah Wildlife Refuge or down to Forsythe Park and back after work a few days a week. They weren't long runs—but long enough for a sedentary Cairn terrier to get some exercise and a welcome addition to the longer runs I often enjoyed in the early mornings.

"Well, go ahead, then." She looked at her watch. "We close in twenty minutes, and I can shut everything down by myself. No worries."

I hesitated. Even a short run would energize me for the evening. "Are you sure?"

She waved her hand in the air. "Of course, sweetie. Go."

"Deal." I looked down at Mungo. "Ready?"

He turned around once on his chair, lay down, and squeezed his eyes shut.

"Lazy," I muttered and saw one eye squint open at me as I turned to go out to get my clothes. I retrieved shorts, sports bra, tank, and trail runners from the backseat of my Volkswagen Beetle and

changed in the restroom of the Honeybee. I
rousted Mungo, slipped on his collar and leash,
and was soon stretching in the alley. Five minutes
later, I took off toward Habersham Street at a slow
jog.

Uncle Ben was a bit of a movie buff, which was
part of why he'd been so interested in working on
the set of *Love in Revolution*. He'd told me more
than sixty films had been made in Savannah,
many of them historical but not all. One reason
was the beautiful architecture and the careful
preservation of so many antebellum buildings.
Then there were the downtown squares designed
by Savannah's founder, James Oglethorpe, and
the beauty of the old riverfront with its tabby side-
walks. River Street and the walkways down to it
still boasted the worn cobblestones that had served
as ballast for nineteenth-century European ships
in the market for cotton and rice.

Love in Revolution was also a period piece, but
unlike so many other films of the old South, it re-
volved around the Revolutionary War rather than
the Civil War. Uncle Ben had told me it was the
story of twin brothers who fall in love with twin
sisters and the ensuing hilarity of confused iden-
tities during wartime. A loose takeoff of *The Comedy of Errors* set against the Revolutionary War.
Althea Cole, as well known for her partying as for
her acting ability, would play both of the sisters,
but from what I'd gathered, the actor who was
playing the twin brothers was not nearly as famous. The result would have to be either pure ge-

nius or utter drivel. Time, and the critics, would tell, I supposed.

At Warren Square, we turned right on Congress and immediately had to dodge around a trio of women hogging the sidewalk. By then I'd found my rhythm, far slower than I typically ran in the cool, four a.m. mornings before heading to the Honeybee around five, but fine for my panting canine companion on an afternoon that had climbed to the mideighties. A rain squall had passed through the night before, leaving behind an inevitable mugginess. I reminded myself that now that I lived in the South, I no longer sweated like a pig when I ran—I glowed like a belle. Whatever you called it, I relished the feel of my muscles moving under my skin, propelling me around the corner onto Houston. Running was one of the things that made me feel the most gloriously human.

I paused on the curb, checked traffic, and continued across Bay to Emmet Park. As I worked my way down toward the water, I reflected that one of the other things that made me feel downright grateful to be alive was practicing magic. Was that strange?

Who cared? Not me. I'd take happy any way it wanted to present itself.

I glanced down at Mungo to check on how he was doing in the heat. He grinned up at me, tongue lolling and little legs churning like the dickens, his previous laziness forgotten. I thought of all the times I'd had to chivy myself into exercising only to be really glad I had.

We veered to the middle of River Street. There were no cars to worry about, but plenty of visitors to fair Savannah who sauntered in front of bric-a-brac shops tempting them with T-shirts, coffee cups, crab crackers, and other assorted souvenirs. The old, rounded bricks could turn an ankle in no time, so I slowed to an even easier jog and kept an eye out where I was stepping.

Two older men stood outside Joe's Crab Shack, lifting their go-cups of beer in salutation as we went by. I smiled and waved but didn't pause. The smell of taco filling, jalapeños, and limes made my mouth water as I passed One-Eyed Lizzy's and headed for the section of the street that threaded under the Hyatt Regency Hotel. When we ran beneath the tall concrete building that arched over the street, the temperature dropped five degrees.

Tantalizing, come-on-in-and-have-a-bite aromas or not, Lucy was making her Low Country pulled pork for supper, and I had no intention of spoiling my appetite. She started with a mustard rub on a massive shoulder roast and then cooked it slow and low for ten hours. That morning, before the Honeybee had opened, I'd baked up a small batch of soft sandwich buns. We'd slather them with more spicy mustard and load them up with the succulent pork shreds and some of Mimsey's homemade bread-and-butter pickles.

Yum. We still had a cabbage and some carrots from my garden after making the movie crew's lunch, so I could make up some spicy coleslaw to serve with—or on—the sandwiches once I got to Ben and Lucy's. It would be a simple but scrumptious feast.

At Whittaker Street I made my way back up to Bay from the riverfront. I increased my speed and we soon came to Broughton. Instead of turning toward my waiting car, however, I continued down and turned left onto Congress. A line of hungry tourists stretched out of the doorway of The Lady & Sons restaurant even this early on a Monday evening.

Reynolds Square came into sight, and I saw what Mrs. Standish had meant about the street—and the square itself. Mungo and I slowed to a walk, taking in the barricades and the asphalt road covered with dirt and straw and groomed to look like a lane might in the 1700s. The statue of John Wesley preaching to the masses in the middle of the square was completely covered by a large blue-green tarp.

Fifty feet away, a boom truck loomed behind an abandoned carriage. The sleek horse harnessed to the carriage turned to survey our approach with a steady brown gaze. Another horse stood in a makeshift paddock in one corner of the square. The sun glinted off two Airstream trailers snugged up to the curb on Bryan Street, and a row of RVs lined up behind them. The chug of an electrical generator sounded from that direction. Air-conditioning for the stars? Or power for the numerous cables that snaked along the ground? Probably both. A half dozen white canvas tents and canopies circled together in the middle of the square, and several of Mrs. Standish's "looky-loos" milled beyond the roped-off boundary of the set. As I watched, a trio of men in crimson British uniforms sauntered toward the crowd and began talking with them.

Motion in my peripheral vision drew my attention as Declan McCarthy rounded one of the Airstreams. He wore jeans and a T-shirt emblazoned with A. DENDUM PRODUCTIONS: SECURITY. His sharp, assessing gaze swept over the onlookers then mellowed with affection when he saw me.

Declan McCarthy: native Savannahian of Irish extraction, the broad planes of his face softened by a kind, blue-eyed gaze. A gardening, cooking tough guy with a heart of honey and the brawn of a seasoned firefighter. My handsome man.

Any lingering weariness forgotten, I ducked under the rope and headed toward him. Mungo pulled at his leash, anxious to greet one of his favorite people.

"Hey!" shouted one of the onlookers, a cranky-looking woman with a big camera slung around her neck. "You're supposed to stay out here. Those security guys are real strict."

I waved. "It's okay. I'm the caterer." I stifled a grin and reminded myself not to get cocky.

Reaching the security guy in question, I slid my arm around his waist as he bent for a quick hello kiss. All the tensions of the day evaporated at his touch. We'd gone through a difficult time recently, but our relationship since then felt like it was solidifying into something even better than it had been before.

"Hey, darlin'" he drawled and bent down to scratch behind Mungo's ears. My familiar wagged his tail so hard I thought his back end might leave the ground altogether.

"Hey, yourself," I said in amusement.

Declan stood. "Simon said you might be stopping by. Thanks for the grub, by the way. Good stuff."

We began strolling toward the cluster of tents. "You're only slightly biased," I said.

A high shriek tore the air, winging through the leaves of the live oaks and seeming to snag in the Spanish moss before fading away. My breath caught, and my steps faltered. Behind us the crowd erupted into conversation.

"What was *that*?" gasped the woman who had chastised me for crossing into the square.

Declan said casually over his shoulder, "It's a movie set, folks. Relax. They're just filming a scene." But he walked faster, and I didn't like the look on his face.

"Deck, that wasn't acting, was it?"

"I don't know." He sounded worried. "But I'd like to make sure."

Mungo growled.

No . . . no, no, no . . .

My uncle Ben came barreling out from between two of the temporary structures, his cell phone clutched in his hand. "That's right, Reynolds Square. Where they're filming." His brown eyes searched the area. "Please hurry." He spotted me with Declan, and his forehead wrinkled.

I approached and put my hand on his arm. Listening to the other party, he squeezed my fingers, too distracted to see the question in my eyes. Declan frowned for a split second, then took off at a run. I left my uncle to his phone call and followed close behind him.

So close that he almost knocked me over when he suddenly stopped and spun on his heel. "Katie. You need to go." He took a step to the side, blocking my view. His voice was calm, soothing. I knew that voice. It was his emergency voice.

"What? Why?" I leaned to one side and saw a plate of leftover pastries on the corner of the table. Only two were left. I would have been pleased at their apparent popularity if my boyfriend hadn't been radiating quiet anxiety. Deep down I knew something was wrong, horribly wrong, but my mind wasn't ready to go there yet.

I jumped when a deep male voice behind Declan let loose with a string of extremely creative swearwords. They were followed by the sound of a woman loudly weeping.

Warning Klaxons rang in my head. "Come on, Deck. Seriously." I gave him a not-so-playful push.

I must have caught him off guard, because, big as he was compared to me, he stepped aside awkwardly to regain his footing. That gave me a chance to take a split-second mental snapshot:

Six open tents around a long table under a shade canopy. Lunch remnants on the table shoved to one side. Bowl of watermelon slices. Five bottles of wine, cheese knife, pile of napkins. A sharp-eyed man with a smoothly shaved head, who looked like Yul Brynner in *The King and I*, still muttering oaths. The dark-haired man next to him was wide-eyed and pale beneath his five-o'clock shadow. A muscular woman with spiked white-blond hair and a silver eyebrow ring stood next to the very recognizable Althea Cole. The star wore a period costume and wept copiously onto the T-shirted shoulder of a man who held his arms protectively around her.

Instantly, I recognized his smooth, honey-colored ponytail, the curve of the lips as he murmured words of comfort. This was no movie scene. Steve Dawes was a columnist for the *Savannah Morning News*, a member of one of the oldest druidic clans in the South, and not so long ago had been Declan's rival for my affection.

He looked up and saw me standing there. Surprise stretched his features taut. "Katie? Why are you . . . ?" He blinked, and his shoulders slumped. "Of course you'd be here." He looked slowly down at the ground.

Almost against my will, I followed suit.

And saw the legs jutting out from under the table.

Chapter 3

His high-end athletic shoes showed little wear on the tread, which happened to be clearly visible since whoever the feet belonged to was lying facedown.

His. Because it was a large shoe, my logical brain reasoned as my mind reeled. A chino pant leg met the top of it. Lots of men wear chinos, right? But I'd seen a pair like those already today.

"Simon?" I murmured and began to push past Declan. He grasped my arm. I pulled, but he didn't let go. I raised my eyes to his face and saw concern quietly overtaken by resignation. We stood there for what seemed like a full minute but was probably only a couple of seconds before he sighed and released his hold. Another second's hesitation, and then I tore my gaze away and took three steps around to the front of the table.

Yep. The fallen man was definitely Simon Knapp. The production coordinator lay diagonally under the corner of the table. His torso was disturbingly visible from this angle, however.

As was the large knife jutting out of his back.

The knife that only hours before Lucy had given him to slice up a watermelon.

A shudder began in my shoulders and migrated down to my toes. My stomach roiled at the crimson stain spreading across the blue T-shirt I'd found so attractive earlier. My peripheral vision blurred, my focus narrowing until all I could see was that knife, the shining strip of steel threaded through its black handle so clear it made my eyes ache and my head throb. Still, I couldn't look away even as my bones melted to jelly. Sparks floated in front of my eyes, and I felt my knees buckle.

"Hey!"

I felt Declan's strong hands grip my upper arms. The sparks turned black. My head felt like a balloon bobbing on a string. I was lifted, and then I was sitting on a chair, and then I remembered to breathe.

Gently, I shook my head side to side. "Whoa." It came out as a whisper.

"Who is that?" It was a woman's querulous voice. "Steve, who is she?"

"You'll be okay, hon. I've got you," Declan said in a low voice. He held out a sweating glass. "Here, drink this."

"Thanks." I took it and raised it to my lips. Quickly, he steadied my trembling hands. "I'm okay, really," I said. The sweet tea slid down my throat, spreading fingers of comfort. I took another swallow, then another before the sugar jolted my system like an electric current. I blinked as the reason I'd nearly passed out came flooding back to me.

Another murder? Oh, good goddess, is this never going to stop?

Quickly, I scanned the area, carefully avoiding the prone figure on the ground twenty feet away.

Steve's brow wrinkled, and his eyes were on my face as he said something into Althea's ear. She wore a simple long dress made of blue calico cotton with a pink overgown tied in front and slippers on her feet. Her trademark waves of ash-blond hair were dyed dark red and stuffed under a white ruffled cap for her role in *Love in Revolution*. It had been her voice demanding to know who I was. I wondered what he was telling her and felt my cheeks color. The others stared at me with curiosity.

Especially the woman with the spiked hair. Her aqua eyes bored into mine, glinting green when she moved her head a fraction. She seemed to make a decision and took a step toward the open-sided tent where Declan had deposited me in a canvas folding chair. As she moved, the air around her seemed to shimmer for a nanosecond, like heat rising from asphalt in the distance.

I blinked.

"Okay, folks," Ben announced. "The police are on their way, so hold tight. I can't let anyone leave—I'm sure the authorities will want to talk to everyone who was here. No doubt the press will be close on their heels, so get ready to deal with that."

I glanced at Steve. Nice for him to have inside access, but he didn't give the impression that he was wearing his reporter hat today. Althea had stopped crying and now contented herself with glaring at me.

The guy with the shaved head was on his phone now, and I heard him say, "Nik Egan here. Is he in? All right . . . Tell him to call me as soon as he gets back. This is an emergency."

Ben had told Lucy and me the director's name was Niklas Egan.

"Whatever you do," my uncle continued, "stay well away from the body."

"*Body*? Oh, my God, oh, my *God*, what *happened*?"

All eyes lasered to the newcomer. Mid-twenties, skinny, pale, and bespectacled, he didn't notice the scrutiny. All his attention was on the ground. *"Simon?"*

"Owen! Where have you been?" demanded Egan.

Bewilderment playing across his features, the young man held up a bag. "The Welsh Wabbit. Simon sent me to get Camembert." He gestured toward Althea. "For her."

The actress rolled her eyes.

The dark-haired gentleman patted her shoulder absently as he stepped forward. His stubbled face and wavy locks rang a note a familiarity, but I couldn't place him. He wore cargo shorts with a Hawaiian shirt and Birkenstocks.

"Who's that?" I muttered to Declan, who still hovered over me.

"Van Grayson," he whispered back. "Lead actor."

That surprised me a little. Althea exuded a combination of haughty confidence that was quite lacking in Grayson's demeanor. He seemed as horrified—and curious—as I felt.

He surveyed the group, speaking for the first time. "Did anyone see what happened?"

There were blank looks all around.

"Simon told me he was going to set up for the after-hours party," Althea said. "I went to my trailer to change; then I remembered something I wanted to ask him and came back about ten minutes later." Her voice broke on the last word, but she soldiered on. "That's when I found him."

Steve said, "I was back there in the property tent, heard Althea's scream, and came running."

Grayson nodded. "I was heading to my own trailer and saw you."

"I was leaving the makeup trailer when I heard the scream," the blond woman with the strange eyes said. Her voice was surprisingly deep. She gestured toward a nearby RV. "Over there."

"Did any of you notice anyone who wasn't supposed to be here?" Ben asked. "A stranger? Or someone leaving the set?"

Of course, they all looked at me. I tried to look innocent, which was harder than it should have been.

"This is my niece," Ben said. "She provided lunch."

"Well, you were all here by the time I happened into this mess." Egan's expression was bitter. "And I sure didn't see anyone running away as I came across the square from Bryan Street."

The blank expressions turned to suspicion as the realization sank in.

"It was probably one of us," Althea breathed.

Declan stroked my cheek with his finger, then tipped my chin up. Worry gleamed from his deep blue eyes. "You okay? I should go make sure no one crosses those barricades."

"I'm fine." I tried a smile.

"Are you sure?"

"And dandy," I managed.

"Katie?" Uncle Ben stepped in front of me and leaned down. His eyes crinkled at the corners as he squinted at me through his frameless glasses. "I've never seen you so wobbly."

I gave a little nod. "I'm okay. At least I will be. But that knife . . ." I trailed off.

He straightened and stroked his short beard. "The knife. Not the . . . ?"

"That, too," I croaked. Though, honestly, I'd seen a dead body—or four—since moving to Savannah, and not once had I felt in danger of fainting. But knives gave me the super heebie-jeebies. Outside of the kitchen, that was. It was a strange phobia for someone who used them in a professional capacity every day, I had to admit.

The spike-haired blond woman had approached and now stood behind Uncle Ben, waiting. I deliberately didn't look up at her, unsure of what she wanted with me. Besides, that whole shimmery thing kind of gave me the creeps.

If it had even been real. My synapses were a little overheated, after all.

Something outside the tent area caught Ben's attention. "Hey, get back on the other side of that rope!" he thundered and took off. Declan took a step, then stopped and turned.

"Go," I urged. Giving in to his training as a first responder, he didn't wait for me to say it twice.

I watched my uncle shoo a bystander back onto the sidewalk and heard his raised voice. Ben was not one to yell—at least not under normal circumstances.

The blond woman stepped forward, and I finally looked up at her.

"I'm Ursula Banford," she said. A blue dragonfly drifted by her shoulder, the iridescent wings flashing. I blinked as a second one followed, and then a third, gliding smoothly along as if they were riding sunshine itself.

Uh-oh. The dragonfly was my totem, and while they sure were handy for keeping Savannah's rampant mosquito population at bay, they also served as a kind of metaphysical tap on my shoulder.

I stood, on guard but glad to feel the muscles in my legs working properly again. "Um, hi." A few beats as I struggled to get some kind of intuitive hit off this Ursula Banford. "I'm Katie Lightfoot."

She inclined her chin slightly and slowly held out her hand. "Nice to meet you."

Was it? I couldn't read her at all. I reached out, ready to flinch when our fingers touched. But there was nothing. Not a hint of anything, even with the physical contact. Her gaze lifted, looking into a distance that wasn't there for a few seconds before her attention returned to me.

She released my hand and smiled. "You're special, Katie Lightfoot. You know that, right? And you know why you're here."

"I'm not sure I—"

"Oh, don't be modest. I've heard on good authority that you will be the one to bring Simon Knapp's killer to justice."

Mind racing, I felt my jaw slacken. Was this woman a witch like me? Or more pointedly, *not* like me? Because I sure couldn't make any predictions like that.

I was about to ask when I heard a voice mutter, "Well, that's *just* what I wanted to hear."

With a sinking feeling, I turned to see Detective Peter Quinn had arrived, accompanied by Ben and Declan. He wore tan slacks and a linen sports coat. His thick gray hair fell in a wave across his forehead, and he was already summer-tan.

I tried a smile, but it slid off my face. "Oh. Hey, Quinn."

He shook his head and held up his palm to me. "Stay right there."

Worry pinched the skin around Ben's eyes, Dec-

Ian had donned a smooth poker face, and Ursula regarded me with unabashed interest. I clamped my lower lip between my teeth and watched Quinn move to where Simon lay, squat down, and take a long look without touching the body. He stood, pulled his notebook from an inside pocket, and made a few notes before returning to where the four of us waited in silence.

Mungo ran to him and gently touched his front paws to the detective's pant leg in greeting before assuming the sit position. Quinn glanced down at him and his narrow lips twitched in a smile—a smile that vanished by the time his gray eyes found mine. "I can hardly wait for you to tell me why you're here."

"We're feeding these fine people." I tried not to sound defensive.

"The Honeybee doesn't cater." His tone was flat.

"We do today," I answered. "Special circumstances." It was true, but not a good enough answer for Quinn. This was the fourth time he'd come to investigate a suspicious death and I'd already been on the scene.

Ursula had taken a step back when Quinn arrived but continued to watch me. I itched to find out more about her—and why she'd made that bold statement about me bringing Simon's killer to justice. After all, I'd never met the woman before. Who the heck was her "good authority"? When I'd touched her hand, there had hadn't been so much as a tickle of energy, which surprised me if she possessed real power. Of course, I'd been fooled before, more than once, by people who were very powerful indeed.

More than one had intended me harm.

Yet her words resonated. The spellbook club had concluded early on that I was a catalyst of some kind, but according to Peter Quinn's former partner, Detective Franklin Taite, I was more than that. He'd called me a lightwitch, a candela. Told me I was drawn to circumstances that involved black magic but was unable to practice it myself—as if I wanted to dabble in the dark arts anyway. Still, during the short time I'd been a witch, I'd found the definition of dark and light magic, like any moral framework, involved a lot of gray that depended on intention and circumstances and abilities and who knew what else.

That had never been as evident as when I'd nearly killed Declan by accident a few months before.

I'd worried about the whole light/dark thing for months, but I'd finally determined to simply do my best and keep in mind the Rule of Three, the part of the Wiccan Rede which states that everything we do comes back to us threefold—kind of like the Golden Rule on steroids. What else could I do? Still, that was a lot easier to say when no one had been murdered.

Now Simon had been. Was I here because there was a magical element to his death?

"Oh, and of course, you're right in the thick of things, too." Quinn narrowed his eyes at Declan.

Before Declan could respond, Ben said, "Security, Peter. Most of the crew is made up of firefighters on their days off."

He'd known Detective Quinn on a professional level for many years. Not that their long-standing working relationship had stopped Quinn from suspecting Ben of murder right after we'd opened the Honeybee. That was water under the bridge now, and Ben was quite willing to forgive and forget. Me? I liked Peter Quinn a lot, but I could never forget how he'd accused my uncle.

The detective nodded. "I guess that makes sense. Makes sense you'd be in the middle of the bunch of them, too, Ben."

"He's head of security," I said and was surprised to see my uncle's face redden. Why . . . ? Then I realized the hard truth: A man had been killed on his watch. Of course he felt responsible.

Not that it was his fault, I felt sure. Still, I knew Ben would torture himself about it to no end. My heart went out to my gentle uncle, a man of great strength but also great pride. This would be hard on him.

It already was.

"Okay, okay," Quinn said. "Enough meet and greet. We have a murder to investigate. What do you know about it?" He looked at me when he said it. Behind him, a van pulled to the curb. Three crime scene specialists exited and began pulling cameras and other equipment from the back of it.

"Simon was dead when I got here," I said. "Which was only a few minutes ago."

"More like fifteen," Declan said. "You lost a few minutes when you almost passed out."

Quinn looked suspicious. "*You* almost fainted when you saw a dead body?"

"Um, sort of." I carefully ignored Ursula's curious gaze. "I don't really care for knives."

He opened his mouth, then seemed to think better of it. Instead, he settled for, "You knew the victim." It was a statement, not a question.

I shrugged. "Not really. I only met him today at the Honeybee. Apparently, he fired the regular caterer this morning, and Mimsey suggested Lucy and I step in. We did our best, and—"

He cut me off. "Mimsey Carmichael." Again, not a question.

"Yes, Mimsey Carmichael. She met Simon when he came into Vase Value looking for passionflowers for Althea Cole." I gestured with my chin toward the actress, who now huddled like a frightened child in the crook of Steve's arm. As I watched, she leaned up and murmured into his ear.

Quinn took a deep breath. "Okay. I'll talk with you more in a little bit. Right now we need to clear this area so the crime techs can get in here. Ben, why don't you gather everyone in that tent over there, and I'll get started on interviews."

"All right, folks," Ben called. "Everyone needs to come with me."

Althea stepped away from Steve's side.

"This"—she indicated the body lying fifteen feet from her quaint shoes—"is unfortunate, but I really don't have any information for you about what happened."

"We'd like to talk with you anyway, Ms. Cole," Detective Quinn said.

"Then I'm afraid you'll need to do it at the house," the actress responded with an imperious toss of her head. "I'm tired and hot and in desperate need of a shower."

You and me both, sister. I glanced at Steve. His face was impassive. *Is he seriously attracted to her?*

"Stevie, will you grab the wine? Where's the Côtes du Rhône? Oh, never mind. Ursula, get the cheese from Owen."

Stevie? I almost laughed out loud. He had an unfortunate propensity to call me "Katie-girl," or at least he had until I insisted he stop. Our eyes met, and his lips twitched. At least he appreciated the irony.

Quinn stepped forward. "I'm sorry, but everything remains right where it is, and everyone needs to stay at least until we get through preliminary interviews."

"You can't force us!" Althea took off her white cap and threw it on the ground. One of the crime scene guys hovering at the edge of the group made a noise of consternation. A tendril of long red hair escaped from the elaborate pinning on the actress's head and snaked slowly down to her shoulder as if it had been scripted.

Steve leaned toward her and said something. She listened, stone-faced, then gave a curt nod. He straightened. "Detective Quinn, would you be willing to speak with Ms. Cole first?"

Detective Quinn was.

Chapter 4

Racks of eighteenth-century clothing surrounded my chair: fancy dress and plain, red uniforms and brown uniforms, wool coats, breeches, and high boots, all interspersed with shelves of pistols and sabers, muskets and rifles, canteens, bags, funny-looking hats, and worn leather footwear. I was sitting in the wardrobe tent with Mungo, waiting for Quinn to finish with me. After he'd learned that I'd nearly fainted—thanks to Declan's spilling the beans—he'd insisted that I "rest" while he interviewed some of the others.

Rest. Sure, Quinn. More like punishment.

As if it were my fault Simon Knapp had been killed. Or that I'd been Janey-on-the-spot afterward. I'd just been in the wrong place at the wrong time . . .

Right. Not even I believed that anymore. Yet how could I tell Quinn his own former partner had informed me that I had a calling to remedy evil in the world? Sheesh.

I still didn't understand how the whole calling thing was supposed to work. It was beyond frustrating that Franklin Taite had dumped that information on me and then up and left town. Quinn had told me Taite transferred to New Orleans after his short stint working for the Chatham County Metropolitan Police Department. No doubt he'd gone to the Big Easy because he'd tracked down another "hotbed of evil," as he'd once called Savannah.

In the brief time I'd know him, Taite had demonstrated quite a flair for the dramatic.

Yet I had to admit I'd encountered some true darkness since my move south. Murder was bad enough without adding in magic. It was spooky to think about.

I sighed and shifted in my chair. Mungo looked up from where he was lying on the floor, his soft brown eyes questioning. I reached down and patted his head. "What do you think about that Ursula woman?" I asked. "Do you think she's like us?"

He blinked. Not much help, that.

The side of the tent facing the dead man was open. I was thankful the crime scene folks had erected walls of plastic sheeting to cut off any view of Simon. A bright light flashed behind it, indicating they were still taking pictures.

Simon Knapp had seemed like a pretty good guy. A little abrupt, maybe, but that was only my first impression. Who knew what he was really like? I'd never find out. Lots of people he would have interacted with in his life would never find out now.

And what about the people who did know him intimately? Parents, siblings, friends? I hadn't noticed whether he wore a wedding ring, but he could have been married, had a girlfriend, or had children who would miss him more than I could even imagine.

Because some jerk had buried a knife in his back.

Sudden rage broke through the resignation I hadn't even realized I'd given in to. Quinn was going to ask me how I happened to witness yet another dead body in the less than two years I'd lived in Savannah. I wouldn't have a good answer for him because I didn't have a good answer for myself.

And now more than ever I wanted one! This was getting ridiculous. The idea of being a light-witch had baffled me, worried me, and made me wonder whether I was worthy of such a thing. It had cast a pall over the delight of learning about witchcraft from the ladies of the spellbook club, of finally feeling like I understood why I'd always felt different, of finally feeling like I'd found a place where I belonged. And the spellbook club couldn't help me, either. Even Mimsey, who would have been our high priestess if our coven had been formal enough to have such a thing, had heard the term only in passing in her youth.

Now it just made me angry. Franklin Taite owed

me an explanation. I deserved to know everything about what it meant to be a lightwitch—including whether it was possible to stop being one.

A fan in the corner turned lazily back and forth, barely moving the stifling air. I got up and began to pace in the small aisle between racks of costumes. Mungo whined and ran to me, stopping in front of me as I turned at the end of the aisle. I paused. "Sorry, little guy. It's just that this whole thing is so upsetting."

He made a low noise of agreement.

Taking a deep breath, I tried to calm down. An elaborate millinery creation sat at eye level on a shelf, a frothy concoction of lace and peach-colored satin. I grabbed it and plopped in on my head. "What do you think?" I asked my familiar.

The look he gave me was answer enough.

"Fine." I took it off and tried on a three-cornered hat. It swam on my head. More than two centuries ago even men had hair longer than my short, no-fuss do.

Voices murmured from the other side of the canvas wall. Recognizing one of them as Quinn's, I moved closer to the sound, hoping he was on his way to interview me.

"Did you see anything unusual when you were returning?" he asked someone. "Perhaps someone within the roped-off area who you didn't recognize?"

"I would have told you that by now." The voice that answered was deep and impatient. I recognized it as Niklas Egan's. "I'd volunteer any of the information you're asking for if I had it. But I don't. End of story. Sorry."

I shuffled up next to the thin wall, listening hard.

"I see," Quinn said. "So I've been told most of the crew had already gone back to the hotel. The only people still around were Van Grayson, Althea Cole, and Simon's assistant, Owen Glade, who was actually off-site purchasing cheese for Ms. Cole."

"Right. Simon sent him to the Welsh Wabbit every bloody day," Niklas said.

"Hmm," Quinn murmured. Then, "Also on the set were Susie Little, the makeup artist, and Ursula Banford, Ms. Cole's personal trainer—"

"And personal psychic," the director broke in.

So she wasn't a witch. But a psychic? Like, a real one?

Quinn's voice came again. "Right. Psychic and personal trainer."

Niklas said, "Then there were the two security guys and that guy Simon talked me into giving a small speaking part to."

"Steve Dawes."

Steve had an actual part in *Love in Revolution*? Well, of course he did.

"And Simon himself, of course," Niklas continued. "He was setting up the wine and cheese dealio Althea insists on every evening. Usually we have it at the house—Simon found an old place to rent for the major players, including myself, about half a block away. Anyway, even though we were done filming for today, I wanted to run over the scene for tomorrow in situ to make sure everyone knew what I expect before we waste a bunch of time with the cameras rolling. And Althea does not like to wait for her wine in the evening, so she told Simon to set up the after-hours party here." His voice lowered so that I could barely hear him, but I did make out the words "bit of a lush" and "keep her away from the hard stuff."

"And you were returning from the rental house," Quinn said. I imagined him scribbling in his notebook.

"I'd gone back to pick up some script changes I made last night. I'd just returned when I heard Althea screaming like a banshee. That sure made me pick up my pace. Lord, that woman can be challenging to direct, but she's even more difficult when she's not working."

Hmm. He'd been there already when Declan and I entered the cluster of tents after hearing Althea scream. However, I'd also heard him swear, as if surprised, and if he'd approached from the opposite side of the square, I wouldn't have seen him.

Not to mention, my memory felt a little fuzzy after I nearly fainted.

Nearly fainted. Good heavens, Katie.

Althea said she'd discovered the body ten minutes after leaving Simon alone. That seemed like a pretty small window of opportunity. I remembered the stain spreading on his shirt and blinked rapidly against the mental image.

"What can you tell me about the victim?" Quinn asked.

"Simon was a combination location scout and production coordinator," Niklas said. "His job was to support the cast and the crew however we needed him to, but Simon was known for going above and beyond. That's why he was in such high demand. I had to pay him double to come work for me on this project, but with a small crew and the limited budget of an independent film like this one, I needed someone who could smooth the way whenever it got rocky. I don't know what I'm going to do now."

"'Smooth the way.' What exactly do you mean by that?" Quinn asked.

"Simon was a . . . a fixer, I guess you'd say."

"A fixer."

"Sure."

"And you knew that before you hired him?"

"Everyone knows it."

"Did he 'fix' situations that were illegal?"

A pause, then, "Sometimes."

"Has he ever fixed anything for you?"

"Sure."

"Care to tell me what it was?"

Another pause. "You're thinking I might have killed him because of it?"

"Keeping secrets can cause a lot of damage in the world," Quinn said.

"Not keeping them has caused some, too." Niklas sounded bitter. "Simon paid off a man whose wife I'd been seeing. Mostly so my own wife wouldn't find out."

"So you're married?"

He snorted. "Not anymore. She figured it out on her own."

I heard rustling then, and the voices grew fainter and then drifted away altogether. Was Quinn done talking to the director? I leaned my cheek against the wall, straining to hear.

Of course, I'd forgotten I was wearing the three-cornered hat, which promptly jammed down over my eyes.

"Ow." As I tugged at the brim, my elbow hit something. I freed myself from the hat in time to see a naked mannequin tipping over. My hand moved to stop it as if in slow motion, and a nano-second later it crashed into a metal shelving unit.

The murmurs of the crime scene techs grew silent.

"Oops," I said to Mungo, who had leaped to the side and now radiated disapproval.

"Hear anything interesting?" Quinn asked from the doorway.

Guilt stabbing my solar plexus, I casually shrugged. "I was looking at the props while I waited."

"Sure you were," he said. "Sit down. I might as well talk with you next."

I sat back on my folding chair, and Quinn took a metal stool and placed it five feet in front of me. Mungo settled between us, and I dove into trying to explain how Ben and Declan and several of our friends had become involved with the filming of the movie while Lucy and I had devoted our time to keeping the bakery running smoothly. I told Quinn again how Mimsey had brought Simon in, that we'd made lunch, and that we had been asked to cater for the rest of the time the crew was filming in Savannah. As I spoke, the light outside grew more angled, and the air inside the tent cooled a few degrees.

"Honest to Pete," I said. "I've never met any of these people before today. I have no idea what happened, why it happened, or who would have anything against Simon Knapp. Except . . ."

His eyebrow rose in question.

"Well, he did fire the other caterer. Seems a pretty weak reason to kill someone, though."

Unsmiling, Quinn made a note. "The director called Simon a fixer." Was he testing me, trying to find out if I'd been listening?

Well, it wasn't my fault I could hear his interview right where he'd told me to wait. He should have been more circumspect if he didn't want me to eavesdrop. So I said, "Yes, I heard him tell you that. Maybe that's a good start for finding a motive for murder."

Quinn looked oddly satisfied. "You say you've never met any of these people."

"Well, of course I know Steve. He was here when Deck and I stumbled onto the scene, all wrapped around Althea Cole." I couldn't hide the scorn that leaked out around my words.

Amusement flickered across the detective's face.

"Whom I recognized but had never met," I finished.

"What about the psychic?"

I pressed my lips together. "Ursula Banford introduced herself to me less than a minute before you arrived."

He leaned back in his chair and regarded me. "Do you think she's really a psychic?"

I lifted my shoulders, then let them fall. "How should I know?"

"Do you believe in psychics?"

I opened my mouth to speak, then closed it. Did I? "I honestly don't know," I finally said.

"What about intuition?" he asked.

Peter Quinn and I had had several conversations, both on his professional turf as a policeman and on mine at the Honeybee. But this was the first time he'd gone down this road.

"Yes," I said. "Of course I believe in intuition. Don't you?"

Slowly, he nodded. "In my job it's helpful. I do all right, but I wish I had more of it. You, on the other hand, seem to have more than your fair share."

Uh-oh. "What's that supposed to mean?" My voice sounded weak.

He leaned forward and put his elbows on his knees. "Katie, I like you."

"Um, I like you, too." The last word lilted up, making my statement sound like a question. What was he getting at?

"And I think you have a good heart. Good intentions, if you will."

I waited.

"But darn it, why are you so often in the middle of my homicide cases?" His voice rose an octave in frustration. "*Why?*"

Mungo scrambled to his feet.

At least I wasn't in the middle of *all* of his murder investigations, I wanted to say. Only the ones with some kind of paranormal activity involved. But then why was I here? Was it because Ursula was a psychic?

I said, "I don't know. I'm sorry, but I truly don't. And furthermore, I don't *want* to get involved. It just seems to . . . happen . . ." I trailed off, the very picture of lame.

He sat for a moment, then shook his head. "Okay. Fine. Call me if you think of anything that might help with this one."

"Really?" I was stunned. "You want my help?"

"So far no one seems to have seen anything, and no one is bad-mouthing anyone else—which, frankly, I find a little odd."

What about Niklas telling you Althea drinks too much?

"We'll see what the physical evidence says, but I can tell this one is going to be tricky." He stood. "I don't know what else to say. Whatever the reason for your involvement, you've given me good information in the past. In fact, you've actually helped find three killers. Even my limited intuition says it would be stupid not to at least listen to you." At the doorway, he turned. "Katie, that's not an invitation to actively investigate. Okay?"

Still speechless, I nodded.

"All right, then. You're free to go."

I picked up Mungo and followed him out of the tent. "Quinn?"

He paused and tipped his head to the side. "What?"

"Have you heard anything from Franklin Taite since he left for New Orleans?"

"Taite? Now, why would you ask about him? As I recall, you two weren't exactly the best of friends."

Which was true as far as Quinn knew. And I still wouldn't call Taite my friend, so much as absent mentor. Now I was trying to figure out how absent he really was.

"He seemed like a pretty good detective, though," Quinn said.

Other than thinking I was the devil's spawn for a while there.

"And he's the last person you were partnered with," I said.

"He was okay," Quinn said. "But I like working alone—and no, I haven't heard anything from him since he left."

"Hmm. Well, I'm sure he's living it up down there in the Big Easy and doesn't have much time to stay in touch." I started off across the square. "See you later, Detective."

He watched me go with a speculative look on his face.

Chapter 5

The late-day sun cast shadows across the walkway leading up to the front door of Ben and Lucy's town house. Pots marched along each side of the path, overflowing with verbena, petunias, marigolds, and geraniums and accented with blowsy ornamental grasses and richly colored sweet potato vines. As I stepped toward the bright rows of flora, Mungo wiggled in the tote bag slung from my shoulder.

"Looking forward to seeing Honeybee?" I asked.

Yip!

But it wasn't just that, I realized a second later when the tantalizing fragrance of slow-roasted pork layered with garlic and savory spices reached my nose. Mungo was always excited to visit my aunt and uncle's home and hang out with my aunt's familiar, but I knew it was the prospect of supper that made him lick the drool off his wee chops. The aroma drifted all the way to the public sidewalk. If my aunt didn't watch it, the neighbors would soon be flocking to her kitchen. Not that she'd mind. She loved feeding people and was an easygoing hostess even with little or no warning.

I felt guilty about the sounds my stomach was making after how swoopy-sick it had felt a mere hour earlier when the police were taking pictures of Simon's dead body. I still felt shaken, but the strange thing I'd learned about when awful things happen is that real life keeps right on happening, too. A man was dead, and I was hungry—and sweaty and tired, to boot.

I stopped in front of the large wreath on the door. Lucy had wired sticks of honey locust together and then woven Spanish moss, or old man's beard, as some called it, and stalks of dried lavender among the thorns to soften their wicked appearance. The trio of plants were attractive together and provided a powerful oomph of protection as well. I had a similar wreath on my own front door.

I skipped the bell, knocked once, and then turned the knob and entered the town house. "Hello?"

As usual, the air inside thrummed with verdant energy from all the growing things: houseplants in pots, a six-foot hibiscus in full bloom, a Mandarin orange tree in one corner, and the thick carpet of ivy gripping the rough brick of the fireplace mantel. The vaulted ceiling rose above, and two skylights offered an abundance of natural daylight. The place had a rich yet airy feel, a welcoming vibe despite the thorns on the front door, and smelled pretty much like heaven right then.

Like an old-time movie star making an entrance, Honeybee came down the steps leading up to the second floor and then to the rooftop garden: graceful, beautiful, and well aware of both. Her orange tabby stripes glowed in the oblique sunlight from the window, and her green eyes flashed a greeting.

I sneezed. Beautiful or not, Honeybee made my eyes puff and my nose run within seconds. Mungo bounced in my tote bag, wanting down. I complied, lowering him to the floor next to the white sofa. His toenails clicked on the dark cherrywood as he ran to meet Lucy's cat. They touched noses while I felt around in the side compartment of my bag for my antihistamines.

I tried again. "Lucy?"

"We're in here." Her voice came from the rear of the house.

We? I left the two schmoozing familiars to catch up and went to find out. The scent of roasting pork was even stronger as I entered the kitchen. Copper pots hung from the ceiling over a large work island, a blue-speckle teapot sighed on the old gas range, and glass-fronted cupboards showed off Lucy's sturdy green stoneware. On the other side of the island, Lucy sat at the scarred wooden table stripping dried thyme leaves from their tough stems into a wide-mouthed Mason jar.

Jaida French sat across the table from where Lucy worked, a book and a steaming cup near her elbow. Her formfitting beige suit testified to her day in court, and her vivid blue blouse glowed like a sapphire against her chocolate skin. She wore a tasteful silver filigree necklace, and matching earrings dangled from her exposed earlobes.

She rose in a fluid motion, reaching to give me a hug as she said my name. Jaida gave the best hugs, warm and enveloping and somehow full of instant comfort. I practically fell into her arms. A second later, I felt my eyes grow hot with tears that almost felt like an afterthought to the day's events.

"Why do you always smell like cinnamon?" I sniffled.

Jaida held me at arm's length, surprise on her face. "I do?"

I nodded, blinking back the moisture in my eyes. "You didn't know? Cinnamon and caramel."

She laughed. "You're the first person to tell me that, but it doesn't sound all bad."

"It's not," I assured her, then realized I hadn't had a chance to shower. "I bet I don't smell like anything sweet right now."

Lucy had risen, too. "Have you been running this whole time? I thought you'd gone home to take a shower." Leaving unspoken that I obviously hadn't.

I sighed. "I wish. Have you talked to Ben?"

Her brow knitted. "I tried to call him, but he didn't pick up. Then I got a text from him a little while later. Said he'd be late and would explain when he got here. Maybe the second security shift didn't show up on time."

Shaking my head, I said, "No, they got there right on schedule. I saw them."

"You were on the *Love in Revolution* set?" Lucy asked.

"I took Simon Knapp up on his invitation to stop by." The last invitation he'd ever extend.

Jaida put her hands on her hips. "You show up for dinner about to break into tears—yes, I noticed—and Ben's unaccountably late. Declan, too."

Lucy nodded, her brow still wrinkled. "He's coming home with Ben."

Our friend gave a decisive nod. "Uh-huh. What's going on, Katie?"

So I told them, pacing from one end of the table to the other as I described what had happened as soon as I got to Reynolds Square. As I spoke, their eyes grew wider, and a few times they turned and looked at each other, but not once did they interrupt me. When I was done, I said, "So that's why Ben and Declan are late. They were finishing up when I left, though, so they should be here pretty soon."

Silence descended on the kitchen, punctuated by the puffs of steam from the kettle and the faint crackling sound of roasting meat in the oven.

"Oh, that poor man," Lucy finally said. "Someone *stabbed* him?"

"With our knife." I shuddered, remembering.

The blood drained from her face. "Why?" she whispered. "He seemed so nice." Of course, my sweet aunt thought the best of everyone.

I shook my head. "Hard to tell." Still, I couldn't help but wonder what sort of situations besides a philandering husband a fixer might fix.

"So," Jaida said, drawing the word out. "You met this Simon Knapp for the first time today?" Her eyes were narrowed in thought.

"Uh-huh. Lucy, too."

"Was there anything about him or the, er, death, that indicated paranormal foul play or dark magic?"

I sighed. "Not that I could tell. He had a kind of . . . spiciness to him but nothing that I'd characterize as bewitching." Not that I'd had a clue Steve Dawes was a druid until he told me. I'd been a real newbie then, though. "Althea Cole travels with her very own psychic. A woman who's also her personal trainer."

"I wonder if that's why you were there." Jaida looked over at my aunt, who slowly nodded.

I sighed. "Yeah. That occurred to me."

"Because it's likely there's something hinky going on, something besides the actual murder of a human being," Jaida said.

Lucy made a noise of consternation. Our friend sat back down and reached across the table to put her hand on my aunt's arm. "I know this is upsetting. Death is always upsetting. But you know what Bianca would say."

My aunt took a deep breath. "She'd say that death is but a transition to the next thing, that it's not a tragedy for the one who dies, only the ones who are left behind." She began reciting as if by rote, but by the time she finished, the thought seemed to give her some peace. Her face relaxed, and her lips turned up in a small smile.

I, on the other hand, felt the jury was still out on

that one. Souls might continue to the next plane, however you defined it, but surely a violent death was a bad send-off.

"Um, about the psychic," I said.

They both looked curious. "Spill," Jaida said.

"Her name is Ursula Banford. She introduced herself to me a couple of minutes after I came to."

"Came to!" Lucy's hand went to her throat. "Katie, what didn't you tell us?"

"Oh. Um, yeah. See, the knife in Simon's back kind of gave me a turn—you know my problem with knives, right? Anyway, I got kind of woozy when I saw it, that's all. No biggie. Declan was right there and grabbed me . . . Anyway, that's not important. The thing is that this Ursula made a—" I paused. "Well, a prediction."

"Really." Jaida's response was flat with skepticism.

"Yeah. I still don't know what to think of her, but she did say I was, er, special and that she had it on good authority I would be the one to bring Simon Knapp to justice."

"Good authority? What's that supposed to mean?" Jaida asked. Still she didn't look as disbelieving as she had a moment earlier. "Who could have told her that?"

Lucy tipped her head to the side. "Many psychics are hedgewitches of another sort, you know. Instead of the traditional hedge on the edge of town that we green witches crossed in the old days to find our medicinal—and magical—plants, they cross the 'hedge' between this plane and the next."

I felt my breath hitch as I caught her meaning. "You think Nonna told her?"

"Your grandmother has reached through to this side a few times before. I wouldn't put it past her to do it through a medium."

Jaida nodded.

"Katie, you've been called again," Lucy said quietly. A strange expression crept over her face. It took me a moment to recognize it as pride.

"I don't *want* to be called again," I grumped. "And you know who else didn't seem very excited about it?" I looked between them. "Declan. That's who. He's put up with an awful lot because of this whole lightwitch thing—"

"Nonsense." Jaida slapped the tabletop and I jumped.

"Of course he has," I protested.

"You two got to know each other in the first place because he helped you with the Mavis Templeton investigation. He's been there all the way through. There was just that one time . . . ."

"Yeah. That one time when I almost killed him. I *did* kill him for a few seconds. I don't know if you remember, but he wouldn't speak to me for days after that. We almost broke up."

One corner of her mouth turned down.

"It's one thing when you live with another witch, like you do, Jaida. But Deck's not one of us."

"Neither is Ben," Lucy said. "It'll be okay. Your Declan McCarthy is a good man, and he loves you. You have to trust in that."

"He sure didn't look very happy."

"Who looks happy at a murder scene?" Jaida asked.

I opened my mouth and then shut it again, stumped.

Taking a deep breath, I leaned against the counter near Jaida. The book by her elbow was titled *Tarot Spells to Enhance Your Love Life*. "Is that the spellbook for the next meeting?" I asked, taking advantage of the opportunity to change the subject.

She nodded. "Brought it by for Lucy on my way home. Bianca chose it, but I already had a copy."

"Poor Bianca. I hope she finds someone soon. Men should be swarming around her."

Jaida shrugged. "They are. She's just picky."

Lucy said, "As well she should be. And honest. She doesn't want the same thing to happen again, not to her and not to Colette." Bianca's husband had left in a huff when he found out she was a practicing Wiccan. Too bad, too. Not only was she beautiful and smart, but she had quite the ability for making money in the stock market.

"Have you heard anything from Cookie?" I asked. Cookie Rios was the sixth and youngest member of the spellbook club. She'd been traveling in Europe for the last three months with her boyfriend, an artist who belonged to the same druid clan as Steve Dawes.

"Got an e-mail from her last week," Jaida replied. "She hinted at some new developments between Brandon and her, but didn't say what."

"Hmm. Do you think she's getting ready to settle down?" Lucy asked.

Jaida gave us a wry look. "Either that or she's finally ready to move on." Cookie was known for flipping jobs—and men—every three or four months. So far she'd spent six months with Brandon Sykes, and none of us quite knew what to think about it.

We heard the front door open, and a few moments later Ben and Declan filled the kitchen doorway.

"Sorry we're late," Ben said at the same time Declan inhaled and said, "It smells *amazing* in here." He approached and slid his arm around my waist. "Hey, you. Feeling better?"

"Yeah. Thanks." I gave him a one-armed squeeze in return and kissed the corner of his mouth. "Everything settle down over at the movie set?"

"As much as it's going to for now," he said.

Lucy stood and brushed thyme remnants from her hands. "Katie filled us in. Horrible. Simply horrible." She embraced her husband, then peered at the two men. "Are you hungry?"

Jaida, too, popped to her feet. "I'll let y'all have your supper."

"You're more than welcome to stay," Lucy said. We all murmured agreement.

"I would," Jaida said. "But Gregory's out of town, which means Anubis goes to doggy day camp. I have to pick him up before they close."

"Bring him back and have some barbecue," my aunt urged.

"Mmm. It's tempting, but I have to finish up a pretrial brief to submit tomorrow. Thanks anyway."

I walked her to the door. "You have no doubt I got caught up in Simon Knapp's murder because of the lightwitch thing?"

She paused with her hand on the brass handle. "Maybe. Or maybe you were simply there because you're a catalyst. Not that you *made* a murder happen, of course, but the confluences of time and events do sometimes swirl around you."

I sighed. At least she didn't think I'd actually caused Simon's death on some metaphysical level.

"What does your gut tell you?" she asked.

I'd spent so much time trying to avoid the idea of my "calling" that I hadn't really checked in with my gut. Now that I did, though, I had to admit the signal was pretty clear.

After she left, I went upstairs to take a quick shower while the others got things ready for supper up on the rooftop terrace. As I dressed again, I finally allowed myself to admit something. There was a part of me that thrilled at the idea of tracking another killer. It wasn't a part I was proud of, but it was there . . . and I had a feeling my nonna, wherever she was on the other side of the "hedge," wouldn't disapprove.

Chapter 6

The rooftop garden at my aunt and uncle's town house was cool, shaded from the lowering sun by a high brick wall Ben had constructed. Trailing nasturtiums and strawberries cascaded from the pots set into the wall, a tangle of edible beauty. More potted flowers, herbs, and vegetables clustered in the corners, along the balustrade, and in the deep wooden box beneath it. Melon vines tumbled down to the stone floor, beans wove up iron trellises, and a huge pot of sorghum reached skyward by the door to the stairs. Tucked here and there were lavender, savory, purple sage, and several varieties of scented geraniums.

The space always smelled lush. Add to it the pungent mustard-pulled pork and vinegary tang of the dressing on the coleslaw Declan had insisted on making while I showered, and I almost hyperventilated trying to take it all in.

Honeybee lounged on her plush bed. Mungo downed the food Lucy served him—a miniature version of our own supper since Mungo refused to eat anything but people food—then joined the tabby for a nice doze. Sitting around the glass-topped table, we humans helped ourselves to the feast and then fell silent in appreciation. I found myself ravenous, mentally flicked away any remnants of guilt about it, and dug in. So did everyone else.

Half a sandwich later, Ben sat back in his chair and took a long swig of sweet tea. He set the glass down and regarded me with concerned eyes. "I heard that psychic said you're the go-to gal for finding Knapp's murderer. When do we start?"

Declan's attention jerked to my uncle. "Ben . . ."

I put down my fork, slowly chewing a bite of slaw. What was going on? My uncle consistently disapproved of my courting the slightest whiff of danger, and as far as I knew, he still considered anything to do with a murder investigation dangerous. I swallowed. "What do you mean?"

His mouth turned down. "Well, I'm sure going to do what I can to find the creep who killed Knapp. I figured you'd be up for it, too."

My lips parted in surprise.

Declan still hadn't said anything, but if the horrified expression on his face was any indication, this conversation wasn't going at all in the direction he'd hoped.

"Why, Ben?" I asked, though I was pretty sure of the answer.

"A man was killed on my watch."

Lucy blanched at the bitterness in his words.

"And I'm not going to stand idly by and let the

murderer get away with it. Between Quinn, Katie, and me, that won't happen."

"Oh, Ben," she said softly.

I looked at Declan. He frowned at my uncle, but said, "You do what you have to, Ben."

"It's my responsibility to make sure things are made right," Ben said defiantly and took another swig of tea.

"Finding who killed Simon won't make it right," I said. "You know that."

"It's a step in the right direction," he said. "I already talked to Peter Quinn. He didn't tell me much, mind you, as he plays things pretty close to the vest. Steve Dawes told me a little about Simon, though."

I felt Declan grow even stiller at the mention of his former rival's name.

"You don't trust Detective Quinn?" I asked.

"He's a good cop. But he goes by the book, and if there's one thing I've learned, it's when this kind of stuff happens around you, Katie, the book goes flying right out the window. I don't understand all this magic stuff, but it seems to give you a leg up on the police."

Beside me, Declan coughed, then took a drink of tea and wiped his lips with a napkin.

"Did you want to weigh in?" I asked him.

He looked at me and pointedly took another bite of his sandwich in silence.

I turned back to Ben. "I thought you didn't like it when I got involved with murder investigations."

"I didn't. I don't. But you're going to anyway, aren't you?" It was more of a statement than a question.

I felt Declan watching me. On one hand, I wanted to live my lovely life with my lovely job and my awesome boyfriend and practice magic and bake for people every day. On the other hand, a man was dead, and it was possible for reasons beyond my ken I might be able to help bring his murderer to justice. Because of that I'd already pretty much decided to do what I could to help. And yes: also because the challenge and thrill of finding the truth appealed to me.

Declan finally spoke. "Of course she is. The resident movie psychic even said so." His tone was part sarcasm and part resignation.

I still didn't say anything, torn more than ever.

A dragonfly drifted over the table and settled near the pepper grinder. Lucy saw it and cocked an eyebrow at me.

I wrinkled my nose and crossed my arms over my chest.

Her lips twitched with amusement.

"Well, I figure this time when you get up to your neck in things, I can be there to protect you," Ben said.

Lucy patted her husband on the arm. "That's sweet of you, Ben."

So while we ate strawberry shortcake made with berries from the hanging plants above us, I told them what I'd overheard Niklas Egan tell Quinn about Simon being a fixer. That turned out to be the same information Steve had passed on to Ben.

"I think the next step might be to find a motive, and that might lie in what sorts of things Simon fixed," I said. "And for whom."

"How do we do that?" Ben asked.

"I'm not sure," I said. "But heaven knows you can charm the shell off a turtle, Ben."

A quick grin lit his face. "Well, thank you, darlin'. Problem is I'm there in a professional capacity, and I don't tend to chat with folks much when I'm being all official."

"Oh, I think you could have a few conversations here and there and still be professional," I said, glad to see he looked a little happier. "And I have an excuse to come onto the set since the Honeybee is catering lunch for A. Dendum Productions now."

"That wasn't just for today?" Declan asked.

"Simon asked us to cater for the rest of the week," I said. "We agreed to at least one more day, but it looks like we have no choice but to step in now that he's dead."

"After all, Simon fired that other caterer, and those poor people still have to eat," Lucy said.

Lucy and I kicked around a few ideas about what to serve for the cast and crew for the rest of the time A. Dendum Productions was in town.

Ben leaned back in his chair. "At least there will be fewer folks to provision."

"Why's that?" I asked.

Declan answered. "After Detective Quinn told

him they couldn't work in the cordoned-off area where they found the body, Niklas Egan made other arrangements for about half the scenes they were planning to shoot in Reynolds Square and sent part of the crew on to set up in the new location. The remaining outdoor scenes here in town will be filmed with a skeleton crew over the next three days."

"Quinn let part of the crew leave Savannah?" I asked.

"They're still in Georgia," Ben said. "Apparently, Simon had already found a second location in Dahlonega, and all the people who are leaving could prove to the police where they were when Simon was killed. Most of them had already returned to the hotel."

"That narrows the list of suspects," I said. "So finding a motive should be a little easier." I pushed a chunk of strawberry around in a pool of whipped cream on my plate. "The problem is everyone who was there when Simon was killed seems to be able to account for their whereabouts."

Or could they? While waiting for Quinn to arrive, the people who were gathered around the body had stated where they'd been when Simon was killed, but any one of them could have lied.

"I wonder why Simon hired Bonner Catering in the first place," Lucy mused. "There are so many wonderful, reputable companies in our little burg."

"Maybe Bonner was cheaper," Ben said. "It's an independent film, though obviously someone with fairly deep pockets is producing it."

"Simon didn't even blink when I gave him our bill," I said. "In fact, he came right out and said money was no object."

Lucy shrugged. "It doesn't matter. If we only have to worry about three days and fewer people, there shouldn't be any problem for the Honeybee to step in."

After we cleared the dishes and cleaned up in the kitchen, Ben suggested we return to the rooftop for a nightcap. "It's been a heck of day, after all. I could use a snort."

Declan shook his head. "Sorry, Ben. I'm tuckered out. Just not used to working seven days a week." He laughed. "I'm not even used to working four days a week."

His typical schedule was to work forty-eight solid hours each week, with the rest of the time free. Many firefighters, especially those with families, took second jobs during that extra time, but other than working some overtime and covering for his friends who were out sick, Declan generally liked to keep his off hours open.

I yawned. "Me too. Tired I mean. And I'm used to working six days a week, you big lug." I punched him playfully on the arm. He grinned and made like he was going to pick me up.

"Don't you dare." I laughed.

Mungo bounced around at our feet. *Yip!*

"See, you're getting the little guy all riled up."

"All right, you two," Ben said. "On your way so we can have our drink and get to bed ourselves." He winked at his wife of over ten years.

I loaded Mungo into my tote. After a long day, a run, and stuffed full of pork and shortcake, he could barely keep his eyes open. We said good night and fervent thanks for supper and went outside.

On the sidewalk, I asked Declan, "My place or yours?"

"Um, do you mind if we each just head home? I'm well and truly beat," he said.

"Oh," I said. "Sure. No problem. Do you need a ride?"

He pointed at his ginormous king cab down the street. "I picked Ben up this morning."

"Okay." I tried to sound noncommittal, but I could feel a distance forming between us. It could be that he really was tired and simply wanted to go home for a good night's sleep. I could understand that. But tonight? After screams and a dead body and a psychic and police interviews and Ben wanting to find a killer? Really?

He kissed me good night and started for his truck.

The only other time Declan had begged off spending time together had been when he was deciding whether to break up with me. Was he doing that again? The thought made Lucy's beautiful dinner sour in my stomach.

"What do you think?" I asked Mungo, who was firmly strapped into the passenger seat of the Bug. "Do I need to worry, or is he simply exhausted?"

I stopped at a red light and looked over at my terrier. He licked his nose.

"He's not happy about me helping Uncle Ben," I said. "I get that. But it's *Ben*. Those two are so close. I'd think Deck would understand how he feels, you know?"

Yip!

The light turned green, and I drove on, mulling over what my uncle had told us about Steve's whereabouts during the murder. Apparently, he'd been in the prop tent on the phone with his father, Heinrich. When he'd heard Althea's scream, he'd quickly ended the call and ran to see what the trouble was—much as Declan and I had.

The four of us had run over everything else we knew, which, frankly, wasn't much. Van Grayson had been walking toward his trailer, but who knew what he'd been doing before that? And Niklas Egan claimed to have just returned to Reynolds Square when Althea screamed, but could anyone verify that he hadn't been there the whole time? I sure hadn't seen him approaching from where Declan and I had been standing, and Ben hadn't noticed him, either. At least we'd witnessed Simon's assistant, Owen, returning from his errand.

And Ursula Banford was still a wild card, in more ways than one. I definitely wanted to know more about Althea's personal psychic.

Personal psychic. Sheesh.

Still, Ben said the makeup artist had confirmed Ursula had been with her during the time frame Simon had been murdered—a time frame Althea herself had defined. She'd alleged that she'd left

Simon alone for only ten minutes or so. He'd supposedly been setting up the wine and cheese soiree.

However, I'd noticed that the wine bottles hadn't even been opened. Even I knew most good wines needed to breathe—and they'd be good wines if they came from Bianca's shop. The remains of lunch had still been on the table, and Simon's assistant hadn't even returned from fetching the Camembert.

"So if I had to guess," I mused out loud to Mungo. "I'd say Simon was killed shortly after Althea left him. Otherwise, he would have been further along in his preparations. Right?"

Yip!

"Of course, she might have been the one who killed him. She could have stabbed him and left for ten minutes, then come back and 'found' his body, or she could have lied about leaving for ten minutes and simply shrieked the alert right after killing him."

Mungo made a sound of disagreement.

"What?" My eyes cut toward him and then back to the road in front of us. "Okay, you're right. I think that woman is a self-entitled pain in the wahoo, but I guess that's not enough to pin a murder on her. Besides, it must take a lot of strength to stab a full-grown man, even in the back."

I pulled into the driveway of my carriage house in Midtown. My next-door neighbors had brought the lawn chairs from the back patio out to their front yard. Redding Coopersmith lifted a hand in greeting as I got out of the car, and his wife, Margie, waved me over.

"Katie, come join us. We moved out here to watch the sunset, but the night is so lovely we don't want to go back inside."

Freed from his seat belt, Mungo bounded to the ground and raced toward them. I followed at a more leisurely pace. The towheaded twins, Jonathan and Julia, ran pell-mell to greet us. When they reached Mungo, they tumbled down and rolled in the grass. He barked and jumped into the pile with them. Their giggles echoed into the evening air, and I couldn't help but smile.

"What a pair!" I said, stepping around them and dropping to the ground in front of the adults. Fireflies flickered in the lawn. "Hi, Redding."

"Hey, Katie." He shared Margie's Scandinavian coloring: light yellow hair, fair complexion, ruddy cheeks. No wonder all their kids were blond, blue-eyed, and sturdy.

"Bart asleep already?" I asked.

"For now," Margie said, reaching toward a pitcher. The light over the porch reflected off its crimson contents. "You want some Kool-Aid?"

I patted my stomach and shook my head. "Still full from supper."

"Okeydoke." Margie sat back. "Anyway, Baby Bart has been waking up at three a.m. for a week now. Lord love a duck, I'd hoped that middle-of-the-night nonsense was over. At least he only stays awake for an hour or so."

"I'll get him tonight," Redding said easily. "I

have to get on the road early anyway." Margie's husband was a long-haul truck driver, sometimes gone for a week at a time. I didn't know how she so often juggled the care of three little ones by herself, but she seemed to do it with a comfortable ease.

"Where to this time?" I asked.

"Oklahoma City," he said.

The cry of a baby crackled from a monitor. Margie started to get up, but Redding said, "I'll check on him. You stay here and chat with Katie."

She watched his departure with an affectionate smile, then turned back to me. "Haven't seen much of you lately, it seems. Work must be busy— and then there's all that hot-and-heavy time with your firefighter."

Margie was always pressing me for details about Declan, claiming that as an old married woman she needed a little vicarious spice in her life. Never mind that she was only a couple years older than my twenty-nine.

"It has been busy at the Honeybee," I said. "Especially since Ben's been spending a lot of time on the *Love in Revolution* set."

She leaned forward. "Ooh! What's he doing?"

I explained about his security teams. As I spoke, the JJs, as Margie called the twins, left Mungo to his own devices and crawled up on the lounge chair with their mother.

"Unfortunately, there was an accident today," I ended, unwilling to get into the gory details of a murder with the twins sitting right there.

"That's too bad," Margie said absently. "Do any of the actors come into the Honeybee?"

"Not so far," I said.

"So you haven't see Van Grayson?"

I cocked my head to the side. "I have, actually. I was on the set this evening and saw him. Althea Cole, too."

She waved her hand and Jonathan grabbed it and hung on. Margie stroked her daughter's hair with her other hand. "I'm sure she's nice enough, but that Van—now, he's a sweetheart! The kids just love, love, love him. We have all his DVDs."

I frowned. "So he's been in children's movies? Maybe that's why I couldn't quite place him."

"Oh, not *movie* movies. He's a . . . what . . . ? Like, a personality, you know? Like Captain Kangaroo or something. Only he's a comedian, really. I read somewhere that he started out doing birthday parties way back when. He had a show on cable for a while, but now I guess he's hit the big time with a movie like the one they're filming here. I'm happy for him, I suppose, but I do hope he doesn't give up performing for the kiddies altogether. He's so talented!"

Her enthusiasm ignited the twins. "Yeah!" they yelled. "Van's the man! Van's the man!" Even in the dark I could make out their hot pink Kool-Aid mustaches.

Margie laughed. "That's his tagline."

"Huh. I had no idea." It was hard to wrap my mind around the idea of the handsome man with a five-o'clock shadow and Birkenstocks delivering jokes to adoring children. Not to mention that he was a potential murder suspect.

"These two would love to meet him," Margie said. "Do you think Ben would let us?"

"Yeah!" the JJs chorused.

I wished Margie hadn't asked right in front of them. "Um, I don't know. I guess I could check. But it's not really up to Ben so much as Mr. Grayson."

"Oh, poo. He's so nice. I'm sure he'd want to meet two of his biggest fans face-to-face."

I half shrugged and lifted my palms. "If I see him, I'll ask. Okay? The Honeybee is providing lunch for them tomorrow, so there's a chance I'll run into him when I bring it over."

She clapped her hands, a gesture immediately mirrored by the JJs, who seemed awfully energized so close to their bedtime. I eyed the Kool-Aid. Oh, well. If Margie wanted to ramp her kids up on sugar, she had to deal with it, not me.

I stood. "I'm bushed. Beddy-bye time for me and Mungo. Come on, boy."

My familiar sprang to his feet, a cloud of fireflies rising with him. They danced around his head as Margie and the kids said good-bye and followed him as we turned to go.

"Now, will you look at that," my neighbor said. "I just can't get over how the lightning bugs flock to that little dog of yours."

"It's funny, isn't it?" I kept my tone casual. Fireflies were Mungo's totem, like dragonflies were mine. His just happened to be a bit more sparkly at night.

I retrieved the duffel full of dirty running clothes from the back of the Bug, and we went inside. In the dark living room, I paused to flip the switch by the door. The floor lamp by the purple fainting couch bloomed into a gentle welcoming light. How I loved this little abode of mine. Once the carriage house for a large estate that was now long gone, it had a single bedroom, a small bath with stacking washer and dryer in the corner, a tiny kitchen, a living room barely big enough for five people to sit in, and a loft above where a futon folded out for guests or provided seating in front of the modest television.

The swooping back of the old-fashioned couch cast a pleasant silhouette against the peach wall across from where I stood, the kitschy lamp beside it decorated with elaborate fringe that normally I wouldn't have said was my style but spoke to me as soon as I saw it. Two wingback chairs sat across from the sofa, the coffee table between them a re-purposed Civil War–era trunk. The wall to my right featured a built-in bookshelf, though my spellbooks were upstairs in the closed secretary's desk, a gift from Lucy where I kept my altar hidden away from casual visitors. French doors led out to the backyard and my gardens.

I dropped the duffel by the entrance to the short hallway so I wouldn't forget to do a load of laundry before going to bed. "Beddy-bye time" had been a bit of an overstatement to the Coopersmiths, as it was unlikely I'd be hitting the sack for another few hours.

My sleep disorder had improved since I began practicing magic. Prior to that I'd slept for only an hour or so each night and still had to run most days in order to burn off extra energy. Being such an early riser was, of course, a boon for a baking professional, and I still regularly awoke around four a.m. But now that I practiced kitchen magic at the bakery and garden magic at home, as well as casting spells with the other members of the spellbook club, I was naturally calmer and sometimes even slept a full four hours a night.

Which still left me plenty of time tonight to try to track down Franklin Taite.

As much as I loved my wee home, I hadn't been there as much as usual because I'd been at Declan's new apartment so much. It was closer to downtown, Mungo was always welcome, plus there was *Declan*. He was fun, sexy, steady, reliable, sweet, a good cook, and he adored me. Steve was also sexy, believe me, and he also adored me, or at least said he did. He was also a practicing druid, so he really understood what magic meant to me. On the other hand, he could be presumptuous, insistent, and he ran with a crowd of other druids with questionable ethics in business and who knew what else. He was more of a bad boy, and I'd had my fill of bad boys. I'd even been engaged to one for a while until he broke it off and broke my heart. The longer Declan and I were together, the more I knew I'd done the right thing. Our relationship had grown, been threatened—by my magic—and then had deepened.

Now it was being threatened again, and again by my magic.

Franklin Taite had to tell me why I kept stumbling into dire situations. And then he had to tell me how to stop it.

He just had to.

Chapter 7

Clothes in the washer, I changed into yoga pants and a tank top and grabbed my laptop from where it perched on the coffee table. I brewed a cup of peppermint tea and settled at the kitchen table, which was big enough to seat three in a pinch.

What do you do when you want to find someone? Google them, of course. I typed in "Franklin Taite."

I'd been hoping for some professional reference to him, but there was nothing—not in New Orleans, not in Savannah, and not in New York, where he'd been before transferring to work with Quinn. There were only links to sites where I could pay for information about my quarry. However, there appeared to be at least one Franklin Taite listed on the first search site I clicked on, so that was a step in the right direction.

Still, that would be my last resort. I tried the New Orleans online phone book next. No luck there, though I couldn't say I was surprised. Since he seemed to move around so much, I suspected Taite would be a cell phone kind of guy rather than a landline kind of guy.

Ah, but the New Orleans Police Department would have a landline, right? I glanced at the clock on the stove and saw it was already after ten p.m. The time didn't really matter, though—the police couldn't care less about Emily Post's guidelines regarding the proper hours to telephone. I retrieved my cell from my tote bag with a frisson of excited dread. Since I could be talking to Taite in mere minutes, I jotted a few notes about what I wanted to ask him.

What is a lightwitch?

Why do you think I'm a lightwitch?

And: *How can I make it stop?*

Pretty simple, but good enough to start a conversation. I put the pen down and searched for the phone number for the NOPD. Right away I ran into a snag, because I didn't know what district of the NOPD Detective Taite had transferred into, and there were eight of them. I retrieved the list from the printer in the loft and returned to the kitchen.

I stared at my choices. *Might as well dive in.*

Beginning at the top, I worked my way down, dialing, waiting, and then running through an exhausting gauntlet of informational runaround at each police district before finally being told that there was no detective by that name working there. By the time I got to the eighth district, I had a bad feeling I was heading straight into a brick wall.

Sure enough, no Detective Taite.

Okay, fine. I'd pay for the information. Plugging back into the site where I'd found references to Franklin Taite, I got out my credit card, justifying the fifty-dollar charge because Simon Knapp, or at least A. Dendum Productions, had given the Honeybee bank account a nice infusion, and there was more to come.

There were three Franklin Taites the Web site wanted to tell me more about. One was a teenager. One was in his late seventies. One was fifty. If any of them was the detective I was looking for, it was the last.

I ran through the pay screen and was awarded with the sterling information that fifty-year-old Franklin Taite lived in Vermont, was married, had three children, and owned a garage that specialized in diesel repair.

That didn't sound anything like the Franklin Taite I knew. It was eleven o'clock by then, certain to earn a frown from Emily if I called. I wrote down the number, thought for a moment, then searched for images of Franklin Taite.

There were photos of three cemeteries, six women, and two males. One was of a teenager in a formal prom photo. The other was of a tall man around fifty next to a Mustang convertible. He had a mane of thick blond hair, a handsome smile, and he and his sports car were in front of a sign that read: BROOKFIELD, VERMONT, POP 1,222.

My Franklin Taite was short, tubby, and had thinning hair he wore in an unfortunate comb-over.

Baffled, I closed the laptop and leaned my bent elbows on the table. Resting my chin on my hands, I considered the pot of purple basil going wild on the windowsill. A soft breeze pushed through the window and the plant's licorice-like fragrance wafted into the kitchen. The number of protections in and around the carriage house had increased over the months I'd lived in Savannah in proportion to the number of threats I'd encountered. The pot of basil was only one.

With garlic, pistachios, olive oil, and lemon juice, it also made a gorgeous pesto.

In this day and age, it seemed like anyone should be able to find anyone else online. Unless, perhaps, if that person didn't exist. But Detective Franklin Taite did exist.

Right?

My mind raced with possibilities. "Have I been misspelling his name all this time?" I asked Mungo.

He didn't respond, other than pointedly staring at the empty dog dish on the floor beside him.

Ignoring his plea for an evening snack, I stood and stretched before climbing the stairs to the loft. Bypassing the secretary's desk in which I kept my altar out of sight, I grabbed the old-school Rolodex off the shelf behind it. Seconds later, I found the business card Taite had given me shortly after we'd met. It looked exactly like Peter Quinn's card, which declared him a detective with the Chatham County Metropolitan Police, only it read "Franklin Taite." So: no spelling error.

What if that wasn't his real name, though? Could he be using an alias?

Could the man I'd believed was telling me the truth about my magical abilities as a lightwitch be an *imposter*?

The thought made my heart beat faster. Agitated, I paced back and forth a few times in the small space before clambering back down the stairs and bursting out the French doors to the back patio. My familiar padded behind me with wide eyes.

Whirling to face him, I said, "What if he lied to me, Mungo? What if . . . I don't even know!" My voiced quavered as a mishmash of emotions cascaded through me. I took a deep breath and looked down into the calming chocolate gaze of my terrier. I bent, scooped him up, and walked out to the dark yard.

The smell of green grass, the fireflies that immediately began to gather in Mungo's presence, the white of the night-blooming moonflowers climbing up the cedar gazebo to our left, and the humid caress of impending dew in the air all settled my monkey mind.

I'd assumed Taite had been telling me the truth, but then again, what had he told me? Not very darn much. So maybe it was the truth and maybe it wasn't. I didn't need him to tell me that I had no desire to dabble in black magic. Nor did I need him to tell me that I had some extra *something* in the magic department. I had my own instincts, and I had the help of the spellbook club when I needed more information or perspective.

"So to heck with Franklin Taite—or whoever he is—and his cryptic declarations," I murmured. "I'll do what I can to help Quinn—and Ben—find Simon Knapp's murderer, but not because some short, bald fibber told me I'm supposed to 'fight evil.' Nope, nuh-uh. It's *my* decision."

I instantly felt a sense of control that I hadn't felt for a while. A smile crept onto my face, and Mungo seemed to sense something, too. He leaned back and opened his mouth in silent doggy laughter.

As I set him down, the pale glow of the moon-flower caught my attention again. True to its name, it reflected the light of the moon from white petals, almost casting its own light in response. I glanced up and saw the waxing gibbous face peering down from the heavens.

"Oh! I almost forgot," I said. "Were you going to remind me?"

Yip! Mungo softly responded.

"Let's go get the tea."

Inside, I retrieved a jar of triple-strength chamomile tea from the counter next to the refrigerator and carefully poured half of it into a mister. I grabbed a flashlight and we went back out, leaving the door open to let the cool night air in, and rounded the corner of the house.

After moving in, I'd carved the vegetable and herb gardens out of the sod by the back fence with a shovel and plenty of effort. I'd arranged water-loving plants along the edges of the small stream that ran across one corner of the yard and had the gazebo built. However, the roses that wound up the iron trellis attached to the eastern side of the house had been there a very, very long time. They exuded a sense of age, even wisdom, from their cracked canes and old-fashioned white flower heads. I'd learned they were Cherokee roses, same as the ones that grew along the Trail of Tears. They were also the Georgia state flower. Perhaps that was why the estate gardener had planted them so long ago, or perhaps it was simply that they could stand a bit less sunshine than other varieties.

Regardless, those ancient flower souls were going through a bit of a battle with black spot and powdery mildew. The mildew had bowed its fungal head to four separate doses of the milk and water solution I'd sprayed on the leaves, but the black spot seemed to be holding out for a shot of poison.

I didn't like poison. First off it was, you know, *poison*. Plus, I felt that as a bona fide green witch, I ought to be able to manage a better cure. Lucy had recommended a superdose of the "plant's physician": chamomile. I'd planted some around the base of each rose—during the dark of the moon, at Bianca's suggestion—and since chamomile was considered a sun plant, I'd asked Archangel Michael, guardian of the South and Fire, to supercharge the healing powers of the fragrant little darlings. Then, again at Bianca's suggestion, I'd been spraying the leaves with the strong chamomile tea during the last quarter of the waxing gibbous moon. Two more days until it would be full, and I was happy to see the black spot appeared to take my ministrations seriously. I imagined creaking sighs of relief from the rose plants as I sprayed them.

Now, that was the kind of magic I loved and the kind I seemed to be quite capable of.

Then I thought of Declan's decision to spend the evening without me, and my satisfaction faded. *That* was a whole other can of worms.

Floral first aid complete, I gave Mungo a bedtime snack of leftover spaghetti and had another cup of tea while he ate. The phone rang as I was rinsing out my cup, and I scooped it off the table.

It was Declan. Relief whooshed through me, and I realized a part of me had been listening and hoping he would call before the night was out.

"Hi," I said with feigned nonchalance. "You're up late." As soon as the words were out, I mentally winced. "Not that you shouldn't be, of course, just because you're tired and all . . ." I trailed off, the hole already deep enough.

"Hi, yourself," he said. "I knew you'd be up and wanted to check in before I hit the sack." Apparently, his response to my babbling was to ignore it. Worked for me.

"Um, about tonight," I started.

"I really am tired. And I needed a little, uh, time alone."

"Oh."

"This murder stuff you seem to attract is, uh, disconcerting, you know?"

"Believe me, I know."

"Not much you can do about it, though, is there?"

"I tried to track down Detective Taite tonight."

"Taite? What for?"

"He's the only one who seems to know why this 'murder stuff,' as you put it, keeps cropping up in my life. I thought maybe he could tell me how to make it stop."

There were a few beats of silence before Declan asked, "And?"

"No luck. He doesn't seem to be working for the New Orleans police anymore. It doesn't matter, though. I don't care anymore."

"I'm not sure I believe that. But I doubt that he can tell you much anyway."

"Why not?"

"Because he didn't tell you before. I mean, why would he keep that kind of information secret?"

I said, "Who knows? Who cares? He always had his own agenda."

"Yeah. Maybe you're right. But, Katie?"

"Hmm?"

"I'll stand with you no matter what you decide you have to do."

My heart warmed at his words. "Thanks," I said in a quiet voice. We changed the subject to sweet somethings for a few minutes and said good night. Soon Mungo and I headed off to bed ourselves, my familiar to dreamland and myself into a thriller I'd chosen from the Honeybee library.

Despite the action-packed pages, the story didn't hold my attention. My thoughts kept ping-ponging between Declan's declaration of support and who might have stuck a knife in Simon Knapp's back. With the novel limp in my hand, my gaze rested on the watercolor of the Irish countryside Declan had given me, charming against the cool Williamsburg-blue walls of my bedroom.

Mungo lifted his head as I got up, retrieved pen and paper from the kitchen, and fluffed my pillows against the wrought-iron bedstead before climbing back in. Within seconds, he was snuggled up against my leg again, and I was making a list.

It started as a list to capture my thoughts about Simon's murder, but soon turned to a task list to tackle first thing at the Honeybee in the morning. Murder or no, we had a lunch to cater and it would be an early morning for me.

I turned out the light but had a harder than usual time sleeping. I dozed in and out, dreaming in fits and starts of knives and blue T-shirts, Ursula's blue-green gaze winging through me as if I were made of nothing more substantial than cotton candy, of lips whispering into Althea's delicate ear, and of the look in Declan's eyes when he realized that he and I were standing next to our second body in less than a year.

At four a.m., I finally gave up and went for a run through the dark streets of Midtown.

Early mornings were sacred to me, and I was lucky to be an early riser who got to enjoy that feeling every day. Unlike the anxious thoughts that sometimes crept unbidden into my brain around two a.m., the dawning of each new day made me feel as if the world was a hopeful, clean slate. Add in the endorphins coursing through my system after my run, and I was a happy camper.

The drive from Midtown into downtown Savannah was precisely long enough to provide the transition from home to work or vice versa. Mungo was strapped into the passenger seat, looking out the window with sleepy, blinking eyes at the silent, dark windows of the buildings we passed, his head nodding as he tried to stay awake. I reached over and stroked the soft patch of fur between his ears and was rewarded with a swipe of bright pink tongue.

Tuesday morning the streets were quiet and calm. Through the open window of the Bug, sixty-four-degree air caressed my skin with the scent of honeysuckle. Then came the faint scent of the Savannah River as we reached the Honeybee. I unlocked the door and carted Mungo into the office. He fell asleep on his club chair within seconds, and I went back out front to flip on lights and rev up the ovens.

Alone in my bakery. Not only mine, of course, but still mine, and still a daily joy. No customers, no sound from the espresso machine, the display case dark, empty and waiting in the silence. I flipped on the lights and dialed up some light classical on the satellite radio. In front of the row of aprons, I stopped and assessed. I didn't feel at all frilly in the wake of a murder, so I bypassed the ruffles and reached for a forest green chef's apron that would go nicely with my simple orange skirt–and–white T-shirt combo. As I cinched the ties behind my back, my mind ran through the list of to-dos I'd written down the night before.

Within twenty minutes, the sourdough loaves that had been slow rising in the refrigerator were baking at high heat in one of the ovens, rounds of rosemary Parmesan scones were sliced into farls on sheet pans, and I was dolloping the batter for peach and molasses muffins into tins. Into another oven with all that, followed by a loaf of pecan sandie biscotti for its first baking. Three batches of cookies came next, the dough prepared the day before so all I had to do was plop mounds onto more sheet pans. The oatmeal cookies were loaded with dried cherries, chunks of dark chocolate, and glazed almonds. The molasses cookies would spread as they baked into thin, slightly chewy discs. The coconut bar cookies spiced with cinnamon and a dash of nutmeg boasted a hefty number of black walnuts. Between them all, Lucy and I had invoked wishes for protection, fidelity, prosperity, peace, and health, depending on the native energy of the ingredients.

Out came the sourdough, in went the next batch of items to bake, and then I dove into the lunch preparation for the movie set. I was finishing the Caprese skewers made with cherry-sized balls of fresh mozzarella, yellow pear tomatoes, and rich purple leaves of basil when Lucy breezed in the door.

"Good morning, Katie!"

"Well, good morning. You seem chipper today."

"New day, new beginning," she crooned, heading for the aprons like I had. I smiled at her reflection of my own earlier thoughts.

"My goodness, you've done a lot already," she said, tying on her favorite tie-dyed pinafore over a hemp skirt and blouse. "Why don't you let me take over the luncheon items and you can start the choux."

I agreed with alacrity. Choux, or pâté à choux, was the simple pastry dough that created the crisp, airy base for profiteroles and éclairs. We'd recently added éclairs to the menu—half sweet and half savory, and with the fillings often changing as we experimented. Today's savory options would be a sweet potato filling with a maple glaze, and a filling of goat cheese and sun-dried tomato with pesto piped on top.

After heating milk and butter to a boil, I took the mixture off the heat and dumped in high-gluten flour. Stirring, stirring, and stirring some more until the dough came away from the edge of the pan gave me a real workout. I added in beaten eggs, bit by bit, and by the time they were all incorporated and the dough looked more like a smooth and shiny batter, I'd broken a sweat.

Er, glow.

As I was piping the éclair-sized lengths of dough onto a buttered sheet pan, Lucy came up on the other side of the worktable.

"All done with that," she said. "I can finish up

the rest of the lunch items after we open. In the meantime . . ." She paused.

I looked up and saw her grin. "Uh-oh. What do you have up your sleeve?"

"I think a new éclair filling might be in order."

The piping bag hovered in my hand. "Such as?"

"Vanilla."

"Vanilla what?"

"Just vanilla custard, with lots of tiny speckles of seeds, strong and classic."

"Isn't that kind of boring?"

"Why, Katie Lightfoot, I'm surprised at you. Vanilla beans come from an exotic orchid, after all. Good heavens. What's boring about that? Besides, we'll glaze the tops with chocolate ganache."

Then I cottoned to her motive. "Who, precisely, are these special vanilla custard éclairs intended for?"

She beamed. "Mrs. Standish."

I smiled and slowly nodded. "Of course. To attract love back into her life."

"It's what we do, sweetie! Now, let me think about the right incantation for her."

Chapter 8

We declared the vanilla-filled, chocolate-topped éclairs the daily special, dubbing them "Black and Tans" and placing them front and center in the display case with tasty little samples by the register. When Mrs. Standish stopped by for her late-morning sugar fix, she took one bite and ordered half a dozen in a bag. Lucy complied with a knowing grin and a glint in her eye.

I had to admit, I was curious about who Mrs. Standish might invite into her life after two years without her Harry. He'd passed away before I moved to town, so I didn't know what sort of man he had been—or whether she'd be attracted to the same again or someone completely new.

She wasn't the only one who grabbed up the Black and Tans, and I wondered how many kindled or rekindled romances might be around the corner for Honeybee customers.

At eleven thirty Bianca and Jaida pushed through the door. Lucy had called them to help out, knowing I wanted to take lunch over to the movie set myself. They settled in at a sun-drenched table by the window as I poured two glasses of sweet tea, garnished them with fresh mint, and took them over.

"Thanks for coming in to help," I said. "I know you're both super-busy."

Bianca waved her hand. "Today I am a woman of leisure. Colette's at school, and I hired another part-time employee at the shop so I'd have more time to play the market."

Bianca Devereaux's wineshop was located near the river on Factors Walk. She tended toward fabrics that flowed when she moved and accented her natural gracefulness. Today she wore a whisper-light linen skirt and tunic combination, and several strands of tiny silver beads wound around her neck, wrist, and ankle. Her black hair was piled up to show her long neck, a few strands curling artfully around her ears. She made being beautiful look so easy, and she was also one of the nicest people I knew. Her focus on traditional Wiccan practices with a special emphasis on moon magic was one of the many aspects of magic the spellbook club had been schooling me in ever since I'd discovered my talents and joined their number.

Now she reached into her big Prada bag, extracted an electronic tablet and opened it. Instantly, what looked like a stock trading application bloomed on the surface. "In fact, I thought I might do a little research before you go."

Jaida smoothed her suit skirt, opened a leather portfolio, and took out a sheaf of papers. "And I brought paperwork I need to complete by end of day, figuring I could step in anytime things get busy."

"Perfect," Lucy said, bringing them napkin and silverware setups. "Hungry?"

"Am I!" Bianca said. "I skipped breakfast, waiting until I got here for one of your éclairs."

Jaida uncapped a pen, laughing. "So did I."

"What kind?" Lucy asked with a grin and listed their options.

"Oh, let's try them all," Bianca said. "Share?"

Jaida nodded.

Well, at least Bianca was eating something substantial. I loved her to death, but sometimes that woman seemed to subsist on nothing but fruit and nuts.

I realized that with all the rushing around, I hadn't eaten, and no doubt Mungo was getting cranky about missing second breakfast—his first being peanut butter toast before dawn. Grabbing a still-warm scone for myself, I set a small dish of Tasso ham and pickled okra on the floor of the office for my familiar.

Mungo eyed me with reproach for feeding him so late, but it didn't last long once he'd launched himself from the club chair to the floor and began chowing down in earnest.

"You're welcome," I said.

He grunted without looking up.

"When you're done with your snack, do you

want to come with me to the set? I have to set up lunch pretty soon."

This time he stopped eating long enough to confirm with a *yip!*

A breeze had freshened off the river, greeting me when I got out of the Bug on Congress Street. Mungo jumped out, and I attached the long lead to his collar. "I know you don't need it, but it's the law, and I don't have enough hands to carry you and the food." As it was, I'd borrowed a collapsible cart from Croft Barrow's bookstore next door to the Honeybee so I could wheel the food onto the set.

As I loaded it with boxes and bags, a movement caught my eye. I looked up to see Declan hurrying toward me from one of the only three tents still standing. I'd called to see if he'd be available to help before I left the Honeybee, alert for any indication of a rift between us. The conversation had been too short for me to really be able to tell.

When he reached my side, he swooped me into a hug, lifting me off my feet, and gave me a firm smack on the lips. "Missed you."

I grinned, pushing my worries back into their brain closet and shutting the door. "Good."

He laughed. "Fine. I guess I deserve that, since I was the one who begged off last night. Tell me what I can do."

I managed the cart across the bumpy road, Mungo trotting at my side, while Declan hefted a cooler full of drinks as if it were full of packing peanuts. My gaze cut sideways to the muscles bulging in his arms, and despite my protests that big muscly guys weren't necessarily my type, the sight sent a quiver of excitement all the way down to my toes.

Everything had been moved away from the crime scene to the far corner of Reynolds Square. It looked like the filming was down to bare-bones: three tents, a much shorter patch of concrete camouflaged to look like an eighteenth-century lane with an unhitched carriage sitting in the middle of it, and only a few people milling around, apparently between shots. Even the horses were gone. Only the number of looky-loos had increased.

"This is all that's left?" I asked.

Declan made a face. "Niklas isn't making much of a secret of how unhappy he is about having to change their plans."

"Yeah—too bad someone died in the middle of his movie," I said. Still, the director's disgruntlement pointed to a possible lack of motive, as did his frank conversation with Quinn about how Simon had stepped in to fix the situation after Egan had cheated on his wife.

Rounding the corner of the resituated catering canopy, I stopped cold. Platters of food marched down the long buffet table, beginning with pimento cheese dip and ending with a sloppily frosted chocolate sheet cake. In between, squares of macaroni and cheese congealed in the breeze, a fancy serving bowl of colorless grits hunched next to a platter of greasy-looking fried green tomatoes with no sauce. Two platters held piles of waffles, one garnished with split sausages and the other plain. My critical eye noted the potato salad looked pretty good, as did the deviled eggs. In fact, all of the food might have been fine if kept warm . . . or cool.

Okay. I was trying to be charitable, when in fact I was really angry. I whirled on Declan. "They already have lunch set up!"

He looked stricken. "Oh, hon. I had no idea. I've been keeping people away from the scene they're shooting in that horse carriage for the last hour or so."

My shoulders slumped. Of course he would have told me if he'd known. "Sorry. I shouldn't have snapped. It's just . . ." My words trailed off as I limply pointed at the table.

He grinned. "If that was you 'snapping,' you need to work on your technique." He gave my shoulder a squeeze. "Maybe you should set up your stuff at the other end and let people decide what they want to eat." Stepping toward the door, he said over his shoulder, "I'll stop back when I can, but curiosity is running high since the murder. We've already had a couple incidents where folks have tried to sneak in, so I'd better get out there." He ducked out, leaving me alone with Mungo.

I grumbled under my breath and turned back to the classic Southern spread. It looked exactly like the fare Simon had described.

"I thought he fired Bonner Catering," I mused

to my familiar while I mentally scrambled. He made a low noise in the back of his throat.

"I hired them back," a high-pitched voice said behind me. Simon's assistant, the one who had arrived so soon after his death laden with fresh cheese and an air of utter bewilderment, entered the canopy. He still looked bewildered, blinking at me from behind his round glasses, head bobbing on his long neck.

"You might have alerted us of that fact, Mr. . . . ?"

"Glade," he reminded me. "Owen Glade. I'm the new production coordinator."

"Right. Of course you are. But even though he's, um, gone, Simon Knapp hired us to provide lunch to your crew today."

Owen put his bony fists on his hips and tried a glare. I felt bad for the guy, but we'd spent a lot of money and a lot of time to put together a small feast for what was left of the cast and crew. Not to mention we'd determined to do the same for as long as the filming was going on.

"Well, he never told me that," the former assistant said. "I don't even know who you are, other than seeing you and that dog on the set last night."

In my sweaty running clothes. Great. I tipped my head. "I'm Katie Lightfoot from the Honeybee Bakery. How exactly do you think your lunch showed up yesterday?"

He started to stick out his lower lip, then seemed to realize what he was doing. "How should I know? Simon never told me anything, just ordered me around. Owen, do this. Owen, find so-

and-so, Owen, pick up the dry cleaning, blah, blah, blah."

"Er . . . isn't that your job?" I asked in as neutral a tone as I could manage.

Owen's face colored, and his eyes flashed behind the round lenses. "Well, it's not anymore."

"So there's a new assistant, then?" I asked.

His nostrils flared in what I took as a negative. I could only imagine what Niklas Egan thought about Owen taking over for Simon. Given what he'd said to Quinn about needing Simon's special skill at getting things done, I doubted Owen would hold the doer-and-shaker position for long.

In the meantime, though, I stood my ground. "I'm very sorry your boss didn't inform you about hiring us, and I'm sorrier than I can say that he's gone now. However, we had an agreement and had to go out of our way to accommodate his request."

Owen's feet shifted, and uncertainty flickered across his features. I straightened my shoulders and opened my mouth to speak again when Althea Cole swept in. Literally. Unlike the day before, when her costume had screamed "simple country girl," today she wore a peach satin brocade gown with full bustle and dripping with lace that swished along the ground with each step. The frothy hat I'd tried on in the wardrobe tent the day before was firmly tied over her cascading red curls, and long fake eyelashes gave her a doelike demeanor.

Until she opened her mouth. "Well, isn't that

too bad. Do you have a signed contract with Simon?"

My heart sank, but I raised my chin. "We had a verbal agreement."

"Which he can no longer confirm. Did he prepay you?"

I shook my head, feeling like an idiot.

Althea sniffed. "Well, it looks like you're out of luck, Miss Lightfoot." Sarcasm dripped from her voice when she said my name.

What's this woman's problem?

At my feet, Mungo emitted a low growl.

Althea's eyes cut to him. "And you'd better get that little beast out of here. I'm terribly allergic to dogs."

I swore my familiar rolled his eyes. I couldn't blame him—the catering tent was open on one side, and even my violent allergies to Lucy's Honeybee wouldn't have been triggered in those circumstances.

"Where is Mr. Egan?" I asked.

"Oh, no, you don't. You haven't got a leg to stand on, so you just take your little bakery stuff and go on home." Althea could do imperious better than most. I was pretty sure she wasn't acting, though.

My jaw set, and I struggled to keep from using my Voice. "Where is Mr. Egan?" I asked Owen this time.

Althea crossed her arms and glared at me, but I ignored her and focused on Simon's replacement. He nervously licked his lips. "I rehired Bonner Catering. That's all there is to it."

"Fine," I said. "I'll find Mr. Egan myself. Because I have no intention of letting you stiff the Honeybee just because Simon didn't keep you in the loop." I strode away, Mungo trotting at my side. Althea's lip curled up as I passed her.

"Wait," Owen said.

I paused and looked over my shoulder.

He made a vague gesture. "This appears to be a simple misunderstanding. Go ahead and set up the food you brought, and I'll cut you a check."

"Oh, for heaven's sake, Owen," Althea said. "Don't be such a wimp."

He visibly flinched at her words. "This one time," he said to me. "But then that's it."

Slowly, I said, "Okay." Reaching into my tote bag, I retrieved the invoice I'd printed out before leaving the bakery.

Owen took it and nodded. "Fine." He stalked off, and I began unloading lunch from the trolley.

Althea watched me, her lip slightly curled as she took in the different kinds of skewers and kabobs.

After several seconds, I stopped arranging the shrimp on their bed of ice and looked her in the eye. "It must be quite gratifying to everyone working on this movie to know how concerned you are with the day-to-day workings of craft services."

She held my gaze; then her eyes narrowed before she whirled around and left without a word.

I stared after her. Why was the famous star of the movie so worried about who supplied the catering? If she'd asked a single question about the food, I might have understood, but she hadn't. Furthermore, her figure was so petite, I doubted that she ate even as little as Bianca did.

It seemed to be all about some kind of power play now that Simon was gone. Puzzled, I began setting up a three-tiered tray for the salad kabobs.

Owen returned with the check and turned to go after depositing it in my hand.

"Hang on," I said.

He paused, looking at me over his shoulder.

"I really am sorry your boss got, well, you know."

"Thanks," he said.

"Were you guys close?"

Finally, he faced me. "I guess." He seemed impatient, or maybe it was simply shyness.

I wished for Ben's ability to put anyone at ease. "I heard Simon was a guy you could go to, to get things done," I tried.

Owen peered myopically at me in silence.

"You know what I mean?" I asked.

"Not really," he said. "You don't really seem to know what you mean, either."

Touché.

"How did you come to work for Simon? Are you from around here?"

He hesitated. "No. I'm from Boulder Creek, California. Simon was working there, for another company. I have a background in theater and talked him into giving me a try. It worked out, and he brought me on his next job."

"You must have learned so much from him." Like how to "fix" things? I wondered.

"I did what I was told," he said. "Now I'll go ahead and do what Simon would have told me to do anyway. It wasn't like he was supersmart or anything. He liked people to think so, but what he did wasn't that hard."

"Oh. Well, okay. Good luck, then," I said.

As he left, I heard him mutter, "Don't need luck."

"Odd little duck," I murmured to Mungo, who concurred with a slight woof. I finished rearranging Bonner Catering's food and fitting in the Honeybee offerings. Mungo watched from under a folding chair as I gathered up all the boxes, bags, and coolers and stuffed them back onto the book trolley. I made a few last adjustments to the presentation and turned to go.

A figure stood in the opening to the tent. The bright sunlight reflected off her white-blond hair, creating a nimbus around her head and obscuring her features. Then Ursula stepped farther inside and the effect vanished. She wore plain khaki shorts and a sleeveless green shirt that showcased the defined muscles in her arms. In that moment, she looked a lot more like a personal trainer than a woo-woo psychic.

Of course, with my short hair and sensible shoes, I didn't exactly look like most people's idea of a witch, either.

"Hi, Katie." She greeted me as if we were old friends. Then she spied the plates of food on the cloth-covered table and made a beeline for one end. "Yes! I was hoping you'd bring more of these." She grabbed two of the loaded oatmeal cookies and promptly took a bite out of one of them. "I ate almost all of them yesterday. Ha!"

"Glad you like them," I ventured.

She reached down with her other hand and scratched Mungo under the chin. He gazed up at her with wide eyes but seemed to enjoy the attention.

"Althea said you were in here," she said, then lowered her voice. "She doesn't really care for you, does she?"

"I noticed. Any idea why?"

Ursula shook her head and took another bite. After she swallowed, she said, "Did you want to talk to me?"

I lifted one eyebrow. "As a matter of fact, I did. I suppose you knew that from your 'good authority,' though."

She laughed. It was a full, free sound, and she looked genuinely delighted. "Nope. Figured that one out on my own."

Two men came in and squirted antibacterial gel onto their hands at the sanitation station. They both wore shorts and T-shirts that read A. DENDUM PRODUCTIONS on the back.

Ursula gestured me toward the exit. "This place is about to fill up with hungry cast and crew. Let's get out of here."

Quickly, I tucked the book trolley around the

corner of the catering tent, and Mungo and I followed her across the square to one of the RVs parked on Abercorn Street. She opened the door on the side and stuck her head inside. I heard her say, "Susie? Lunch is ready. You might want to grab some before the good stuff is gone."

Susie Little. Her alibi.

Thirty seconds later, a curly-haired woman wearing a loose white jacket over a bright yellow sundress stepped out, nodded at me, and headed for the catering tent. Ursula waved me inside. Picking up Mungo, I went up the steps and ducked through the doorway.

The place reeked of hair spray. A long row of round lightbulbs illuminated the mirrors running down one wall. Deep, comfortable chairs at each of four stations hinted at the long periods of time actors spent being coiffed and made up for their screen time. A shelving unit boasted a dozen wigs perched on plastic forms, ranging from elaborate updos for women to men's neat ponytails and gray curls. Cases of makeup ranged down the counter, and more peeked out from drawers. Hair-taming implements hung from hooks at regular intervals: dryers, curlers, flatirons, and diffusers.

Ursula plopped into one of the chairs and swiveled it in my direction. "Take a load off. The little dog can wander around. He won't hurt anything."

Mungo looked a bit insulted as I set him down and snapped off his lead. "Of course he won't hurt anything," I said, and he wagged his tail once in thanks. I sat in the chair next to Ursula and regarded her in silence.

"So . . . ," she prompted.

"You tell me. After all, you're the one who came up to me out of the blue and said I'm supposed to find Simon's killer."

"Yep, that's true," she said with a grin.

"What, exactly, is so funny?"

"Well, you are, to start. That wasn't news to you. I could tell. There's something about you."

She doesn't know I'm a witch.

I took a deep breath. On one hand, I liked Ursula's easy manner. On the other, I wasn't sure she needed to be so darn amused at my discomfort. Putting my ego aside, I asked, "So? Who told you?"

The humor faded from her expression. "Not one of my usual crew of spirit guides. Someone I've never had contact with before."

"So you're saying a spirit told you?"

"Well, yeah." The way she said it made it sound like, well, *duh.* "You know that's what I do, right?"

"I heard you were a psychic, but I don't know how that works."

A decisive nod. "Right. Okay, so I hear dead people." She grinned again. "Sort of. Sometimes. I have a crew of three spirits who I have regular access to. But sometimes others come to me unbidden, and I can often call on spirits for others."

"Like for Althea?"

"Althea—well, that's probably covered by

something like psychic/client privilege, but that's part of why she keeps me around. The other part is keeping her skinny ass skinny."

I smiled.

"Anyway, yesterday as I'm standing there with everyone else, staring at poor Simon, I felt a new presence. And it told me about you. That's all."

"Do you know who it was?" I asked.

She shrugged. "Someone who knew you in this life, that's for sure."

"Nonna," I breathed.

"Who's that?" Ursula asked.

"My grandmother. She's, uh, made herself known before."

Her eyebrow arched. "Is that so? Interesting. Still, it wasn't her this time."

I blinked. "Then who was it?"

She frowned and looked out the window, seeming to hear something I couldn't. As I watched, a shiver ran down my back. Mungo made a low noise in his throat and trotted back from where he had been exploring to lean against my leg. Another nod and Ursula returned her attention to me.

"My guides say the name started with an F. Francis? Fitz . . . No, I think it's Frank. Did you know a Frank?"

I started to shake my head, then stopped and stared at her. "Franklin?"

She pointed her finger at me. "Bingo. That's the guy."

"But you only communicate with the spirits of those who have passed over, right?"

Realization dawned in her eerie green-blue eyes. "Oh, honey. You didn't know?"

Thoughts racing, I picked up Mungo and held him close to my throat. Franklin Taite was *dead*?

Chapter 9

I wanted to ask Ursula what else she knew about Franklin Taite, but the hair and makeup artist returned with Steve Dawes in tow. He looked at me curiously as she settled him into a chair and began working his long hair into a ponytail, complete with a little bow to hold it back.

"Very nice," I muttered as I carried Mungo to the door where Ursula was waiting. I was still reeling.

He grinned. "Thanks."

The woman working on his gorgeous tresses didn't crack a smile, however. Apparently, getting that bow right was serious work.

Then Steve got a good look at my face and drew his eyebrows together. "Katie? Everything okay?"

I shook my head. "I don't know. I'll tell you about it later."

Back on the sidewalk, Ursula said, "So you two know each other pretty well, I take it."

"We're friends." I reattached Mungo's leash,

and we began walking back toward the catering tent.

"Althea seems to like him a lot," Ursula said.

"Bully for her," I said, still distracted. I had so many questions I didn't know where to start. I settled on, "What else can you tell me about Franklin?"

Her grimace carried a note of apology. "Sorry. Only the name and the information he told me to pass on to you. He hasn't returned since that initial contact."

"He didn't say anything else about me?" *Like I've been known to glow when under pressure?*

She looked curious. "Nope. Anything you want to tell me?"

I sidestepped her question with, "He specifically said to tell me that I'd find Simon's killer? That wasn't your idea?"

"Oh, no. I hear things about people all the time, but I usually keep them to myself. Hearing news from a psychic isn't always . . . welcome." She looked at me sideways. "He was pretty clear that I needed to pass that message on, though."

We walked a few steps in silence.

"I'll help you load up your car if you want," Ursula offered.

"That would be great." My biggest question was one I couldn't very well ask the psychic herself: Should I trust her? She was personable and engaging, and I felt an unexpected kinship with her. Still, conmen—and women—were known to be quite personable, and while I wasn't exactly naive, I knew I could be fooled. It didn't seem like it would be that hard to fool Althea Cole, either.

Yet why would Ursula try to deceive me? What would be in it for her? She already had her paying gig with Althea and barely knew me from Eve. Plus, it was hard to be skeptical since I wholeheartedly believed in magic and had actually talked with my dead grandmother on more than one occasion.

So there was that.

I retrieved the wheeled cart, and, Mungo trotting ahead, we pushed out to my Bug on one of the walkways that crisscrossed the square. Niklas Egan hurried past with a sheaf of papers in his hand, heading toward where Van Grayson stood waiting with a cameraman next to the horseless carriage.

"Oh, I have a Volkswagen Bug at home," Ursula exclaimed when we reached the car. "It's one of the old ones, though, from the sixties. Red convertible. I adore it."

"It's been a good little car, seen me through a lot. Yours sounds like fun, especially the convertible part." I found myself wondering if she really had a Volkswagen. Could it be a ploy to try to bond with me?

She grimaced. "Not that I get to drive it much. Althea travels a lot, and she always wants me to go with her."

"How long have you been working for her?" I asked.

"Almost three years now." Her strange eyes cut

toward me. "The money is a lot better than working at the gym or my private practice."

"Your practice as a psychic?"

She nodded.

"I heard Simon was good at taking care of
things. Someone used the word 'fixer.'"

Ursula laughed. "I bet they did."

"Did he fix anything for Althea?"

She stopped and put her hands on her hips.
"You don't like her very much, either, do you?"

"I was just wondering who might have a motive to kill Simon."

"Hmm. Guess you're taking Franklin's message
seriously. I can honestly say I don't know of any
reason why Althea would want Simon dead,
though."

I hesitated, then plunged ahead. "Do you think
you could contact Franklin again?"

We reached the car, and I opened the door.
Mungo jumped in and then wiggled over to the
passenger seat.

"Maybe," Ursula said in a musing tone as we
stacked the empty containers on the seat.

I snapped my fingers and suddenly stood upright. "Oh, my goddess," I said without thinking
how that might sound. "Why couldn't you simply
contact Simon and ask him who stabbed him?"
Talk about streamlining the investigation!

A speculative look crossed her face. "You know,
that's not a terrible idea. I felt his spirit hanging
around right after he died, and he knows what I
do. He might be willing."

"Why wouldn't he want justice?" I couldn't keep the excitement out of my voice. Grabbing a couple of garbage bags, I rolled down the window for Mungo and shut the car door.

"You want me to take those back to the catering tent?" she asked, eyeing the plastic bags.

"I'll do it. Might as well do some of the preliminary cleanup."

"I want to snag another one of those cookies, so I'll go with you." We started back. "If I contact Simon, I want to do it right," Ursula said.

"Meaning?"

"A séance. It will help to have the energy of other people to reach to the other side."

"Makes sense to me," I said as we reentered the tent. The tables were littered with paper plates and napkins, but I was pleased to see the majority of the Honeybee's lunch had been decimated.

"When would be a good time?" I asked. "Tonight?" Then I saw Althea still sitting at one of the tables with Owen Glade.

Great.

She had a square of cold macaroni and cheese on the plate in front of her. When she saw me looking, she stuffed a big bite in her mouth and chewed with great gusto. Glancing at her tiny waist, I wondered if she might be wearing a corset. Owen sat next to her, nibbling on a flaccid fried green tomato. He gazed at her like a puppy with a new and particularly shiny toy.

"Tonight should be fine," Ursula said, grabbing another oatmeal cookie.

My stomach clamored. Woman could not live on scone alone. I took one of the loaded oatmeal cookies, too.

"Come over to the house where we're staying," Ursula said, then louder, "I bet Althea will happy to help, won't you?"

"Help with what?" The movie star sounded suspicious.

"A séance tonight. We're going to try to contact Simon on the other side to see if he'll reveal who murdered him." Ursula said it as if contacting the dead was the most natural thing in the world, like going to the grocery store or mowing the lawn.

Althea came to her feet. "At *our* house? Are you out of your mind? I'm not inviting a stranger into our house for a séance."

"Well, honey, it's not exactly ours," Ursula said. "Simon only rented it for two weeks." And then, in an aside to me, "It's haunted as the dickens, too."

Steve entered and steered a direct course to the food table. I could tell he was listening, however, and wondered whether he might have been eavesdropping outside.

"Actually, I'm hoping I can invite a few friends," I said. "Since you said the more people are there, the more likely you'll be successful." I wanted as many members of the spellbook club at the séance as possible. It would be harder to fool all of us if Ursula was a fraud, and if she wasn't, then I figured our natural affinity for working together would add extra oomph to the proceedings.

"Absolutely not." Althea actually stamped her foot. Owen blinked up at her.

I struggled to keep from laughing at her antics as Steve took his plate, piled high with satay and melon skewers, to the place across from Althea. He sat down and snagged her gaze. She stared down at him for a long moment before finally taking her seat again. Owen directed a petulant look at Steve, got up, and went to the food table.

I was lifting the cookie to my mouth when Ursula's fingers gripped my wrist and pulled my hand away. With her other hand, she took my cookie away.

"What the—?" I said.

She shook her head curtly and laid the cookies down on an empty plate, surreptitiously covering them with a napkin.

I frowned at her. Who did she think she was?

She leaned toward me and said in an undertone. "There's something wrong. I don't know what, but trust me."

Wrong? With my cookies?

"Althea, why wouldn't you want to help find Simon's killer?" Steve asked in a gentle voice, redirecting my attention back to them.

"It's not that," Althea said.

"Don't you believe in Ursula's abilities?" he asked.

"Don't be silly. Of course I do. She's *my* psychic."

I glanced at my companion, but she appeared unperturbed by her employer's possessiveness.

"Then what's the problem?" Steve asked.

Althea pointed at me. "She is."

He turned and looked at me. "Really? What did Katie ever do to you?"

"I, uh . . ."

"Nothing at all, right?" He didn't seem to be using his Voice, the one that literally compelled people, but Althea nonetheless responded. "I guess not."

His voice lowered so that we couldn't hear the words, but Althea seemed to soften further. "Althea, what do you say?" Steve said in a normal tone.

"You can have the séance at the house, of course. We all want justice for Simon, after all." She smiled at me, the very picture of graciousness.

I smiled as well. "Thank you so much, Ms. Cole."

"Althea, please."

"Um, okay," I said.

All of a sudden, I heard Ursula cry, "Owen, *don't*," from beside me.

He'd taken one of the oatmeal cookies and was about to take a bite. Waving it in her face, he asked, "Why not? Are you such a big fan of that Honeybee place that you don't want anyone else eating what the other caterer brought?"

I was about to point out that those cookies, even though they were sitting next to Bonner Catering's chocolate cake, were actually from "that Honeybee place" when he stuffed half the cookie in his mouth.

"No!" Ursula reached for his arm.

He chewed with a defiant look in his watery eyes.

"There's something wrong with it!" the psychic insisted.

Fear suddenly brightened in Owen's eyes, and a strangulated groan came from his throat. I watched with horror as his face crumpled with revulsion. He clamped his hand over his mouth and bolted from the tent.

"Oh, dear," Althea said, dabbing at the corner of her mouth with a paper napkin.

From outside, we heard the sound of loud retching, then worse as Owen was sick. The sound repeated over and over. Steve jumped to his feet and ran out. To my amazement, Althea took another bite of congealed macaroni and cheese. I swallowed hard and looked away.

Puzzlement creasing her brow, Ursula pushed the napkin-covered plate on the table behind us to one side. "We should put aside the rest of those cookies."

"Indeed," Althea said. "It seems the Honeybee Bakery could poison us all."

I felt the blood drain from my face. "But . . ." I gestured toward the disgusting noises still coming from the other side of the canvas. "Ursula, you had two of those oatmeal cookies earlier, and you're fine."

"There's something wrong with these, though, and with the one that Owen ate."

My breath hitched in my throat. "How do you know?"

"Let's just say I have it on good authority." She shook her head. "I only wish my guides gave me more complete information sometimes."

Yeah, I thought. *Me too*.

The assistant production coordinator was so violently ill that Ben called an ambulance. Steve stayed with the poor guy until it got there, but Althea seemed to have evaporated. I'd have speculated that her sensibilities were too delicate for such distasteful goings-on if I hadn't seen her stuffing her face right in the middle of it all.

Niklas Egan had added to the festivities with another string of epithets directed at no one in particular, and Van Grayson had lived up to his name, his face turning a sickly shade of wallpaper paste when he'd heard Owen dry heaving.

I shuddered, remembering. "Will he be okay?" I asked my uncle as they wheeled Simon's assistant away.

"I think so," Ben said. "Whatever disagreed with him didn't stay in his stomach for very long."

My appetite had flown and didn't seem inclined to return anytime soon. Funny how hearing someone be violently sick was almost worse than seeing a dead body.

"Ursula said there's something wrong with the cookies." After she'd said that, she strode out of the tent with a firm sense of purpose, but I had no idea where she'd gone.

Ben looked surprised. "From the Honeybee?"

I nodded. "The loaded oatmeal cookies. I can't

imagine what I could have done wrong. All the ingredients are innocuous. The most unstable thing would be the butter, and if that went bad for some reason, it would only taste unpleasant, not make anyone ill like that. At least I think so. Besides, the cookies Ursula ate earlier today were perfectly fine."

His brow furrowed. "That's pretty suspicious, don't you think? Especially the day after someone is murdered. I've never known you to make mistakes baking, and I'd think if something wasn't right, the whole batch would have been affected. No, I'm sure you didn't do anything wrong, Katie," he said. "And we can't afford to have the Honeybee's reputation sullied. I'm calling Peter."

The ambulance drove away. Declan was busy keeping people out of the square since so many had been attracted to the sketchy perimeter of the set after yesterday's swarm of police and then today's visit from the ambulance.

I couldn't really blame them. I wanted to know what the heck was going on, too.

In the empty catering tent, I opened a garbage bag with the intention of cleaning up, but slowly sank onto one of the benches instead. Once more I mentally ran through mixing the oatmeal cookies. It had been a huge batch, which we then kept for a couple of days in the refrigerator so we could easily bake fresh cookies throughout the day. Portions of that same batch had been served to Honeybee customers already. Other than a small incantation to give an extra kick to the prosperity-

producing aspects of the cinnamon and the healing and love contained in the chunks of dark
chocolate, no strange ingredients had gone into
those cookies.

Either something else had made Owen sick, or
someone had tampered with the cookies. In the
latter case, I doubted the police would want me to
touch anything.

Great. First I'd lost the catering job for the Honeybee for the rest of the week, and now the catering tent itself was a potential crime scene.

Ursula opened the side of the tent wider and
came to join me.

"Where did you run off to?" I asked.

"I was awfully vocal about how much I liked
those cookies," she said. "I wanted to see who was
hanging around."

I tipped my head to the side. "You think someone was trying to poison you specifically?"

She shrugged. "Like I said, I ate most of those
cookies yesterday."

"But why would anyone want to do that?" I
asked.

"Perhaps they overheard us talking about the
séance tonight."

"Oh," I breathed. "Of course the murderer
wouldn't want Simon to reveal who killed him.
But how would anyone have time? We'd just come
up with the idea."

She shook her head. "I don't know. We'd have
seen anyone around the cookies once we were in
the catering tent talking with Althea and Owen. I

suppose Steve could have slipped something into the cookies when he was getting his lunch . . ."

I gave a definitive shake of my head. "It wasn't Steve."

Her eyebrows rose. "Then it would have to have been someone who heard us talking by your car."

"Niklas? Or Van? Were they close enough to hear?" I asked. "Because I don't remember anyone else being around."

"I'm not going to accuse anyone until we find out what's in those cookies," Ursula said. "I saw the police cars arriving. I assume you called them?"

"Ben did." I touched her forearm with my fingertips. She felt cayenne hot, and I realized I could physically feel her anger. "Are you still up for the séance tonight?"

Her jaw set. "You bet I am."

Peter Quinn came in then with a couple of uniformed police officers carrying their own bags.

"Leave everything as it is," he said.

"Don't worry." I rose. "I know the drill."

"Ben said someone was poisoned."

"Owen Glade," Ursula said, also coming to her feet. "He's already on his way to the hospital."

"What happened?" Quinn asked.

We took turns telling him. "And those are the two cookies we were about to eat when Owen got so sick." I indicated the two oatmeal treats Ursula had covered with napkins. "I've racked my brain and can't see how it could be the Honeybee's fault."

He removed one of the napkins. "I hope not. My wife brought home half a dozen of these a few days ago." His face was serious as a tomb when he looked up. "Don't worry. We'll get to the bottom of this."

"Do you think this incident has anything to do with Simon Knapp's death?" I asked, daring a glance at my psychic companion.

"Sure would be a coincidence if it didn't," Quinn said.

Beside me, Ursula pressed her lips together.

Chapter 10

I'd been gone from the Honeybee a lot longer than I'd planned, so while I walked back to my car, I called Lucy to check in.

"Jaida had to go file her paperwork at the courthouse, but Bianca is still here and we're doing fine," she said. "When do you think you'll be back?"

"I'm on my way," I said.

"Did you find out anything?"

"Not anything very useful." Except that Franklin Taite might be dead. "There was a rather . . . unsavory development, though. The new production coordinator became ill after eating one of our oatmeal cookies."

"Oh, no! Is he allergic to chocolate or nuts?"

My steps slowed. "I don't know. I guess it's a possibility. He got really sick to his stomach, though. Don't food allergies typically give people hives or make it hard to breathe?"

"From what I know, yes."

"Well, he's at the hospital, so they'll know what to do," I said.

"Oh, no! It was that bad?" she asked.

"Definitely that bad. Ben thinks someone tampered with the cookies." As did Ursula, but that was a little harder to explain.

"What? Why would anyone do that?" Lucy asked.

"I don't know. Detective Quinn is looking into it. And there's more bad news—at least for us," I said. "Before he got sick, the new production coordinator hired the old caterer back. I barely managed to get paid for today's meal."

"Oh, sweetie. I'm so sorry."

"It would have been a challenge anyway," I said. "A lucrative one, but still."

There was a long pause before she tentatively asked, "They don't think you did something to the cookies out of spite, do they? To get back at the new guy for rehiring the other caterer?"

My stomach sank. "Honestly, that never occurred to me, Luce. Quinn didn't give that impression, but then again, he might not know we got fired this morning. Darn it. I hope he doesn't pull the same kind of nonsense he did when he accused Ben of murder last year."

"I'm sure that won't happen," my aunt soothed. "You two are friends now."

"Hmm," I murmured, noncommittal. "There is one other thing I want to give you a heads-up about."

"More?" She sounded wary now.

"It's a good thing. At least I think so."

"Katie," came my aunt's gentle voice. "Just tell me."

"Remember me telling you about the psychic?"

"The one who said you'd find Simon's killer."

"Well, she agreed to hold a séance tonight to try to contact Simon Knapp himself," I said.

"Oh, honey! That's a wonderful idea." Lucy's voice trilled with excitement.

"Will you come? She said I could invite some friends."

"Of course she did! Contacting the dead must be like any other spell, and as you well know, we are more powerful as a group than alone. You can count on me to be there. Shall I contact the others?"

"If you don't mind. But keep in mind that Ursula knows I'm bringing reinforcements, but she doesn't know we're a practicing coven."

"Got it."

"Thanks, Lucy. I'll be there soon."

I hung up and opened the car door. "Hey, little guy. Thanks for hanging out here. It got a little crazy there for a while."

Mungo shot out of the car.

"Oh, sorry," I said, assuming he had to use the lawn facilities. But he kept running frantically toward an azalea bush on the other side of the square. A squirrel's tail twitched from the underbrush. "You little stinker," I muttered under my breath.

Shutting the door, I retraced my steps for what felt like the umpteenth time. When I got to the bush, my familiar was nowhere to be seen, however.

"Mungo," I called.

Steve rounded the corner, still in full eighteenth-century regalia. "What's wrong?"

"Have you seen a Cairn terrier in the last few seconds?"

He grinned and shook his head. "It's not like he's a runner. He'll find you if you don't find him."

"It's not like him to take off at all, even after a squirrel, and I need to get back to the bakery."

"Do you want me to watch for him and bring him to you when he makes himself known?"

I shook my head. "No. I wouldn't feel good about that. I'll find him soon."

"Okay. But I'm happy to help," Steve said.

"I know. Thanks." And I did know. Steve had steered clear when Declan and I started getting serious, and then he'd pursued a platonic friendship because he wanted to be in my life. It had been a little awkward at first, but I wanted him in my life, too. Declan didn't love the idea, but he wouldn't presume to choose my friends for me.

Steve continued on his way, and I went looking for Mungo. I finally spied him sitting near the relocated wardrobe tent Detective Quinn had made me wait in while he interviewed other, more important people after Simon's murder. When I approached the little dickens, he threw a glance over his shoulder and trotted around the corner.

I started to call for him when I heard voices inside. Rounding the edge of the canvas, I saw Mungo waiting for me in the opening. He came toward me, but when I reached down to pick him up, he ran back toward the tent with another backward look. *Come on*, he seemed to be urging.

Something about his manner told me to be quiet. I slipped into the tent, recognizing the racks of clothing and hats, even the mannequin, which, though now dressed in a frumpy nightdress, still sported a slight dent in her cheek from our encounter the day before.

And there, at the rear of the tent, stood Althea Cole, still wearing the elaborate peach satin gown. She was embracing a man with a neat blond ponytail, and in the dim light, I immediately thought of Steve. A pang of something arrowed through my solar plexus—concern? Wonder? Certainly not jealousy, I began to tell myself before realizing I'd just seen Steve, and he'd been in full costume down to the bow in his hair.

Squinting, I could now see the man with his arms around the testy leading lady was taller than my friend by several inches, had a pale complexion, and wore casual shorts and a plain white T-shirt. His hair was a few shades darker than Steve's, too.

He looked up, and our eyes met over Althea's shoulder. "Can I help you?" He sounded irritated.

"Er, sorry," I said, backing away.

Althea stepped back from him, whirling to see who had interrupted her tryst. I was surprised to see something very like fear drawn across her fea-

tures before she masked it with an imperious toss
of her head and a slight sneer.

"Don't mind her," she said. "She's a bit of
snoop, that's all. And just leaving. Weren't you,
Miss Lightfoot?"

I bit back a reply and bent to pick up Mungo,
who watched our exchange with eager interest.
"Indeed." I gritted my teeth, gave her the widest
smile I could manage, and said in a chipper tone,
"I'll see you later tonight, though!" I bestowed a
vestige of my smile on her paramour and high-
tailed it back to my car with my familiar.

"What was that all about?" I asked as I deposited him into the passenger seat. "Do you think
Althea's dalliance is relevant to Simon's death?"

Yip!

"How so?"

But my familiar only grinned his doggy grin
and left me to mull over the possible answers.

Before I pulled away from the curb, I texted Declan: *Hey, big guy. Have to get back to the Honeybee.
Check in when you get a chance?*

He called as I was parking the Bug in the alley
behind the bakery. "That was quick," I said.

"Hey, darlin'. I'd hoped to see you before you
left."

"Sorry. I've been gone much longer than I expected and felt like I needed to get back."

"No problem. No one expected all that drama
this afternoon. I wanted to see if I could take you

out to dinner tonight, though. To make up for last night."

"Er . . ."

"You're not mad at me, are you?"

"Oh, no. Of course not. But I kind of have plans for tonight," I said.

"Another date?" he asked, teasing.

"Not exactly." Should I tell him? Well, it wasn't going to be a secret. "We're having a séance at the house where the movie muckety-mucks are staying."

"A . . . You're kidding."

"Nope. I figure if Ursula Banford is the real deal, then why not ask Simon himself who killed him?"

"Wow."

"Yeah. Crazy, huh?" I opened the back door of the Honeybee and carried Mungo, hunkered down in the bottom of my tote, through to the office. Lucy waved at me from where she was chatting with a customer at the register.

"I don't know that I like you going into that house by yourself," Declan said. "Most of the people who live there are suspects."

"Don't worry. Lucy is going to come, too, and she's checking with the other members of the spellbook club to see who else can make it. I want lots of support, and even Ursula says the more energy she can draw on, the better luck we will have."

"What about me?" he asked.

"What about you?"

"Were you going to ask me to come with you?"

"Honestly, I hadn't thought about it," I said. "I'm surprised that you'd even consider coming to a séance."

"Maybe it's time I learn more about that part of your life," he said. "And it's not like you're going to invite me to one of your spellbook club meetings, right? Not even Ben gets to go to those."

I had to give him credit for making the effort. "Do you really believe we can communicate with those who have passed on?" Ursula hadn't said anything about participants needing to be believers, but it couldn't hurt, right? Plus, I had to admit I was testing him a little.

"I'll do my best," he said.

That was good enough for me. "Okay, then. I'll pick you up at your place at seven," I said. "We can grab a quick bite and then head over to the house where the cast is staying. Festivities are slated to begin at eight thirty."

I found Jaida and Mimsey seated at a bistro table by a front window.

"I came back as soon as I was done," Jaida said. "I want to hear more about this séance you have planned."

Mimsey beamed at me. "It's an excellent idea, Katie."

Bianca came out from behind the espresso counter, scanning the Honeybee for customers. A couple sat next to each other on the sofa, heads together as they looked at something on the laptop screen between them. A dreadlocked dude rocked out silently to whatever was streaming through his earbuds, reading a copy of Khalil Gibran from the bakery's library. In a far corner, a mother tended two little girls dressed up in lace and petticoats, bright patent-leather shoes on their swinging feet.

No one paid us any mind, so I sat down as Lucy left the register and joined us. Quickly, I outlined the plan and gave everyone the address.

"Declan wants to come, too, so I'm going to pick him up on the way," I said.

Lucy looked satisfied. "See. I told you he'd come around."

"He was never antimagic," I said. "He just didn't get it."

"Tonight could change that." Jaida's lips twitched. "If your psychic manages to reach the murder victim, that is. I'm still not convinced."

"Well, I'm not either, not all the way. But I can't figure out why Ursula would try to hoodwink me, and heaven knows we understand there's a lot more happening on this plane—and the next— than most people realize."

"True," Bianca said. "And I'm willing to believe."

"That's called faith," Mimsey said with a decisive nod.

Jaida shook her head. "It might be called something else. What if Ursula is the one who killed Simon? Then she'd have a good reason to try to misdirect you, Katie."

"Sure," I agreed. "But telling someone they've been chosen to solve his murder sure isn't the first step I'd take in that situation."

Jaida made a moue of agreement.

I dropped my voice to a low murmur, and they all leaned forward so they could hear me. "Besides, someone must believe that Ursula can really talk to the dead, because it looks like she might have been the intended victim of the poisoned oatmeal cookies."

Exclamations at that. Lucy hadn't had a chance to tell them that part of the story, so I caught them up. "But if that was the idea, then it only made her angry. She's even more determined to go on with the séance."

"Good for her!" Mimsey said.

Lucy's head bobbed. "Let's just go with it and hope. What's the worst that could happen?"

The spellbook club members looked around at each other. What indeed?

"Just so you know, I don't think Ursula knows I'm a witch," I said. "Or that you are. Until we know more, we might want to keep it that way."

"Oh, poo," Mimsey said with a wave of her hand. "A psychic isn't going to care one way or the other."

Before I could respond, the door swung open, and Mrs. Standish burst in. "Helloooo, darlings! How are we this fine afternoon?"

Lucy and I both came to our feet. "Fine and dandy," I replied.

"Twice in one day?" Lucy said. "You flatter us, my dear. Or perhaps you're simply thirsty?"

"Nonsense," Mrs. Standish boomed. All the customers, including earbud man and the two patent-leather princesses, turned their heads toward us. "I simply must have two more of those Black and Tan éclairs. Samantha—my daughter, you know?—confiscated the last two from those I bought this morning. I'd been saving them to share with a friend of mine this afternoon, and as much as I love my darling girl, I still want those éclairs."

Lucy bustled behind the counter and shook out a bakery bag.

"Can I get you any more whoopie pies to go with those?" I asked.

"What? Oh." She waved her hand in a gesture of dismissal. "No, thank you. I've had enough whoopie pies to last me for a while."

As she left, Lucy winked at me. "I have a feeling that any whoopee in Mrs. Standish's future will not involve red velvet cake."

"Why, Lucy Eagel. You're enjoying this matchmaking a little too much," I said.

"Not matchmaking, my dear. Only . . . facilitating."

Chapter 11

At six thirty I packed up Mungo and took him over to Declan's apartment. We left the little guy contentedly tucked into an afghan on the sofa to catch up on his soap operas. The house where the séance was to be held was within walking distance from Deck's, but we didn't want to rush supper at the casual and kitschy Toucan Café. He folded himself into the Bug with nary a complaint, his knees jutting up and his head almost brushing the roof of the compartment. My car was easier to park downtown than his extended-cab pickup, and as he put it, he was literally along for the ride.

After a rib eye steak for Declan and the jerk tilapia for me, we motored the short distance to the address Ursula had given me. Given my aunt's terrific parking karma, I wasn't surprised to see Ben and Lucy's baby blue 1964 Thunderbird convertible already squeezed into a convenient space, but I was surprised to see Ben get out of the driver's side.

"Fancy meeting you here," I said, approaching and giving him a hug.

"Declan told me about what you had planned for tonight, and Lucy said it would be okay if I came, too."

"Of course it is. I just didn't expect, well—"

"I know," my uncle broke in. "But I'm willing to do whatever I have to in order to find this murderer. Believe me. I've seen your aunt pull off some pretty strange stuff—you, too—and I have to at least admit it's possible that this might work." He looked uncomfortable in his dress shoes and sports coat, and I wondered whether he'd ever enjoyed wearing his dress uniform or if over the last two years he had simply grown used to the freedom of retirement.

Retirement—or whatever you called working at a bakery nine to ten hours a day.

Lucy greeted me with her own hug as Bianca's red Jaguar pulled up. A flushed Mimsey rolled out of the passenger seat. She was resplendent in a pantsuit of eye-popping yellow, white alligator pumps, a string of oversized pearls, and a yellow ribbon in her hair. Bianca swirled out of the driver's side wearing a sleeveless watered-silk blouse, dark slacks, high-heeled gemmed sandals, and a row of silver bangles halfway up her forearm. Jaida arrived next, wearing jeans, a Stonehenge T-shirt, a black jacket, and knee-high boots.

I had changed into a long skirt and silky tank top, and Declan wore a collared shirt and jeans. Yes, I decided, we were all dressed nicely enough for a visitation from the spirit of Simon Knapp.

Squarish and tall, the house was three stories high, with three sets of windows on each floor. Those on the top floor were set back and smaller, as if the top layer of the cake had come out a bit smaller than the first two. Brick trim studded all the vertical corners and set off the creamy white exterior. Wrought-iron balconies outside the middle windows matched the fence that enclosed the small front yard. More iron, decorative spikes this time, ringed the flat roof and probably served to deflect the attentions of pigeons as much as anything.

The building certainly gave off an effluvium of *age*, so much so that I felt sure it was an original antebellum home. Of course Simon wouldn't have stinted on finding the best Savannah had on offer for his A. Dendum charges. It was quite beautiful, and certainly not the kind of place you'd find for rent on Craigslist. I guessed it was a private residence whose owners were off in St. Moritz or some such, and Simon had arranged with them for the cast to stay there.

It couldn't have been cheap, though, and the only people staying there were, as Niklas Egan had put it, "major players," while the regular crew stayed at the Hyatt. It was a very nice hotel, of course, but nothing like this. I wondered whether this evident hierarchy between cast and crew was typical for film projects or specific to *Love in Revolution*.

I hadn't been in many true antebellum homes and looked forward to seeing the interior. Althea answered the door wearing a little black dress. Make that a *tiny* black dress, cut low on top and high on the bottom and cinched around her wispy waist with a wide magenta belt. It was further accessorized by glittering diamond studs in her ears, stiletto heels, and a goblet of red wine in her left hand. Her hair, which I had thought might be a wig, hung in luxurious tresses down her back.

"Come in," she intoned as if trying to emulate a female Vincent Price with a Deep South accent. Séance in the offing or not, it didn't quite work.

I glanced at Declan. His eyes sparked with amusement, and I barely managed to control my urge to giggle.

Ben stepped forward. "Ms. Cole, I'd like you to meet my wife, Lucy."

Althea gave a regal nod. "Ms. Eagel."

"Lucy, please."

"Oh, my stars and garters, what a pretty girl you are!" Mimsey stepped forward before anyone could introduce her. "Of course, I already knew that having seen every single one of your pictures, but you're even lovelier in person!"

Althea's ice appeared to fracture.

Mimsey barreled on. "You are just the nicest thing, too, to let us invade your home like this so we can have a little confab with Mr. Knapp. Just the most generous, sweetest thing ever."

Man, she's laying it on kind of thick.

But Althea loved it. Her prim little smile grew into a wide, genuine grin. "You are most welcome, my dear."

"I'm Mimsey." She suddenly embraced Althea, who looked stunned for a moment before the older woman stepped back. In fact, I'm pretty sure we all looked stunned. "Mimsey Carmichael. Your passionflowers come from my florist shop. And this here is Jaida French."

"Nice to meet you," Jaida said.

"Sure. You, too." Althea replied, more interested in the fawning Mimsey.

"Hello, Althea," Bianca greeted her. "I think you know everyone else."

The actress glanced at the rest of us, gaze lingering for a moment on me before moving on. "Mmhmm. Well, come on in." She stepped back and waved us inside.

We stepped into a wide entryway, where a fountain trickled water from lily pad to lily pad. The sound was soothing, as was the indirect lighting that extended into the large open space. Indirect but bright, spilling from sconces, exploding from torchères, and sneaking from uplights hidden behind furniture and potted palms.

Niklas Egan appeared at the top of the stairway to the right. He ran lightly down the steps, Van Grayson behind him. They were dressed designer casual, and both paused when they saw us.

"Ah, the spiritualists have gathered already," Niklas said. "We'd better vacate the premises ASAP unless we want to become ensnared in their silliness."

"Well . . . ," Van said.

"Poor Nik is jealous of those who believe in

something beyond what can be seen with the naked eye," Althea said in a frosty tone. "It must be difficult to get through life believing in nothing but your own ego."

The director treated us to a full-throated laugh. "Actually, it's surprisingly easy." He quickstepped down the last few stairs, Van on his heels. As they approached the door, Niklas paused in front of Bianca. The corner of his lips lifted in a wry half smile. "You, too?"

"I'm afraid so," she said. They gave the impression they knew each other rather well, and Jaida and I exchanged a quizzical glance.

"Well, you all have fun, hear?" Niklas said to the group. "But we're going to wash our hands of this shindig and see what kind of rocking nightlife we can find in Savannah on a Tuesday night. I doubt it'll be much, but with Grayson here as my wingman, it shouldn't be too bad." He winked at Bianca, waved dismissively at the rest of us, and left through the still-open door. Van's smile faltered before he ducked his head and tagged along behind.

Althea sniffed her distain before leading us through the main hallway. Waist-high wainscoting ran around the perimeter, and we craned our necks to take in the high ceilings and eggshell walls. The floor was whitewashed wood, as was the towering fireplace mantel. The carved moldings along the edges of the ceiling were a darker ecru. The furnishings were understated and appeared, frankly, uncomfortable, the hall not a place for lingering but transition. The dark wood settee and chairs looked even darker against all the white backgrounds.

And everywhere, passionflowers punctuated the decor, singly and in groups, in small and large vases.

"The séance will take place in the dining room," Althea said, and we trailed behind her like so many baby ducks. Her expensive perfume wafted behind her. She missed her step once, smoothly catching herself on the back of a Queen Anne chair. It was a subtle move, though possibly well practiced, and I wondered whether it was the stilettos or the wine.

We shuffled into the dining room. The table was an impressive slab that sat fourteen people easily. Four of the chairs had been moved to the edge of the room so that ten remained, four on each side and one at each end of the table. The space was large, the walls high, but not so high as the main hallway, and they were mostly covered in tapestries. I recognized some of the scenes from mythology: Diana and the stag, Zeus visiting Leda as a swan, and right over Althea's shoulder, Narcissus gazed adoringly at his reflection in the water. The air smelled of lemony furniture polish, a whiff of patchouli incense, and the delicious scent of golden beeswax that somehow negated Althea's strong perfume without overpowering it.

The honeyed atmosphere was because of the candles. More than a hundred of them, already lit, the flames wavering as we passed by. I exchanged approving looks with my coven mates and inhaled a deep, appreciative breath. As it sighed out, I saw Steve standing under Leda and the Swan, his usual casual attire replaced by slacks and a sports coat similar to Ben's. His lips curved up in a small welcoming smile.

I was oddly glad to see him and realized with surprise that I was a tad nervous about what might happen. A glance sideways, however, revealed Declan watching Steve with narrowed eyes, his lips firmly pressed together. Steve refused to look at Declan altogether. I stifled a sigh.

Ursula stood behind the chair at the head of the table. She wore a simple shirtwaist dress, loose and comfortable-looking and the same color as her eyes. Her right ear sported a large silver cuff beneath her spiked hair, and she had added some understated gloss to her lips. She seemed to assess each of us as we filed in the door, often looking off to the side as if listening to someone.

The fine linen cloth that covered the table was a dark blue that set off the color of Ursula's eyes. I wondered if it was part of the house furnishings or if she carried it as a prop because of the numinous effect it gave her gaze. Declan bent down as if to retrieve something from the floor and took a good hard look under the tablecloth—and under the table. If the psychic noticed it, she didn't give any indication.

Once we were all inside, Althea waved her arm toward the back of the room and said, "There's plenty of wine and cheese to sample. Help yourselves."

Ben moved toward the sideboard, no doubt thinking a bit of the grape might help calm his own jitters. I joined him and snagged a nugget of deeply golden cheese off the board. Popping it in my mouth, I nearly swooned. It was rich and chewy, the texture similar to Parmesan, but the flavor was a complex combination of nuts, fruits, and, of all things, butterscotch.

"Welcome, everyone," Ursula said. "Thank you for your generosity, Althea, but I really must advise against drinking alcohol until after we've completed the séance."

The actress gave her a dirty look.

Ursula calmly ignored her. "It can interfere with the high vibrational energy required to communicate with the spirit world." She smiled. "However, wine can be marvelously grounding afterward, so do feel free to imbibe after we're finished."

Her employer approached and sat down in the chair to Ursula's right. She patted the chair next her, then crooked her finger at Steve.

"Althea," Ursula said. "Since you have experience contacting the other side, I was hoping you would anchor the table at the other end."

"Not sit by you?" Althea asked.

Ursula simply smiled.

"Well, okay. Come on, Stevie."

Oh, Lord.

She stood and put her hand on his arm, and he steadied her with his other hand. She wrinkled her nose, all cutesy, and batted her big fake eyelashes. I looked away. Declan leaned down and said into my ear, "I wonder what she was like before she was a big star?"

Lucy leaned in on my other side. "She seems awfully unhappy and insecure, doesn't she?"

I opened my mouth to scoff, then closed it. Instead, I put my arm around my aunt's shoulders and squeezed. "Trust you to look past appearances."

"Come sit here, Katie, so you will be available to speak to Simon should he grace us with a visit," Ursula said, indicating the seat to her left.

Now I got the dirty look from Althea.

Ursula arranged the rest of us around the table to her satisfaction. Declan sat next to me, and next to him was Jaida and then "Stevie" on Althea's right. On her left, going back toward the head of the table, sat Bianca, then Ben, Lucy, and, finally, Mimsey directly across from me.

"Has anyone heard how Owen is doing?" I asked.

Ben said, "I checked after the relief guys arrived for the night, and he's still in the hospital under observation."

"But he's going to be okay," Lucy said.

"It sounds like they plan to release him tomorrow morning," my uncle confirmed.

I sat back, relieved.

Ursula's skirt swirled as she rose and moved to close the double doors to the hallway. She twisted the round light switch on the wall, and the chandelier above us darkened. The sudden contrast made the candle flames seem to grow brighter. They cast dancing shadows over the walls and up to the ceiling.

With calm, measured steps, Ursula returned to her seat at the head of the table. Her eyes smiled at me before her attention flicked to Althea, who was saying something to Steve. I couldn't make out the words, but her tone was edged with complaint. She took a big swig out of her wine goblet and turned her attention back to the rest of us.

Without warning, the loud chirps of crickets filled the room. We all looked around in surprise, and then the sound abruptly ceased. Ben ducked his head over the cell phone in his hand.

"Er, sorry," he said.

"That's okay," Ursula said. "It's the perfect reminder that we all need to turn off our cell phones."

Ben flashed a white-toothed smile at Ursula and nodded before returning the phone to the inside pocket of his sports coat.

Declan retrieved his cell and began pushing buttons. Out of habit, the members of the spellbook club had already turned ours off the same way we did before casting together. Steve, no doubt, had done the same, and Althea would already be aware of her personal psychic's preferences.

Including not drinking wine before a séance, which apparently she didn't feel was all that important.

Mimsey leaned toward me. "It feels like we should cast a circle," she whispered. "To keep everyone safe."

Ursula's eyebrow arched; she'd heard.

I reached across the table and patted the older woman's hand. "I'm sure it will be all right."

Ursula murmured to me, "You're a witch? Suddenly a few things make more sense. Are these friends of yours . . . ?"

I gave a little nod, glancing around to make sure no one was paying attention to our conversation. No one except Althea down at the other end of the table appeared to be, but she was too far away to hear our low tones. "Are you okay with that?"

Her smile was wide and genuine, but she spoke so quietly I had to scoot my chair closer in order to catch the words. "Absolutely. I wanted extra power in order to reach Simon tonight, and a coven of witches is just the ticket." She laughed, the notes falling like crystals into the air. Heads turned.

"Shh," I said, my eyes cutting subtly toward Althea.

The actress took a drink of wine, her eyes never leaving my face. Despite her apparent curiosity, however, I was relieved to note she didn't seem to be aware of what we were talking about. Her interest struck me as proprietary, given how she'd referred to Ursula as "my psychic," perhaps with a little jealousy in the mix.

Mimsey was leaning over to hear Ursula, too. Now the psychic whispered to her, "Don't worry. I'll invoke something very similar to your protective circle. My guides will guard us as well as serve as conduits to the other side."

Mimsey sat back with a satisfied nod.

Ursula clapped her hands twice, and the low undercurrent of whispers around the table quieted. "It's time to begin. It's not imperative, but if you're comfortable with the idea, please take the hand of the person next to you. If you don't want to, for whatever reason, don't feel obligated and no one will judge you." She looked each person seated at the table in the eye, conveying the order they were not to judge.

Declan's fingers already gripped mine, and I held my other hand out to Ursula, who took it with a smile. No one else seemed to have a problem with holding hands except Althea, who seemed more than fine with holding Steve's hand but refused to offer her other hand to Bianca, who sat on her other side.

Did I judge her for it?

Yep.

Bianca merely pressed her lips together for a moment, then shrugged and held her hand out to Ben, who readily enveloped it in his own.

Ursula looked around at each of us before nodding to no one in particular, closing her eyes and leaning her head against the high back of the chair. "I respectfully ask my spirit guides to honor us with their presence this evening, to surround this gathering and protect us all from harm and undue influence." She waited. We all waited. I could sense the heightened awareness as the entire group strove to hear or see something from beyond.

She began to sway, and her eyelids fluttered. "Now, settle down, everyone."

Was she talking to us?

The atmosphere in the room seemed to thicken, the smell of beeswax sharpening in my nostrils. The slightest of breezes moved through my hair and made the shadows cast by the candle flames cavort crazily across the walls, ceiling—and us.

Ursula's eyes opened, and a grimace quirked up one corner of her mouth. "I was afraid of this."

"What's wrong?" Declan asked with obvious skepticism. Althea immediately made a loud shushing sound.

Ursula waved away her employer's concern, however, not noticing how furious her gesture made the actress. "This house is inhabited by many ghosts, both those who have not completely passed the veil for whatever reason and those who have come back to protect or communicate with those still living. I've known of them since we began staying here, but didn't feel it was my place to remedy the situation, instead asking my own guides to—well, run interference, if you will. But so many of you have strong psychic powers, and the spirits are clamoring to be heard."

"You never told me about all these extra spirits," Althea protested. "And you've read for me here twice."

"They weren't relevant to our work," Ursula answered patiently. "Now they are."

"Are they here for us?" my aunt asked, and I knew she was hoping to talk to my nonna.

Ursula shook her head. "No. These spirits are attached to this property, either to the house itself or to the land before it was built."

Lucy quickly wiped the disappointment from her face.

"Now," the psychic continued. "I'm going to ask them to let us go on with our work tonight without interruption." She bowed her head, and while her eyes remained open, they went vacant as she stared at the expanse of tablecloth. Her fingers tightened over mine. It felt like a signal. I closed my own eyes and concentrated on funneling power through our locked hands. Ursula jerked slightly as if shocked; then she seemed to lean into what I was offering. Additional power from the others around the table joined ours, and I recognized the signatures of the other members of the spellbook club.

And Steve. We'd worked together only a few times, but they had been significant, and I knew the feel of his power the same way that I knew his smile.

Another vibration was familiar yet not, tentative and inconsistent. I made a note of it and moved on, narrowing my focus to Ursula and the task at hand.

The impression of winging entities, vaguely human, flitted through my mind. At least a dozen of them. Others, a much smaller group of three, joined our effort. One of the smaller group felt very inhuman, though I couldn't have said how. Lighter. Brighter.

These are her guides. I reached out to the one that felt so strange. *Who are you? What are you?*

An impression of a word, not even the word itself came to me.

Angel.

And then from that entity: *Employ your power, Katie Lightfoot.*

Chapter 12

I joined the others and *pushed* the house spirits away. Not far away, though. Out of the room, but, I suspected, not even out of the building.

Ursula opened her eyes. "Okay. We've established a perimeter within which we can work."

Much like the spellbook club would have cast a protective circle. *Nice.* In our work, we even invoked the help of the archangels. Not that I'd had a chance to actually communicate with any of them. *Was that really Ursula's personal angel? Or something else? Could I have imagined it?* I shook my head.

"Now I'm going to attempt to summon Simon," the psychic said. "Again, I'll need your help."

We looked around at one another, and I sensed Declan's apprehension.

"We're going to focus our attention on the Simon that each of us knew," Ursula went on. "That means we will each be focusing on something a little different because no one is the same person to everyone."

"What if we didn't know him at all?" Jaida asked.

Ursula answered, "Then focus on the Simon you've heard of, or, if you have experience with focusing in a group, you can employ whatever technique you use then."

Jaida blinked. She flashed a glance at me, and I gave her a barely perceptible nod. Yes, Ursula knew we were witches and therefore assumed we'd worked together in the past. Jaida's lips parted briefly, but she quickly recovered.

"Does everyone have an idea—an image, an impression, even something you've heard about Simon Knapp that you can tap into?"

Murmurs of agreement all around, some more enthusiastic than others.

"Okay. Now close your eyes to better concentrate."

One of Declan's eyebrows lifted, and I doubted he'd follow her directions. Not that it mattered. He might think she was trying to pull one over on us, but after linking with her posse of spirit guides, I was convinced Ursula was the real deal. Closing our eyes would only help.

"Now, with that idea of Simon in mind, I want you to repeat after me," she said. Her voice took on a dreamy intonation. "We respectfully call upon you, Simon Knapp, to grace us with your presence tonight."

Dutifully, we repeated her words. She said them again, and again we repeated, "We respectfully call upon you, Simon Knapp, to grace us with your presence."

Over and over, until it was no longer a call and repeat but all of us chanting together. An objective part of me realized we sounded like a roomful of idiots. I peeked at Declan, whose eyes were wide open and darting around the room and at the participants. His lips moved, but I was pretty sure he wasn't vocalizing. Steve, too, opened his eyes, noticed Declan, then looked at me. Understanding passed between us at the same time I felt the intention that was riding on our words grow stronger. No longer did I care if we looked crazy.

Whatever we were doing was working.

Suddenly Ursula grew quiet, and our final call to Simon trailed off at the end. The room grew weirdly silent after the myriad voices mingling together, saying the same words again and again. Into that quiet, Ursula said, "Hello? Simon?"

We all waited. A breeze shifted through the room again, and the candles flickered.

She nodded. "Yes. Simon is here."

I felt Declan tense beside me. I squeezed his fingers and realized I wasn't exactly breathing normally, either. Excitement and curiosity trilled through me. I inhaled deeply and then let the air out.

Ursula's eyes were still mostly closed, but I could see them glitter through her long lashes. Her face was calm, her expression alert and expectant. "Simon wants to know why we summoned him."

"Seriously?" I muttered, then cleared my throat when no one else answered. "Um, hi there, Simon. Katie Lightfoot here. Remember me?"

Ursula's face remained impassive.

"I'm sorry I only got to meet you the one time, you know, before you got killed and all," I babbled. "Kind of funny that I'm even here, trying to get ahold of you, I suppose. Maybe you're wondering about that." My words tumbled over one another, and I felt awkward with a capital *A*. Who was I to ask Simon who murdered him, anyway? I couldn't very well refer to Ursula's prediction in front of everyone. I stared hard at the psychic, trying to let her know I needed her help, but she seemed completely unaware of my presence.

Or anyone else's.

"Mr. Knapp, can you tell us the name of your murderer?" Ben asked, bypassing all my blithering.

Thank goodness.

There was a long, tense silence as we waited for the answer.

Ursula's hand gripped mine harder, and the muscles in her neck flexed. "Simon has something he wants me to pass on," she intoned. If I hadn't known better, I would have thought she was being overdramatic. Heck, maybe she was, out of habit. There had to be a certain amount of showmanship associated with her profession.

"Simon says . . ."

We all leaned toward Ursula.

"Simon says . . ."

"Oh, for heaven's sake," Althea said in a loud voice and suddenly stood. "I know you used to like to play *Simon Says*, Knapp, but this isn't a children's game!" She emphasized her words with an unsteady jab of her finger. Unfortunately, that hand also held her glass, and a crimson dollop of wine splashed out to land on the tablecloth. We all stared at her with varying expressions of horror.

"Lord have mercy," Mimsey exclaimed under her breath.

"Althea," Steve hissed, reaching for her elbow.

She jerked away from him, miraculously avoiding another spill. "You be quiet, Stevie. Ursula has worked her magic. Now we need an answer. Who killed you, Simon? Just *tell* us so we can call up the police and let them know your ghost told us who they should arrest." Sarcasm dripped from her words.

Ursula's eyelids fluttered and then popped open. "He's gone."

"Oh, sure," the actress said, throwing her arms wide. Steve grabbed her glass and set it on the table. "He's just kidding around, aren't you, Simon? Never did like being told what to do, did you?"

The psychic released my hand and Mimsey's at the same time while gaping at her employer. "What is the matter with you, Althea? Were you trying to make him leave? Because I assure you Simon Knapp's spirit is long gone now."

My shoulder slumped. *Gone.* "Can you get him back?" I asked. Nods all around.

"Well, I'm afraid you can do it without me," Althea said, taking an unsteady step toward the door. "I've had a very long day and have to get up early in the morning." With that, she tossed her head and strode out of the room as fast as her stilettos would carry her.

Looking an apology at all of us, Steve rose and followed her, closing the door behind him.

The room erupted into conversation. "What was that all about?" Bianca asked, while Lucy wondered, "Do you think she purposefully drove him away?"

Why would Althea disrupt the séance? Did she think Simon would reveal her as his murderer—or was she afraid he might reveal something else, something only a fixer would know?

The image of Althea with her mystery man in the wardrobe tent flashed across my mental movie screen, and I guiltily wondered if I should tell Steve. We were friends, after all, and he'd look out for me the same way if the situation was ever reversed.

Declan squeezed my hand. "Was there really a spirit here?"

"I think so." My eyes met Ursula's and she nodded. "Will he come back?" I asked.

"I can try. He seemed awfully angry, though. Quiet, everyone. Let's give this another go."

Althea's querulous voice cut through the door, making it that much harder to concentrate.

"Good goddess," I muttered before closing my eyes again. "That woman is a first-class pain."

We tried the chanting again, but it felt lame all over again, falling on dead air. It soon became apparent Simon's spirit was too offended to grace us with his presence again. Ursula opened her eyes and shook her head. Our voices trailed off.

Suddenly her eyes darted to the left. "Hello?" she asked. "May I ask who you are?" She seemed to listen; then her eyes cut to me. "Yes, I've heard of you."

Taite? My heart pummeled my ribs.

Then I smelled the sweet fragrance of gardenia. *Not Taite. Nonna.* The floral scent grew stronger.

"Smell that?" I asked Declan.

Frowning, he shook his head.

"Lucy? Do you smell it?" I asked.

My aunt leaned forward, her face shining. "Mama?"

Ursula's lips curved up in a smile. "Yes, it's your mother. Is there anything you'd like to say to her?"

Lucy's eyes welled. "Only that I miss you, Mama. And I hope you're happy over there."

A pause, then Ursula said, "She says she is. She says she watches over you as well as Katie and . . . Mary Jane?"

I nodded. "That's my mother."

"She says to pass on her love to Mary Jane and that's she's sorry she hasn't been in contact with you directly, Lucy, but that you haven't needed her in the same way."

A tear spilled down my aunt's cheek, and she whispered, "Oh, that's okay, Mama. I understand."

"Nonna," I called. "Can you tell us what happened to Simon?"

The psychic paused before shaking her head. "She can't help us with that. She says she simply wanted to say hello, given this opportunity."

I laughed. "Figures."

Ursula took a deep breath and distributed a look between Lucy and me. "She's gone."

Uncle Ben, looking a bit baffled, scooted his chair close, put his arm around Lucy, and pulled her to him. She leaned her head on his shoulder, still beaming.

Mimsey patted her hand. "I told you," she said, and I wondered whether Lucy had confided her disappointment that Nonna had contacted my mother and me but not her youngest daughter.

"I think we're done for tonight," Ursula said. "I'm sorry it didn't work out—" She stopped. "*What?*"

Her gaze swung to Declan, who, I realized, no longer held my hand. I turned to look at him, and what I saw made my heart stutter. He gripped the arms of his chair so hard, his fingers were white. His head leaned against the back of the chair, lips parted, eyes rolled back so that only the whites showed. I heard Jaida suck in a surprised breath as I thought: *seizure.*

There were gasps around the table. "Deck!" Ben exclaimed and leaped to his feet.

"No!" Ursula said. "Don't touch him."

But I did anyway, putting my hand on his arm. The contact blasted power through me, and I lurched in my chair. The familiar-yet-not signature I'd felt earlier swept over my psyche, and I realized it was Declan.

Declan? My Declan?

He blinked, his head dropped, and his baby

blues found mine. They sparkled and danced in a way I'd never seen, and I found myself unable to look away. "Katie, m' darlin'! How I've admired you from afar!" Gone was my boyfriend's sorghum-laced accent, replaced with the playful lilt of a native Irish speaker. His voice was much higher, as well, and disturbingly nasal.

"Who are you?" Ursula asked. My heart spasmed again. She was right. This was my boyfriend's body, but no longer was Declan running the show.

"Connell O'Donohue, at your service! I'm this boyo's great-great-uncle, don't you know. Been watching over him since he was a wee lad."

Like Nonna. Only Connell felt . . . different. And unlike Nonna, *he was possessing my boyfriend*. I gripped Declan's arm tighter.

Those blue eyes I knew so well flashed, and he let loose a high-pitched chortle. "Now, don't you worry, Katie. I'll only be a moment—or two! Ah! It's such a luxury to be what you would call corporeal again, though. How I've missed it!"

"Is that why you're here?" Ursula asked in a tense voice. I didn't like the worry that pinched the skin around her eyes. "Or did you have a message for one of us?"

He sighed. "Only for my great-great-nephew. To tell him I'm glad he finally found a woman worthy of his attention, who will embrace his gifts even if he won't." He winked at me. "And that now he has to make sure he's worthy of her attention, as well."

"All right. Thank you." Ursula's tone was gently dismissive.

"Oh. I see. You don't want me to stay!" Connell sounded angry now.

"Please," I said. "Where is Declan?"

"Well, begorra! Did you think I wouldn't be lettin' yer man come back to you? Ah, Katie darlin'. I see I've worried you unnecessarily. All right. I'll go now."

Declan's head arched against the back of the chair again and then fell forward. He gasped for air, and when he looked at me again, panting, it was my sweet guy looking at me from his eyes. I threw my arms around him and held on tight. Jaida reached over and rubbed his shoulder, instinctively murmuring words of comfort.

When I let go, everyone was staring at us in alarm except Ursula, whose concern had turned to amusement. "Well, that was quite the show, Mr. McCarthy."

He licked his lips.

"Do you remember?" she asked.

He finally managed, "I think so. Connell." He shook his head as if to clear it. "What the hell happened?"

"You," she said with satisfaction, "are one of those rare people who can not only hear the spirits, but can actually channel them. I can't even do that."

"No." He shook his head again. "That's not possible."

"A true medium," she said. "Very rare, indeed,

to have the precisely right vibrations to allow a spirit to occupy your physical self."

Declan blinked at her in disbelief. I knew the feeling. I'd felt the same way when Lucy had told me I was a witch.

Ben was still standing. Lucy pulled him back to his seat. "He's okay," she said. "Aren't you, Declan?" She was still riding high after the contact with Nonna.

"That was horrible," he said with a shudder.

The smile dropped from my aunt's face.

Mimsey, who had been uncharacteristically quiet, make a *tsk*ing sound. "A glass of wine, a nice hot bath, and a good night's sleep. That's what you need, young man."

Bianca got up and went to the sideboard. She poured a glass of wine and brought it to Declan, who drank it down like so much of Margie Coopersmith's Kool-Aid.

"Whoa there, big guy," I said. But when Bianca brought me a glass, I didn't hesitate to take a swig, either.

Mildly fortified, I leaned close to Declan's ear and murmured, "Are you okay?"

"No," he shot back. "I'm not okay."

"You will be," I tried to assure him.

"Can we talk about this later?"

"Of course," I agreed.

Someone turned on the chandelier, and soon everyone was milling around the room, subdued conversations murmuring in the corners, the occasional glance at Declan full of wonder.

"Here. Finish this." I handed him my wine. "I'm going to check in with Ursula, and then we can go home."

She was standing by the sideboard next to Bianca. My stomach growled, and I realized I was starving. Reaching for a slice of that succulent cheese, I asked, "Is Declan really okay?"

Her smile was weary. "Should be. The spirit who visited him was friendly, a relative who has been with him for his whole life, it sounds like. There shouldn't be any lasting effects. Your friend there"—she indicated Mimsey—"prescribed exactly the right thing."

"Do you think it will happen again?"

She shrugged. "I don't know."

I took another bite of cheese. "Do you know what this cheese is?"

Ursula snorted. "I ought to. Althea made me go get it since Owen is, shall we say, indisposed. It's called Mimolette."

I had another quick nibble, eyeing the selection of wine that was supposed to go with it. An empty bottle of Côtes du Rhône stood next to half-full bottles of Cabernet Sauvignon and Malbec. "Guess that must be what Althea was drinking," I said, pointing to the empty bottle.

"Just as well," Bianca said. "That was to be paired with the Camembert yesterday. Not quite as suitable for this lovely Mimolette. Here, try the Cahors." She held out a bottle.

"No, thanks. I'm driving—and I think Declan's about ready to go."

The door to the dining room opened, and Steve came back in. I heard him say to Jaida, "I didn't want to interrupt if you were trying to contact Simon again."

Her fingers gripped his arm, and she pulled him to a far corner, talking rapidly. He listened for a few moments, then shot a look at Declan and then me. She was telling him what had happened, though I doubted Declan would appreciate her sharing.

Ben approached Ursula and me. "So much for finding Simon's killer." Disappointment hummed under his words.

"I'm sorry, Mr. Eagel. We did try."

"I'll say," he said, eyes widening as he turned to look at his firefighting protégé. "I still can't quite believe what happened."

Lucy threaded her arm through her husband's. "See what happens when you get involved with the spellbook club?"

Chapter 13

We left Jaida and Ursula talking about tarot layouts and walked out to the street with Mimsey and Bianca, Lucy, and Ben. Steve followed close behind, heading for his Land Rover. I wanted to ask him about Althea's ridiculous display, but my priority was getting Declan home. We called good night to each other as we made our way to our vehicles, started them up, and went our separate ways.

It was almost eleven by the time we got back to Declan's. Mungo bounded off the sofa to greet us at the door, and I bent down to pick him up. Nuzzling his dark fur, I murmured, "Boy, did you ever miss an interesting evening."

He whined and licked my neck.

"I'll tell you about it later," I said, putting him down. I shed my light wrap and laid it over the back of one of the barstools next to the high counter that separated the kitchen from the living room.

Declan's laugh sounded tired. "I think he really understands you."

Yip!

"Of course he does," I said. "I told you he's my familiar."

"Yeah, but what does that . . . ?" He trailed off, staring at me. "Oh, my God. You mean he really does . . . ?" He wagged his head as if trying to dislodge something from his brain.

"Talking with the dead give you a different perspective?" I teased and reached for him.

But Declan turned his shoulder toward me and went into the walk-through kitchen. He stood for a long moment in front of the open refrigerator before selecting a can of soda and closing the door. Still, he didn't move. The under-cabinet lighting provided the only illumination, casting the strong planes of his face into shadow.

"Oh, hon," I said softly from the doorway. "Tonight really threw you, didn't it?"

He looked up, his public poker face melting into the bewildered expression of a child who has been told there is no Santa Claus.

Except in this case it was more like the opposite.

Taking a few tentative steps toward him, I asked, "Are you okay?"

Finally, he spoke. "Honestly, Katie? I'm not sure."

I crossed the distance and wrapped my arms around his waist. I laid my head on his chest. The crisp fabric of his shirt crinkled against my cheek, and his heartbeat thrummed in my ear. His hand moved to the back of my neck and rested there, but he didn't return my embrace.

Letting go, I stepped back and looked up into his eyes. "Come on."

I led him into the living room, pushing aside Mungo's afghan on the sofa. Sitting, I patted the cushion beside me. "Let's talk about this."

Instead of joining me, he said, "Stay here. I'll be right back." He handed me his sweating soda can, walked into the bedroom, and flipped on the light.

Flummoxed, I waited. Took a sip of his drink. Orange, sweet, and tangy. Mungo jumped up on the sofa beside me. We heard a door open and some rattling noises, then a *thunk*. Silence, then a rustling.

I got up and turned on a couple more lamps. Whatever was going on, it didn't seem like there was romance in the air, so we might as well have some light. I sat back down, and Mungo crawled onto my lap.

Declan's newly renovated apartment was charming. However much he cooked and gardened, though, he had not absorbed much in the way of decorating sense from his strong mother or his four sisters. An unframed Guinness poster was the only art on the blond brick walls, and the Mexican rug tossed onto the gleaming wide oak planks of the floor was worn and frayed from foot traffic. Most of his furniture looked like he'd picked it up from the curb back in college and never bothered to upgrade. The pull-out sofa was an unfortunate brown plaid, the coffee table pitted and scarred from hard use at the firehouse, which had been its original home, and the red Scandinavian rocking chair was weirdly out of place.

This abode needed some tender loving care. It needed, in short, a woman's touch. However, when I'd made a few suggestions, Declan had started talking about moving in together. I wasn't ready for that, so I'd dropped the subject. If Declan wanted to live with ugly furniture, so be it.

Now he returned from the bedroom with a large, leather-bound book in his hand and a serious expression on his face. It was an album, I saw as he settled onto the sofa beside me. Putting his arm around me, he opened it across both of our laps. I snuggled into his side, and Mungo wiggled in even closer.

"What's this?" I asked.

"It's one of many family scrapbooks. My mother was crazy about keeping records of things, and when she went back to Ireland to explore our roots, she got a bunch of photos from a cousin of ours. See? This is my great-great-grandfather from Connemara."

I leaned forward, drinking in the details of the black-and-white photograph. An elderly man clad in tweeds and a short jacket squinted into the camera from under the brim of a felt hat. The pipe in his mouth trailed a barely discernible stream of smoke.

"He has a gleam in his eye," I said with a smile. "Did you know him?"

Declan shook his head. "No. My mother's

mother is still alive, but this man was long gone by the time I was born. And I've never been to Ireland. There's a whole branch of the McCarthy clan there."

I leaned my head back and looked up into his face. "We should go sometime. I probably have some kin there, too. Lucy would know."

"We should." His eyes searched mine.

"Did, uh, talking with your uncle spark this sudden interest in your heritage?" I asked, feeling my way.

His face darkened. "You mean talking *for* my uncle?"

"I guess it was more like that, yes."

A few moments of hesitation, and then Declan said, "I wanted to show you something in particular." He flipped a few pages, stopping at another photo. It was a group of four men and three women. The men's clothing was similar to his great-great-grandfather's, which made me think the photos were from the same time period. The women wore dresses reaching almost to the ground and boots almost as heavy as their male counterparts, but one in particular had a fresh face and held her head at an angle as if she were questioning the whole notion of having her picture taken. A light spot had developed in one corner of the paper, though, which bleached out some of the finer details.

Declan pointed to the man on the end, at the edge of the group. My eyes narrowed. "Who's that?"

"That," he said, "is Uncle Connell."

I sipped a quick breath of surprise and leaned forward. He was short, considerably shorter than the other men. Than the other women, for that matter. His dress was a bit different, too, as he wore breeches, a coat, and boots that looked more suited for riding horseback than working in a field. He wore his hat at a rakish angle. And his face—well, his face looked ancient, wrinkled and wizened as a dried apple. His eyes were bright, though, even in the somewhat bleary photo.

"So that's who visited you tonight. Holy crumb, Deck!" I grinned up at him. "That's exciting, don't you think? That you have this picture, so you know what he looked like. Are there more?"

Wordlessly, he flipped the page to reveal two more pictures of Uncle Connell. Both had those light spots in the corners, too.

With my thumb, I swiped at them. "Must have been a reflection in the camera lens." I cocked my head, studying the old gentleman. "He's an odd-looking duck, isn't he? A bit different from the others."

He snorted, and Mungo jerked his head up in surprise. "That's one way to put it, I suppose."

I raised my eyebrows in question.

"He's supposed to be a leprechaun."

I grinned up at Deck, then saw he wasn't kidding. My smile dropped. "*What?*"

Mungo wriggled in closer, his nose almost touching the album.

"That's what the cousins told my mother when

she was staying with them. Uncle Connell was a leprechaun who fell in love with my great-great-aunt Avril." He pointed to the young woman with the skeptical expression. "He was considerably older than her, and she naturally resisted his affections. But he continued to pursue her over the years until she finally gave in and married him. Despite their age difference, he outlived her. After she passed, he disappeared, and they never saw him again. And they said he looked as old when he met her as when he left after her funeral."

I stared at him. "You mean he . . . No." I shook my head. "That's not possible."

He shrugged. "You believe in magic. And if that's possible, why isn't the existence of a leprechaun?"

"Well, for one thing, leprechauns are immortal. Right?" A part of me marveled that we were even having this conversation, but still I scrambled to piece together a logical argument. "And your uncle Connell came to you from the other side of the veil tonight. So he has to be dead."

A slow grin spread across his face. "So you're saying my uncle couldn't be a leprechaun because he's a ghost?"

"Uh—"

"Where do you draw the line, Katie?"

My shoulders slumped. "You do have a point." My head came up. "Wait a sec. You had this secret in your family all along, and you question my heredity as a hedgewitch?"

He frowned. "I didn't question anything. I took

you at your word. I just didn't know you could go
all abracadabra on my ass."

"Abra . . . Declan!"

"You know what I mean."

And I did. It had been an unfortunate incident,
and I'd thought it was water under the bridge.

He pointed to the pictures still on our laps.
"These smudges are supposedly lights that were
often seen near Connell at night. There isn't a
photo of him where they don't appear."

"Amazing."

Declan snapped the album shut. "Or not. It's
just a family legend." He stood, displacing Mungo,
who jumped to the floor. "Who knows how much
of it's true? I mean, leprechauns? I think my
mother was making up fun stories for her kids, to
tell you the truth."

"But Connell was real, right? You knew the
name when he . . . came to you?"

He paused on his way back to the bedroom,
met my eyes. "Yes."

"So there's that."

"Yes," he said. "There's that." And he turned to
put the pictures of his great-great-uncle and the
other McCarthy ancestors back in the closet.

Mungo jumped back onto the sofa and regarded
me with questioning eyes. "Do you think it's true?"
I whispered, hugging the afghan around me.

Yip!

Chapter 14

Once the morning baking was well under way, I went into the office and closed the door. Our Web designer had sent updates to our Web site that I wanted to review, and there were new e-mails in the Honeybee in-box to answer. Those bits of secretarial duty attended to, I sat back and took a sip of strong coffee before reaching into my tote bag and retrieving my cell phone.

My mother, Mary Jane Lightfoot, and I had had our differences since I'd learned from Lucy that I came from a long line of hedgewitches. At first Mama had been really upset that her younger sister had not only spilled the beans but was instructing me in the Craft. However, after a surprise visit in the middle of a murder investigation, my mother and I had finally reconciled after a year of estrangement.

Trial by fire, I supposed, but the result was we were not only speaking to each other again, but were in frequent contact.

Now my mother answered on the second ring. "Katie! I'm so glad you called, sweetie. How are things in fair Savannah?"

I leaned back in the desk chair and reached over to scratch Mungo under the chin.

"Unseasonably hot today, humid, mosquito-y, and when the wind drifts from the wrong direction, it smells like the pulp mill."

"You sound kind of grumpy."

"Oh, and you know that film they're making over in Reynolds Square? The romantic comedy set during the Revolutionary War?"

"You mentioned it." She sounded wary.

"Well, someone died on the set. Was *killed* on the set, I should say, and right after he hired the Honeybee to cater lunches."

"Killed . . . Oh, dear." I heard her take a deep breath. "Were you the one who found him?"

"No. Althea Cole did. At least that what she says. But Declan and I got there right after we heard her scream." I braced myself for my mother's dire warnings against using magic or putting myself in danger.

Instead she said, "Althea Cole? Really?"

"Sure. She's the female lead. Both of them, actually, since she's playing twins."

"And you don't believe she found the body?"

"It's not that, not really. I just don't trust her."

"Why is that?"

"For one thing, she sabotaged the séance last night."

"Séance."

"Oh. Right. So Althea travels with a personal trainer who's also a psychic. This woman—her name's Ursula Banford—apparently has this trio of spiritual guides that help her talk to dead people. So a bunch of us got together last night and tried to reach Simon—that's the victim—to see if he could tell us who killed him. Althea disrupted things, though, right as Simon showed up, and he left without telling us who stabbed him."

There was a silence, and then she said, "I see."

"And get this: Franklin Taite apparently told Ursula I would be the one to bring Simon's killer to justice, which means he has to have passed to the other side, only I don't see how he could be dead without anyone knowing about it, so that doesn't make any sense, except I can't find any record of him on the Internet." Mungo stood up and stared at me, and I realized I'd been talking at breakneck speed. I inhaled and said, "Oh, and Nonna showed up at the séance. She said to pass her love on to you."

My mother snorted out a very unladylike laugh. "Oh, Katie. You've been called again, that's all."

"That's all? You sound like Lucy."

"Well, it's pretty obvious."

"Yeah," I agreed. "And Ben asked me to help, too, since he's angry that someone got killed while he was working security for the area. Declan was working at the same time, and he doesn't seem to take the murder personally. Ben was in charge, though, so he feels responsible."

"I imagine he does." Her tone was light, neutral. I pictured her sitting on the Queen Anne chair next to the telephone table she insisted on using despite the phone being cordless now. Her ankles would be crossed beneath her pencil skirt, and her blouse would be crisply ironed, her hair perfectly coiffed, and her makeup light but precise in the even sixty-nine degrees she and Daddy kept their home at year-round.

"Aren't you going to tell me to butt out?" I asked.

"Of course not. I have all the confidence in the world in you and your ability to fulfill that psychic's prediction. And if my mother came through for her, you can bet this Ursula is a bona fide medium. Anyway, your father and I are only a phone call away if you need us. Plus, you have those wonderful ladies in the spellbook club. They are quite the impressive coven of witches, and you'll be well advised to ask for their help."

"Wow," I said. "You've certainly changed your tune."

She paused and then said cheerily, "You'd be surprised how much. Your father is, at least."

"How's that?" I asked.

"I worked with him to cast a fertility spell on our garden seeds this year. It worked! The vegetables are growing like mad, and the frost-free date was only a few weeks ago." She giggled. *Giggled.* "We're thinking of boosting all the seeds down at the store."

My mother might come across as a prim-and-proper lady of society, but she and Daddy owned the hardware store in the little town of Fillmore, Ohio. And when I say little, I mean little—fewer than six hundred residents. Which was one reason why my mother was so careful about practicing magic, especially since her mother had been caught casting a fertility spell in her backyard there.

In the nude.

"Mama, I'm so proud of you."

"Thanks, honey. I must say it felt really good to cast again."

"Maybe we could try a spell together some-time."

"I think that would be fun," she said. "Something light, though, not any of your crazy light-witch stuff."

Crazy lightwitch stuff. Well, mothers would be mothers, wouldn't they, even if they also happened to be witches.

Still, I felt better after talking with her. Clear and focused after the confusing evening with Declan had muddied my thoughts.

"Mama?" I asked. "Do you believe in lepre-chauns?"

"Do I . . . what?" she asked. "What do lepre-chauns have to do with anything?"

"I don't know. Probably nothing. Last night Declan was at the séance with us, and his great-great-uncle came through. I mean, actually came through Declan himself. Ursula said it's rare that someone has the right vibrations to physically channel a spirit, but he did."

"Oh, my," my mother said. "How did he take that?"

"Er, not very well, actually. But afterward, Deck showed me old pictures of this uncle Connell of his, taken back in Ireland maybe a century ago. More, even. He's a strange-looking guy, and Deck said his mother was told by his Irish cousins that Connell was a leprechaun."

My mother blew a raspberry. "Just because someone looks odd doesn't mean they're another— I don't know—species. Good heavens, Katie. Leprechauns are only a myth."

"What about water spirits or tree spirits?"

"Naiads and dryads are different," she said, but I could hear the doubt in her voice.

"How?"

"I don't know. They're nature spirits, for one thing, not little men who run around in green suits. Seriously, Katie. Declan's uncle was not a real leprechaun."

I let the subject drop. We talked for a few more moments, and she promised to update my father on the murderous doings in Savannah.

As I hung up the phone, I reflected that she was probably right that leprechauns weren't real. But Declan was right, too: Once you believe in magic as a reality, once you proudly call yourself a witch, talk to ghosts, and admit that water and tree spirits are actual entities in the world, how much further does your belief have to stretch to include a wee leprechaun or two?

*　　　*　　　*

At ten thirty I was restocking the pistachio cream éclairs, and the air was filled with the spicy scent of carrot 'n' apple cake baking in the oven. Jaida sat over in the reading area perusing back copies of *Cosmopolitan*. Today she wore skinny jeans and a Che Guevara T-shirt, so I knew it was not only not a court day but also not an office day. I was glad to see her take some time off since she'd been working so many hours lately. Mungo was hanging out in the library, too, keeping an eye on the goings-on from his comfy new bed on the bottom shelf of a bookcase.

The door opened and Detective Quinn stepped through.

"Hey there," I called and waved him in. "Can I interest you in a piece of lemon sour cream cake?"

He came over and leaned his elbows on the espresso counter. "I don't suppose you have any of those big oatmeal cookies left?" His eyes twinkled.

Lucy shooed him off. "Those aren't on the menu anymore." She lowered her voice. "Just in case, you know?"

"Mmm. You're right, of course. But I do have news on that front." He turned to me. "You look nice, Katie. That color suits you."

I glanced down at my indigo-and-plum-striped skirt and sleeveless plum crinkle blouse, all covered with a navy apron. "Um, thanks." But I was suspicious. Why was he being so nice to me?

Quinn, of course, looked cool and collected in blue slacks and a crisply starched white shirt that looked like it was fresh from the cleaners. I knew, however, that when he was working on a murder case, the detective tended to work around the clock. He probably kept a drawer full of shirts in his office.

He did look tired, though. The beginnings of half-moons darkened the area under his eyes, and he'd missed a slight bit of stubble the last time he shaved. For the first time, I wondered how old Quinn was. Though his face had its share of lines and his hair was almost solid gray, I'd always thought he was in his late forties. Today he looked at least a decade older, and I reminded myself to ask Ben if he knew Quinn's age.

"The lemon cake sounds good. It's one of my favorites." He lifted a hand to Jaida, who returned the gesture, and then he promptly chose a seat as far away from her as possible. As far as I knew, he didn't have a problem with Jaida personally, so I put it down to police instinct regarding defense attorneys.

Sliding onto the seat across from him, I asked, "How's Owen Glade?"

"He spent quite a few hours at the hospital, but he's okay. They released him late last night."

I blew out my breath in relief. "So what happened?"

"Someone definitely tampered with those cookies."

My stomach dropped, even though I'd suspected Quinn would say that. "Only those cookies? From the Honeybee?"

"Yes. All the oatmeal cookies we tested from the

movie set had a little special addition to them. No other food item did, however, and neither did the cookies we picked up here and took to the lab. It was obvious sabotage."

I thought of poor Owen, as sick as anyone I'd ever seen. "Sabotage of what, though? The movie? It was a *poisoning*." I rubbed my hands over my face. "What will people say about the Honeybee?"

"It's not your fault someone slipped a powerful emetic into something after you served it. And I can't imagine you did it yourself. The last thing you'd want is to make people sick with your cooking."

"Emetic? Like ipecac syrup?" I made an up-chucking motion.

"At least it wasn't ex-lax," he said.

Ugh. "So it was some kind of prank?"

"Hmm. I wouldn't call it that," he said. "An over-the-counter emetic might have counted as a prank, but whatever was used was strong. Prescription strong."

"People get prescriptions for emetics? For what? I mean, I've heard of *antiemetics*, sure." I thought of a friend who'd gone through chemotherapy. "But trying to be sick? I don't get that."

Wait a minute. My fingers crept to my lips as I thought of Althea and her tiny waist and thin arms. Sure, she traveled with a personal trainer, and Ursula had said she kept Althea skinny, but I'd seen her tuck into macaroni and cheese with great gusto, and she apparently drank wine and ate cheese every single day.

"You look like you might have something to tell me," Quinn said.

"I wish I did, at least something definitive. I was just wondering how Althea stays so thin."

Understanding dawned on his face. "Ah. You think she might use an emetic as part of her 'Hollywood diet'?" He tapped his fingers on the table. "You know, that's a good place to start looking."

I shrugged. "I must say that for someone so famous, Althea seems to have her fingers in the middle of everything, from finding Simon's body to influencing Owen Glade's choice in caterers to being right there when he got so violently ill." Not to mention she'd ruined a perfectly good séance.

Lucy brought Quinn's slab of lemon cake over, along with a complimentary cup of coffee. He dug in, still listening.

"Plus, she's obviously involved with Steve Dawes but still fooling around with another man."

He swallowed. "And how do you know that?"

I told him about chasing Mungo into the wardrobe tent and finding Althea embracing the stranger. "He has a ponytail, too, like Steve. Maybe that's her thing." I raised my palms to the ceiling. "I don't suppose there were any fingerprints on that knife?"

Like mine? Or Lucy's?

"Wiped clean," he said.

"So tell me, how much strength would it take to drive a big knife like that into a grown man's body?"

"A grown man the size of, say, Simon Knapp?" Quinn asked.

"Precisely that size."

"Quite a bit, actually. However, it would take less force if he were to be on the ground, already unconscious." He took a sip of coffee and sat back in his chair. "Which Simon probably was."

"Really?"

"His skull showed signs of blunt force trauma. It looks like he was struck on the head, went down, and then was stabbed."

I leaned forward and put my elbows on the table. "But no idea what he was hit with?"

He shook his head. "Something round, maybe like a baseball bat? We didn't find anything that fit the bill on that set."

"Did you search the house Simon rented for the cast?" I asked.

"Simon's room only. We didn't have probable cause for the other parts of the house since the murder took place a couple blocks away."

"A baseball bat, huh. So about this big around?" I formed my fingers into a circle and peered at the detective through it. "Oh, my God!" My hands dropped to my lap. "Quinn, could you hit someone with a bottle of wine hard enough to knock them out?" I asked. "Without breaking the bottle, I mean."

His lips parted, then formed an *O* as he considered the idea. Then he slowly nodded. "I've seen it myself, back when I was still a patrolman. Guy tried to rob a liquor store and the manager clocked him with a bottle of Night Train. It was sitting on the counter when we got there." He sipped his coffee. "We confiscated all the wine bottles at the scene. I don't know if they've all been tested yet, though."

Lost in thought, I barely heard him. There was something, if only I could remember. I closed my eyes and ran my hands over my face; then suddenly it came to me. I looked up. "The Côtes du Rhône."

He looked puzzled.

"Althea demanded 'Stevie' get the wine after Simon was killed and asked where the Côtes du Rhône was. So she expected it to be there on the catering table, but it was gone."

"Okay." He drew the word out.

"There was a bottle at their rental house last night, though." Oh, God. Was that what Bianca had poured for Declan and me? No, it had been empty by the time we were done. That must have been what Althea had helped herself to so generously.

His eyes narrowed. "You were at the house last night?"

Uh-oh. "Ursula invited us—er, me—over," I sidestepped. "Stay here for a sec? I have to call Bianca."

I went behind the register to use the Honeybee's landline. A quick conversation with my wine-savvy friend, and I returned to the table, where Quinn sat looking impatient.

"Bianca told me Côtes du Rhône pairs with Camembert, but not with the cheese they were having last night. There were wines there to pair with that cheese, but the Camembert Owen picked up at the Welsh Wabbit was to be served the evening before—with the Côtes du Rhône. Bianca can confirm that was the intention because the wine came from her shop."

One side of Quinn's mouth turned up in a wry smile. "Well, isn't that interesting. But how did the wine bottle get to the house from the movie set?"

I shrugged. "The killer could have hidden it and taken it there later."

"I'd throw it in the river," Quinn said.

"*Mmmph.* Yeah. I would, too. Or even in a Dumpster someplace." I held up a finger. "Unless there wasn't time. What if Niklas Egan was coming back from stashing the murder weapon at the house?"

Slowly, he nodded. "It's worth looking into," he said. "And I wouldn't have known to check since I wasn't invited into a houseful of possible suspects like you were."

I forced a smile and changed the subject. "So no real suspects?"

"The alibis of the major players, such as they are, check out. We can't find anyone who wasn't supposed to be on the set, though it turns out the key grip—the guy in charge of equipment—and his best boy were still packing away the lighting used that day. They confirm they were both in one of the RVs when Simon was killed. They had the stereo on, so they didn't even hear Althea scream."

"And what about the things Simon fixed for people?" I asked. "Are you checking into all the suspects' backgrounds?"

He gave me a look. "Why, yes, Katie. We are."

I ducked my head. "Of course. Sorry."

When I looked back up, he was smiling. "You're right that something Simon Knapp 'fixed' might have bit him back. Nik Egan's story about his wife checks out, but he didn't seem to be too worried about keeping it a secret. As for the others, we're still doing background checks to see what we can find." He finished the last of his coffee. "I'll follow up on whether Ms. Cole has a prescription for an emetic and check with the ME about the wine bottle. If she says it's a possibility, I might convince a judge to give us a warrant to search the house where the movie folks are staying." He stood. "Nice job, Katie. But if I might offer a bit of advice?"

"Sure."

"Don't go into a houseful of murder suspects alone again."

I smiled, wanting to tell him I wasn't stupid but unwilling to go into details about the séance. So I simply said, "Noted."

Chapter 15

I waved good-bye to Jaida as she left, and Quinn went to use the restroom, but I remained at the table, mulling over what we'd discussed. The bell over the door announced a new customer, and out of habit I glanced over at Lucy to see how busy she was. She was refilling the basket of napkins nestled in among the coffee condiments and looked up, smiling at whoever had entered. When I saw her eyes widen, I turned to see who it was.

Althea Cole stood in the open doorway, Owen Glade hovering on the sidewalk behind her.

"Oh, my gosh!" a young woman seated at a table near the reading area said to her companion. "Is that . . . ? Oh, my *gosh*, it *is*!"

The starlet swept inside. Owen followed with a scowl on his face. There were dark circles stamped on the translucent skin under his eyes. Why was he back at work so soon after his ordeal and hospitalization? There wasn't anyone else to do his

job now that Simon was gone, so perhaps he
didn't have any choice.

Lucy stepped forward, reaching for her hand
with both of her own. "Oh, Ms. Cole. I'm so glad
you stopped into the Honeybee for a treat. We're
honored."

I felt my nostrils flare, but I held my tongue and
stayed right where I was.

Althea pulled her hand away from Lucy's and
looked around. She wore a white sundress with a
flared skirt and tightly cinched waist to show off
her twiggy figure, along with ballet flats and a hat
with a wide brim that flopped adorably to one
side. Long, glossy ringlets cascaded down her
back. Owen carried her brown leather Marc Jacobs
bag.

The customer who had instantly recognized the
movie star rummaged in her backpack, pulled out
a small notebook, and then looked wildly around
the room. "I don't have a pen," she practically
wailed. "Does anyone have a pen?"

Lucy reached behind the register. "Of course."
She held the instrument out toward her. The
woman bolted out of her chair and snatched it out
of my aunt's hand. "Oh, thank you, thank you.
Ms. Cole, oh, please, Ms. Cole, won't you please
sign your autograph for me?"

"Of course, dear," Althea said with a genteel
curve of her lips. "I'd be delighted to."

The woman held out the notebook to Althea.
"Can you write, 'To my bestie Kortney, with

love and kisses. Stay in touch'? That's Kortney with a 'K.'"

Althea's eyebrow lifted an infinitesimal amount, and I wondered whether her subdued reaction was from self-control or Botox. She bent her head and wrote, saying, "To Kortney with a 'K'. Althea Cole." She signed with a flourish and handed the notebook back.

Kortney's face fell as she read her idol's abbreviated autograph. "Um, okay. Thanks." She returned the pen to Lucy and joined her companion with considerably less verve.

Lucy watched her with pity, though a part of me could understand why Althea didn't want to be bossed into what to write to an adoring fan, and at least she'd handled the situation with a certain amount of grace.

"What can we get you, Ms. Cole?" Lucy said. "On the house, of course."

I frowned. Really? It wasn't like my aunt to be starstruck, and she sure hadn't acted this way the night before.

Althea drew herself up to her full height, which was only about five-six. "I would never eat anything made in this establishment after what happened to my friend." With a sweeping gesture, she directed everyone's attention to Owen, pale and blinking behind his round glasses. "He ate a cookie, just one little cookie, made by these women and ended up in the hospital!"

Lucy's fingers went to her lips and her eyes

widened. Solid silence lowered over the bakery. I felt my face grow red.

"Now, hold on, Althea." I stood, and her attention focused on me.

"No, you hold on, Katie Lightfoot. I have a bone to pick with you."

"That cookie—"

"This is about Ursula. How dare you usurp my own private psychic?"

A few customers exchanged glances.

"Usurp? I—"

"You know what I'm talking about. That little séance of yours. It didn't work, now, did it? But it wore her out, and I need her. I need solace from beyond to help me cope with that horrid murder, and you used her up."

My lips thinned. "I hardly think your psychic is used up. She just needed a good night's sleep, like we all did."

Her fists went to her hips. "I pay her, and I'll decide what she needs. You stay away from her."

What was her problem? But I could feel the eyes of our customers on me, and I knew word could spread—of this ridiculous accusation about Ursula, but more important, about the Honeybee's food safety.

I spread my hands in front of me, palms up. "Okay. I'm sorry, Althea."

She glared at me, but my apology seemed to have taken some of the wind out of her sails. Finally, her shoulders slumped a little. "Well, all right, then." She turned to go.

"But let's be very clear about something," I said. "That cookie that sent Owen to the hospital had been tampered with."

She crossed her arms over her chest. "Sure it was."

"The police discovered someone had added a prescription drug to it." I kept my tone even and straightforward. "In fact, they are looking for people associated with the movie who might have filled that particular prescription."

Althea blanched. "But Owen—"

I looked at Simon's assistant. "I'm sorry you got sick, Owen, but they tested the same cookies here at the Honeybee. They were fine. Whoever poisoned the cookie you ate did it on the *Love in Revolution* set."

Althea harrumphed, a sound so strange coming from her that I almost laughed.

"Ms. Lightfoot is correct," Quinn said. I hadn't heard him come out of the restroom. "I'm a police detective, and I can assure you there is nothing wrong with the baked goods here at the Honeybee, folks. In fact, I just treated myself to some of the lemon sour cream cake."

Althea's jaw clenched and the muscles in her throat worked, but her face remained impassive. Yep: Botox. "I'm sure poor Owen here is comforted by that information," she said and yanked the door open.

Poor Owen followed her out to the sidewalk without ever having said a word. Probably hadn't had the energy for it.

Conversations began again, and I went over

and hugged Lucy. "Sorry. You tried to be nice, but I'm afraid that woman isn't very good at being nice back."

Detective Quinn walked up.

"Thanks for standing up for us like that," Lucy said. "Hopefully, that will nip the rumors in the bud."

"Only told the truth," he said. "Besides, this is my favorite bakery, and I want to make sure you guys stick around for a while."

I grinned. "Glad to hear it."

His smile faded. "Now, what was that about a séance?"

Lucy looked worried.

I shrugged. "You met Ursula Banford. And I did mention she invited us to the house where she's staying."

"I met everyone remotely associated with that movie set." He said *movie set* the same way you might say *cockroach*.

"So you know she works for Althea."

He glanced at Lucy. "And I heard her very convenient prediction that you'd find Knapp's killer. But really, Katie. A séance? I'd think you'd take murder more seriously than that."

"Hey!" I protested.

"Keep your voice down," Lucy warned.

"Right. But Quinn, I *am* taking Simon's murder seriously. Very seriously. Enough so that if Ursula is the real deal and could possibly contact Simon himself to tell us who killed him, then it would be remiss not to at least try."

Quinn shook his head. "You are a lot of things, Katie, but I wouldn't have said one of them was gullible."

"Gee, thanks."

"Until now."

"Now, listen—"

He cut me off. "What did Simon's ghost have to say?" Sarcasm dripped from the question.

Lucy spoke up. "He showed up but didn't stay long enough to tell us."

Thanks to Althea.

Quinn looked at her with surprise. "You were in on this, too?"

"Even Ben was," she said. "He agreed that when it comes to murder, all avenues should be explored."

"Good Lord," Quinn said. "How much did Banford charge?"

"Nothing," I said.

He looked nonplussed. "Oh. Well, did you get any information?"

Lucy and I silently shook our heads. "But it didn't hurt to try," I insisted.

A customer came up to the register then, and Lucy took his order. I accompanied Quinn to the door, stepping out to the sidewalk with him. He paused and tipped his head to the side. "What?"

"I don't know if it makes any difference or not, but Althea sure didn't seem to want her personal psychic to get any answers from Simon Knapp. And whether you believe in Ursula's powers as a medium or not, Althea Cole most certainly seems to."

His eyebrow quirked up. "I'll take that under advisement, Ms. Lightfoot."

After Althea's little visit to the bakery I thought it was high time I talk to Steve about his new love interest. Bianca was slated to appear as an extra, and that gave me a good excuse to go back and look around. Besides, I wanted to check in with Ben because I knew he'd been keeping an extra-vigilant lookout for anything unusual.

Declan saw Mungo and me coming and waved us inside the roped-off area. "I have standing orders from my boss to let you in."

Smiling, I resisted the urge to indulge in a nice big public display of affection and simply squeezed his hand. "I wonder what Ben's boss thinks about that executive decision."

Declan gestured toward the group of people several yards away. "Owen? I don't even know if he considers himself anyone's boss."

Sure enough, the acting production coordinator hovered near Niklas Egan, waiting for orders.

"I can't believe he's back at work already," I said. "Quinn stopped by this morning and told me the oatmeal cookies had been laced with a strong emetic, something you can only get with a prescription. There's no question it was deliberate, though what the motive was, I can't imagine," I said.

"To make the Honeybee look bad," my boyfriend grumbled.

"Maybe. Either way, I'm surprised Owen feels

chipper enough to fetch and carry for Niklas," I said.

"Chipper isn't the word I'd choose to describe him today. But I have to give him credit for bucking up," Declan said.

"Poor guy," I said. "Getting a job with a movie production company like this must be pretty competitive. Plus, he told me Simon brought him in from another job. Owen is probably afraid someone will step in and take his job if he doesn't show up."

Van Grayson, in his crimson uniform and with a wicked-looking bayonet in his hand, leaned over Niklas Egan's shoulder. Althea was nowhere to be seen, and I guessed she was still in the makeup RV, since she'd so recently been at the bakery making her feelings about me and mine loudly known to all and sundry. Bianca and Steve stood near Grayson, listening to Egan, who moved his hands in the air and spoke with sharp-eyed intensity. I couldn't hear his words, only his tone.

Bianca looked up, saw me, and waved. I lifted my hand in response.

"Since they're actually paying me to hang out here, I'd better get back to chatting with the fans," Declan said.

"Seriously? That's what a security guy does?"

"Sometimes. Ben and I have found that if we make nice with them, we have a lot fewer problems."

Trust my uncle to find the friendliest way to deal with people. "Okay, I'll be fine on my own."

"No troublemaking, you hear?"

I laughed, despite the fact that he couldn't quite hide that he half meant it. "Cross my heart. I was hoping to see Bianca in her walk-on role."

He glanced over at her. "Should be pretty soon. Niklas is winding down, and that usually means they're about to get started." He kissed me on the cheek and returned to patrolling the perimeter of the square. I noticed he had to work his way around the crime scene on the Congress Street side.

The group dispersed, and Niklas Egan walked rapidly toward the boom truck behind me. He slowed when he saw me. "Afternoon, Ms. Light-foot," he said with a curt nod.

I blinked. "You know who I am?"

"This is my set. I make sure I know who everyone is on my set."

"Oh."

"Nice job on the food, by the way. Not sure what Owen was thinking, bringing back Robin Bonner, but the little putz went and signed a contract—something Simon was way too smart to do. Sorry."

"That's okay," I said.

"So why are you here?"

My hand fluttered in the general direction of Bianca, who was now deep in discussion with Steve. "My friend . . ."

Egan turned his hawkish gaze their way. "Which one?"

"Well, both really. But I came to see Bianca's walk-on."

Another curt nod from the director. "She's a beauty, she is, and so very sweet." His affectionate look in her direction belied the rest of his all-business attitude. Then she looked up and they exchanged a tender smile. My mental alarm bells clang-clanged as I remembered their familiar exchange before the séance.

My distraction blurred the director's next words, and it took me a moment to realize he'd asked if I wanted to be in the movie.

"In . . . ?"

"As an extra. Like Bianca. We could pay you a little something—and I do mean little—if you wanted to join her. It'll be your last chance. We're almost done with the scenes we can complete here."

"What's your hurry?" I asked.

He frowned and rubbed his fingers together. "Money, honey. So, yes or no? You'd have to hurry, though."

My instinct was to politely refuse, but then I thought, why not? "What do you want me to do?"

"It's literally a walk-on, as in, you walk through the shot in the background. Moving window dressing, really." He lifted his chin toward the makeup trailer. "Get in there and have them do you up. We'll start in ten minutes." And off he went to talk to the camera operator, who waited nearby.

Bianca was coming toward me by then. I ran to her. "Looks like I'm going to be joining you."

"That's wonderful!" she said, her Georgia accent seeming to run thicker than ever since *Love in Revolution* had come to town.

"So, about Mr. Egan," I began.

"Ten minutes, Ms. Lightfoot," the director called, then turned to Owen. "She needs a dress, too." The young man shot a long-suffering look my way before blanketing it with an obsequious smile. "Yessir. I'll get right on it," he said before scurrying toward a woman holding a clipboard.

"Oops. I'd better scoot," I said to Bianca. "See you in a few."

Chapter 16

It took almost twelve minutes, but the smocked woman who had vacated the makeup RV the day before so Ursula and I could talk turkey about spirits transformed me into a lady from the past. She told me her name was Susie, plopped a blond wig on my head, stuffed most of the hair under a white cotton cap, and applied what seemed like four tons of makeup with a deft, lightning hand.

She whipped off the bib from around my neck and said, "You'll do for a background shot. Try not to smear your face when you change."

"Thanks," I said meekly. "I'll do my best."

Owen burst through the door, staggering under petticoats and crinolines. "Here. Get into these, quick!" He tossed a pair of pointy-toed satin shoes on the floor and ran out.

All the bossing around was making me regret saying yes, but I stripped down to my underwear and Susie helped me wiggle into the dress. "Where is wardrobe when you need them?" she muttered as she tugged the dress down over my bosom and began tucking and pinning around my waist. Moments later she stepped back. "Okay. I think you're set." She looked at her watch. "Better get a move on. Nik's not the most patient man."

I stumbled down the steps in the too-tight shoes and hobbled across to where Bianca stood waiting. Althea's jaw dropped when she saw me, and her eyes blazed under the big satin hat she'd been wearing the day before. Same outfit altogether, in fact.

Flustered, I looked away—right into Declan's delighted eyes. He stood next to one of the onlookers, and I saw him lean over and say something. The man listened, then clapped my boyfriend on the shoulder and nodded at me.

I would have loved to have known what was said in that exchange, but Niklas was already barking at me to stop limping.

Not at Bianca, I noticed, however. To her he said, "Sweetheart, remember what we talked about? You start down at the corner and stroll along the pathway. Stroll. Simply out for the afternoon, no hurry, and, if you like, perhaps the mildest, most genteel curiosity about the handsome man in uniform here."

Van Grayson grinned.

"Of course, Nik."

"Ms. Lightfoot, you follow her lead, okay? And whatever you do, do *not* look at the camera lens."

"Okeydoke," I said. How hard could it be?

Not hard at all, it turned out. At least the first

time. Or the second. But Althea kept flubbing her lines, or Niklas didn't like her delivery, or Van's uniform was crooked, or, or, or. Between takes, Bianca explained that the scene, which frankly looked pretty boring to me, held more depth than met the eye. It might *look* like a whispered agreement between the fancy lady and the British officer to meet later that night. Only the fancy lady was really the twin sister, who was bent on sabotaging the fancy lady's love affair after a lifetime of jealousy over the fancy lady's fancy life. *However*, little did the twin know the British officer was also an imposter!

Oh, yes. Great hilarity would ensue, Bianca assured me.

I took her at her word.

By the time the director was pleased, we were on the seventeenth take and my feet were killing me. With relieved gratitude, I sat down on the grass and slipped off the offending shoes. A closer look revealed they were rather well worn, and I wondered with a shudder how many sweaty-footed extras had worn them before me. I felt a trickle of sweat work down my side and was pretty sure all Susie's carefully applied makeup was turning into a melted mess on my face.

Bianca, looking cool and lovely, grinned down at me. "So how do you like acting?"

I flapped my hand at her. "Bah." I began to massage one foot, trying to regain some feeling. "This is your second time, right?"

She nodded, a weirdly happy expression on her face.

"You and Niklas Egan are involved, aren't you?" It was more of a statement than a question.

"I guess you could say that," she lilted.

I nodded. "Just be careful. I don't want to see you get hurt."

She stood and pulled me to my sore feet. "I'm a big girl, Katie. Don't you worry."

"Bianca!" Speak of the devil. "Coffee?"

"Sure," she said. "Let me get changed."

He lifted a hand in agreement and began speaking with a female member of the crew.

I turned toward the RV where I'd abandoned my street clothes in a heap on a chair. As I did I saw a figure with hunched shoulders duck between the catering tent and the area where the props and costumes were kept. He paused by the corner of the catering tent, looking over his shoulder as if making sure he hadn't been seen.

It was the man I'd stumbled onto in the tent. The one who'd been wrapped around Althea. The one I'd at first mistaken as Steve.

"Bianca," I hissed, though he was too far away to be able to hear me anyway. I pulled her into the shade of the boom truck.

"What?" Her gaze followed mine.

"Who is that guy?" I asked.

"That's Robin Bonner," Bianca said.

My chin jerked in surprise. "Really?" For some reason I'd imagined the caterer as an older, portly gent. This guy was younger than me.

"What on earth is he doing?" she asked.

I shook my head. He'd been hired back, after all. Even had a contract and every reason to be on the set of *Love in Revolution*. So why was he acting so weird? He took one last look around and furtively moved toward the crime scene tape. As we watched, he crossed the tape and bent to the ground. Seconds later, he'd retraced his steps, straightened, and walked into the catering tent as if he owned it.

"That," Bianca observed, "did not look quite kosher. Do you think Peter Quinn would want to know about the curious caterer?"

The corners of my mouth turned up. "I bet he would. But Quinn isn't here right now. I'll see you later."

I fast walked to the tent. Inside I found Bonner bundling up a bag of garbage.

"Hi!" I said.

He looked up, but when he saw me, the smile that had begun to form dropped from his face. "What are you doing here?"

"I'm in the movie," I said brightly.

His eyebrows shot up.

"As an extra," I clarified. "Don't worry. I'm not trying to take your job away."

His eyes narrowed. "Good."

"In fact, I don't really understand why Simon fired you in the first place."

He shrugged and turned back to the garbage. "We had a scheduling conflict."

Meaning you didn't show up on time.

"So just now," I said. "Before you came in here?

It looked like you crossed the crime scene tape. That's pretty brave. I'd be too scared of what the police might do if they found out."

He whirled and stared at me. "I picked up a candy wrapper." He reached into the bag of garbage and pulled out the torn packaging from a Baby Ruth bar. "Althea is right about you," he said, stuffing it back into the bag and cinching the ties.

Feeling chastised, I watched him stride out of the tent with the bag in his hand. Robin Bonner had been picking up litter.

Unless, of course, Robin Bonner was lying.

Not long after changing into my street clothes, I saw Steve stepping out of the makeup RV. He was back in costume, hair tied with a bow, his muscular legs well defined beneath the tight breeches. Did men really wear their breeches that tight back then—or ever? I had to admit, if anyone could pull it off, Steve Dawes could.

He paused when he noticed me hurrying across the corner of the square toward him. "Hey," he said when I reached him. "You look like you're on a mission."

"Er, sort of." Now that I was standing in front of him, I felt terribly guilty. I wanted him to know Althea was stepping out on him with, of all people, Robin Bonner, but I didn't want to hurt him. As far as I knew, Althea Cole was the first woman he'd shown interest in since he and I had been sort of, kind of, but not really dating. Sometimes things were awkward between us, and it might not really be my business, but he was my friend, and I wanted the best for him.

The best couldn't be a woman who dallied with other men behind his back.

"Are you on the way to film a scene?"

He shook his head. "Just finished. Last time. I'm only in a couple of scenes, but Niklas is a bit of a perfectionist. I never dreamed it would take so much time."

"So is Heinrich waiting for you to get back to the office?" I asked. Maybe he didn't have time for me to give him the bad news.

Amusement tugged at his lips. "Nope. I'm all yours. What's up?"

Taking a deep breath, I plunged in. "I think Althea is messing around with someone else."

He blinked. "Really?"

"I didn't mean to, honest, but I stumbled into them in the wardrobe tent the other day. It didn't look good. Althea and the man who I found out later is the caterer Owen hired back were all sneaky and chummy. I've been debating whether to tell you or not, but I think you deserve to know." I put my hand on his arm. "I'm so, so sorry."

Steve looked down at the ground. He put his hand over mine. I felt him tremble, then heard a small sound. Oh, no, was he going to start crying? I was searching for the words to comfort him when he raised his head and I saw he wasn't exactly weeping.

He was laughing.

"I'm sorry," he said with a little snort. "You're

just so darned earnest. Thank you for looking out for me, but I think you might have misconstrued the situation. I don't think you saw what you think you did."

"Oh, really." He must really have it bad if he didn't want to hear anything against his new girlfriend. *Idiot.*

Except.

Except the Steve I knew was far from being an idiot. He knew something I didn't. Something about Althea. Could it be something Simon had known about, too? A secret the fixer had to fix?

Fists on my hips, embarrassment forgotten, I demanded, "Okay. Spill it."

"What do you mean?" The picture of innocence.

"It could be important."

"Aw, Katie, c'mon." He reached out a hand toward me.

I backed away. "Really important. And if it's not, then I promise not to tell a soul. Cross my heart."

"It's not mine to tell," he said.

"Do you care for her so much you can't tell me?" Even as the words left my mouth, I knew it was dirty pool.

"Of course not." He sighed. "I'm not dating Althea Cole, for heaven's sake. I couldn't care less who she spends time with or what they do. I'm pretty sure she and Robin Bonner weren't doing anything untoward in the wardrobe tent, though."

I digested that information for a few seconds. If he wasn't dating her, why was he hanging out with her and letting her call him Stevie? And how did he know so much about the caterer?

"Okay, let me ask you one thing," I said. "Do you know Althea well enough to be sure that she wouldn't kill Simon over whatever this secret is that you won't tell me?"

He opened his mouth, hesitated, then shut it again. He thought for a moment, then said, "No, I guess I really don't."

I waited.

"Come on." He waved me to the edge of the square by the Airstreams. We ducked under the rope, and he led me to a bench tucked under the overarching branches of a live oak. The succulent aromas of seafood, garlic, and grilling meat wafted from the direction of the Olde Pink House restaurant.

Once we were seated, he said, "Althea isn't even aware that I know who Bonner really is."

My curiosity ratcheted up another notch.

Steve gave me a long look, then seemed to make a decision. "He's her son."

I blinked. "What?"

"Simon came to Father to help find Althea's son. She gave him up for adoption when she was sixteen."

"Good heavens. How old is Althea now?" I asked.

"Forty-one. Her son is twenty-five. Anyway, she knew he was adopted in Savannah, and since they were going to be filming here—and she knew of Simon's ability to get information and to keep his mouth shut—she decided to track her son down."

"So . . . how do you know all this if she didn't tell you? Oh, wait." I snapped my fingers. "Your father." Heinrich Dawes was a powerful mover and shaker in Savannah, with tendrils everywhere and no compunction in using his druidic magic for business ends. "But how did Simon know to contact Heinrich?"

Steve shrugged. "Father has all kinds of contacts. And Simon was the kind of guy who knew people with lots of contacts. Father delegated the task to me. I tracked down Robin Bonner and told Simon Knapp. He's the one who reunited mother and son."

"Then you met Althea, and she took a shine to you," I said. "Got you a speaking part in the movie."

He grimaced. "Not quite. Oh, she took a shine to 'Stevie,' all right, but I only met her after Simon had arranged for me to be in the movie, and it worked out well that she likes me. See, Althea is apparently known to be difficult, and Niklas wanted things to go smoothly. Simon had too much to do to micromanage the leading lady, so he asked Father if I'd step in."

And true to clan and Dawes family policy, you did what you were told.

"You agreed to help," I said.

He tipped his head to the side. "In case you're wondering, I haven't been seriously interested in any woman since you turned me away. I guess I'm still hoping you might . . ." He trailed off as my eyes widened in alarm.

"Steve—"

He held up both his palms to me, moving them like erasers on a chalkboard before dropping them back into his lap. "Never mind. Forget I said anything."

"But—" I sighed and let it go.

He grinned easily and returned to the original subject. "It's been fun working on the set and seeing how movies are made." The smile dropped from his face. "Fun except for, you know, the murder."

I sifted through what Steve had told me about Althea. "It wasn't just happenstance that A. Dendum hired Bonner Catering."

"Nope. Althea insisted Simon hire her son the budding culinary art student, and since Simon wanted to keep her happy, he agreed." He made a face. "It wasn't horrible, but the guy has a lot to learn. Apparently, he had a food truck for a while that specialized in waffles."

"The Waffle Baron?"

Steve nodded. "He should have stuck with that."

"He's back to work now that Owen Glade re-hired him." I met Steve's eyes. "I bet Althea made Owen hire her son back, just like she did Simon."

Steve made a noise of agreement and stood. "It's kind of hard to watch her order him around, actually. I'll be glad when they all move on to Dahlonega and I can get back to writing my column and doing my part for the family biz."

We made our way back toward the white canopies flapping in the breeze.

"Do you think Althea would have gone so far as to kill Simon for firing her son?"

Steve considered the question. "That would be pretty crazy, especially since she had just met him recently as an adult. But who knows? Stranger things have happened, and Lord knows Althea is unpredictable. It was an ugly scene when Simon fired him in front of everyone. Embarrassing. He had a good reason, though. Even if the star actress was his mother, Robin couldn't seem to show up on time."

I veered toward the catering tent, curious about what Bonner Catering had on offer.

"Katie?" Steve touched my shoulder.

I stopped and turned.

"Are you going to tell anyone about Althea's son?"

I licked my lips. "Honestly? I won't tell people . . . except I think it's important that I tell Detective Quinn, if that's okay. It doesn't seem relevant, but at some point it might prove to be."

"Okay. But just him. Althea doesn't want anyone to know about Robin," Steve said.

"Well, okay. But I'm a little surprised she'd be so secretive. There's no such thing as bad publicity, right? And she's certainly had her share of scandal over the years—like the rest of Hollywood."

"Has it occurred to you that she's not thinking about herself?" Steve asked. "That she's thinking of her son? Not everyone wants their family to be seen as a tacky reality show."

It hadn't, actually. And maybe he was right.

Or maybe there was still something we didn't know.

Chapter 17

"Katie! You *are* here."

I whirled at the voice. Margie Coopersmith walked slowly toward us. Jonathan's fingers were clasped in one hand and Julia's in the other, while baby Bart gazed with wide-eyed wonder at the world from his backpack carrier.

Declan held Julia's other hand, and as they approached, she skipped and let the two adults swing her through the air for a couple of steps before her flip-flops kicked up and then touched grass again. Deck watched her antics with gentle affection. He didn't talk about it much, but I knew how much he loved kids and that someday he wanted a passel of them.

Hopefully, that someday would fall around the time my biological clock finally kicked in—which, at the rate it was going, would be a few years down the road. Though, honestly, a "passel" seemed like one or two too many to me.

Deck's expression turned stony when he looked

up and saw my companion. However, when I smiled a welcome, his features softened a little.

In a low voice, I said to Steve, "Thanks for letting me know about Althea. I'm glad she's not, you know, cheating on you . . ." My words trailed off as his eyebrow lifted in amusement.

"I appreciate you looking after me," he said.

I shrugged. "You're my friend, right?"

A single decisive nod. "Right." He lifted a hand to Margie, who smiled in response without letting go of the twins' hands. "I'll see you later . . . friend." I watched him walk away for a few seconds before turning back.

Margie, looking her usual robust and tanned self, flashed a white-toothed grin at me as they approached. She wore oversized sunglasses, a sleeveless camp shirt, denim shorts, and Keds. A messenger-style bag was slung across her ample chest, another way she kept her hands free to manage three kids at once.

She stopped in front of me.

"What are you all up to?" I asked.

"Mommy says we're running 'rands," Jonathan said.

On the other side of her mother, Julia solemnly nodded her head. "It's boooring."

Margie rolled her eyes with a grin. "Ah, my little darlings love to help their mama."

Declan let go of Julia's hand and looked to me. "Margie said you wanted her to bring you something." There was a questioning lilt at the end of the sentence.

"Um," I said.

"You know," Margie said, and I thought I saw a twinkle behind the dark lenses of her Jackie O's. "That *thing*."

"Oh, right. That." What was she up to?

Declan's eyes narrowed in suspicion.

I gestured for my neighbor to follow me. "Over here," I said, stopping to buss Declan's cheek. "Thanks, hon."

He didn't protest, but kept an eagle eye on our progress as we made our way toward the catering canopy.

"Katie Lightfoot, was that your good-looking reporter who waved at me?"

"Not mine, but yes, it was Steve," I confirmed. "Now, what on earth would make you"—I glanced down at the twins—"er, prevaricate to the security guard."

"Well . . ." Margie drew the word out. "Like the JJs said, we had some errands to run downtown, so I thought I'd stop by and show the kiddos how they make movies."

Julia's eyes followed a man wearing a lace cravat, breeches, and a powdered wig hurrying toward where Niklas Egan consulted with a cameraman "This doesn't look like our movies," she said.

"Uh-uh," Jonathan said, his nose wrinkled.

"I bet most of your movies are made on a computer screen," I said.

Margie let out a full-bodied laugh, startling Bart into his own chortle. "Hadn't really thought of that. But you do like Mr. Van, and he's not a cartoon character," she reminded the twins.

"Van's the man!" they shouted.

My neighbor turned the full wattage of her smile on me. "Think we might be able to . . . ?" She wisely did not say, "Meet Van Grayson," in front of the young fans by her sides.

"Uh . . . ," I said. "I really don't know. I guess I could find out. I saw him earlier."

Her head jerked up like a pointer's when a bird is flushed. "Yoo-hoo!" she called. "Mr. Grayson!"

He was a hundred feet away, strolling toward his RV. His steps slowed, and his eyes cut toward Margie, who was now hurrying toward him as fast as she could with multiple offspring in tow. He picked up speed, pretending not to hear her.

"Yoo-hoo!" She let go of the twins' hands to give the actor a double full-armed wave.

He'd have to be deaf not to hear her.

The JJs recognized him then, squealed like only five-year-olds can, and ran pell-mell across the lawn, shrieking, "Van's the Man. Van's the Man."

From my angle, I saw his lip curl up as if he smelled something unpleasant. Then he looked up and saw me watching him. Instantly, his distaste morphed into a big, happy smile. He stopped and turned, eyes as wide and delighted as the kids'.

"Oh. My. Goodness! Are these a couple of my very own Vanimals?"

The two children squealed again, more high-pitched than ever.

I caught up with Margie. "Quite the showman," I commented.

"Oh, isn't he wonderful with them? I can't tell you how many hours they've spent sitting in front of the television watching his videos. I swear, they love Van the Man as much as Simba or Ariel."

"Ariel?" I asked.

"You know. *The Little Mermaid*."

Ah. Vaunted company, indeed.

Julia held two of Grayson's fingers in an iron grip, grinning up at him like the little imp I knew she was. As a smile crept onto my face, he pulled back, but she held on, screeching with laughter. His smile slipped, revealing a sneer. With his other hand, he peeled her fingers off his own and leaned down to say something to her. When he stood back up, her features had transformed from joy to tragedy. He patted both of the JJs on the head and turned toward their mother.

"Delightful children you have here, ma'am. And who is this little darling?"

Margie practically preened, swiveling so Bart was hovering over the man like a thoroughly seat-belted cherub from on high.

Instinctively, I mentally reached out toward Grayson with my senses, searching for clues like an aardvark searching for ants.

Bitterness. Revulsion.

I managed to control my features just as he looked at me, pasting a big smile on my face.

"Gotta go get dressed for the big scene, little Vanimals. Will you be sticking around to watch me?" His question was directed at me and was none too friendly.

"Not today," I crooned. "Come along, guys. Let's leave the big movie star to get ready." I nodded at Grayson, and understanding flashed between us.

Margie gushed the whole time I led her and her miniature entourage back to where Declan stood. "Oh, my God, isn't he wonderful? So good with the kiddos. Kind, gentle, such a touch with the little ones. Of course I knew that from seeing him on television, but I hadn't realized that he's *so* handsome! It must be awfully hard for you to work around such a good-looker. . . ." She trailed off as we reached Declan.

I snaked my arm around his waist and smiled at her. "Oh, Margie. If you only knew."

Never mind that I wasn't exactly working on the set.

And never mind that I'd just learned Van the Man abhorred children. It certainly made me wonder what other secrets he might have.

That evening, Aunt Lucy and I closed down the Honeybee and got things ready in the kitchen for the next morning's work. I'd called Uncle Ben and asked him to stop by after he and Declan had turned over the daytime security of the abbreviated movie set to the next shift. Declan had agreed to fill in for a friend at the firehouse who wanted to attend her daughter's piano recital for a few hours. We'd get together for supper after he was finished.

Now my aunt and uncle and I, supplied with the requisite drinks and a plate of molasses peach muffins, lounged in the Honeybee library to chat about where things stood in Simon's murder investigation. Ben had pulled over one of the bistro chairs, straddling it and leaning his forearms on the back. Mungo padded over from his bed on the bookshelf and put his front paws on my leg. I lifted him up to my lap, where he promptly curled into a canine comma and began to snooze.

"Okay," I said. "I know we're all busy, but I need to bounce some ideas around and I don't know anybody I'd rather do that with."

Lucy smiled and took a sip of peppermint tea. "Of course. Anything we can do."

"Well, mostly I wanted to talk about the possible suspects in Simon's murder and ways that Simon might have fixed things for them. Because I still think that's why he died. I think in his fervor to get something done, he pushed someone too far. Either that or someone he fixed a situation for decided they didn't like that he knew so much about them."

Lucy nodded. "Secrets. The longer you keep a secret, the more power it has over you."

"And the more you'll do to protect it," Ben said. "You wouldn't believe some of the things I saw when I was working in the firehouse before getting into the administrative aspect of the department. Nothing like a fire to expose how people live."

"I bet," I said, curious but wanting to stay on

track. "There were only a few people left on the set that evening: Althea Cole, Van Grayson, Steve Dawes, Niklas Egan, Ursula Banford, and the makeup specialist, Susie. And, of course, Simon himself and Owen Glade."

"And there was a key grip and his best boy," Ben added.

"Right," I said. I passed on Quinn's assessment to my aunt and uncle. "But they vouch for each other and Quinn can't find any evidence that they had anything to do with Simon."

"He didn't hire them like he did Ben?" Lucy asked.

"Nope. Niklas hired his own crew. Now, everyone seems to have been away from the catering tent when Simon was killed, but no one has a bona fide alibi except those two crew members and Ursula and Susie the makeup lady."

"And Owen Glade. We all saw him come back from the Welsh Wabbit well after Althea screamed the alert."

"So that leaves Althea, Van, and Niklas," Ben said. "That's a pretty short list, really."

I frowned. "And they all have secrets of some kind, all right."

Lucy settled back against a cushion. "Do tell."

"Well, Niklas Egan told Quinn right off the bat that Simon had paid off the husband of a woman he'd been seeing on the side," I said. "Quinn told me earlier today that he'd confirmed the story."

"What about the others?" Ben asked around a bite of muffin.

I hesitated. "I did find out something from Steve today about Althea. He didn't want to tell me at first, because it's kind of gossipy, if not actually scandalous."

Lucy frowned.

"Still," I went on. "It might be relevant. Otherwise I wouldn't pass it on."

My aunt glanced at her husband. "If you're asking whether we can keep whatever you're about to tell us mum, you can count on us to be discreet."

I looked at Ben, and he made a get-on-with-it gesture. So I told them about how Simon had enlisted the Daweses to reunite Althea with Robin Bonner.

When I was done, Lucy was already shaking her head and *tsk*ing. "That poor girl."

I almost protested that Althea was hardly a girl, but then I realized what Lucy meant. She'd been only a teenager when she had given up her baby.

I sobered at that. "Yeah. I guess she's had her share of heartbreak."

"Okay, so we know what Simon did for Althea," Ben, ever the practical one, cut in. "What about Van Grayson?"

I pointed my finger at him. "Funny you should ask, because I'm pretty sure he's hiding something pretty juicy. I just don't know what."

"You should ask Jaida what she can find out about him," Lucy said, eyes flashing.

"Can she do that?" I asked.

She shrugged. "She knows her way around

public records. And one time she told me that it doesn't always take that much digging to find secrets, once you know they're there to find."

"Maybe," I said. "Though even after only one encounter, I'd say Simon wasn't one to leave things to chance."

"Meh. She can at least try."

I nodded. "That's a good idea. Anything she can find out about Van Grayson would be helpful. Ben, is there anything else at this point?"

He shook his head. "Nothing you don't already know about."

I stood. "I'm going to call Jaida, then." Mungo followed me into the office. Jaida answered her cell on the second ring.

"Any idea where I should start?" Jaida asked after I explained that we needed help digging into Van Grayson's background.

"Well, my neighbor, Margie Coopersmith, told me he used to be a children's comic. A TV personality with a show on cable, the whole bit," I said.

"Really? Well, that will give me a good place to start."

"The strange thing is that now that he has his foot in the door of grown-up movies, he doesn't have the time of day for little kids. At least he didn't seem to today."

"Do tell."

"Margie brought her twins to the set this afternoon. You should have seen Grayson with the JJs and little Bart. He was really grumpy about having to deal with them. And he said something to

Julia that made her look like she was about to burst into tears."

"That's horrible," Jaida exclaimed.

"I know," I said. "I could sense his distaste, but when he saw me watching him, he turned on the full-wattage charm. The look on his face before that, though . . ."

"Hmm," Jaida said. I heard her Great Dane, Anubis, bark in the background. "Well, I'll see what I can find out about Mr. Grayson."

"Thanks," I said. "And while you're at it, maybe see what you can find out about Owen Glade. I know we saw him return from the Welsh Wabbit well after Althea found Simon's body, and he told me Simon hired him after working on some movie in Owen's hometown, but he's such an odd guy for Simon to hire as his assistant."

My phone buzzed then, and I shifted my familiar in order to retrieve it from my tote bag on the floor. It was Declan. *Supper at your place? I'll grab takeout.*

"Let's check in tomorrow," I said to Jaida. "I have a date with my fireman."

Chapter 18

I agreed with alacrity to Declan's suggestion, sending him a quick text and then buzzing home to quickly run a broom and dust rag through the carriage house and tidy a few things here and there. By the time he arrived, I'd also swept out the gazebo in the backyard, lit a few candles, and loaded a couple of beers into an ice bucket. Not exactly champagne, but perfectly suited for the Low Country grub he'd brought from The 5 Spot.

"Oh, yum!" I said by way of greeting, ushering him and his take-out containers into the kitchen before bestowing a big smacker on his lips. "I can't tell you how much I appreciate this."

He grinned. "Sure you can. Over and over, if that's how you do it."

I lightly slapped his arm with the back of my hand. "Get the plates. I have beer outside."

We loaded my fried green tomato BLT and his chicken and waffles with red-eye gravy onto bright Fiesta plates and carried them outside with silverware and napkins tucked under our arms. Mungo trotted ahead, ready to partake as well. Declan had brought him his own order of biscuits and gravy, of which I'd dished out a minor portion. When I put it down on the floor of the gazebo, my familiar spared me a brief look of consternation.

"A half biscuit is plenty," I admonished. "Save the rest for tomorrow's breakfast."

He huffed a sigh for effect before digging in.

Declan shook his head and took a seat in one of the thrift store chairs I'd put in the gazebo. Truth be told, the mishmash of seating in the small space looked more like my boyfriend had been in charge of it. However, I'd wanted kitschy casual, and the other, more important touches he was probably unaware of.

I'd had the structure built shortly after moving into the carriage house—and shortly after learning I was a green witch. It was my sacred space for gardening, for casting outdoors, and the bare cedar of the walls, the bundles of angelica tucked into the five corners of the ceiling, and the crudely painted white star in the middle of the floor outlined in purple all added to its power. Even the broom leaning against the wall was really a besom, a tool I'd made myself from willow branches and an ash handle. I used it to ritualistically clear the space before casting a circle.

Never mind that we witches were supposed to be able to ride brooms like those. I hoped that bit of lore never came true; I'm not that fond of heights.

As the sun went down, we joined my familiar

in filling our bellies, sipping beer, and chatting about anything except murder or magic. As we finished, the crickets started to chirp and the fireflies came out to play with Mungo. He raced to the lawn, chasing them for a while before rolling onto his back and looking at us upside down.

"Yes," I assured him from where we sat watching. "You are well and truly adorable."

He licked his nose and, belly full of biscuits and gravy, his eyes drifted shut in the gloaming. The fireflies drifted down to form a circle in the grass around him.

Declan pointed. "He's the only dog I've ever seen attract lightning bugs like that. It's downright weird."

So much for staying on neutral subjects.

"Not really," I said. "It's a familiar thing. They're his totem."

"Totem?"

"Mine are dragonflies."

He turned to look at me, his eyes catching the last of the light so they glowed ice-blue in his handsome face. "What else am I going to learn about you and this hedgewitch business?"

"I don't know," I answered honestly. "I'm still learning myself."

We sat in silence for a moment, thinking about that.

"And it doesn't sound like I'm going to learn anything more from Detective Taite if he's passed on," I said. "But Quinn doesn't seem to know anything about him. Including that he's likely dead."

"You don't know that for sure, either."

"Do you have another explanation for why someone named Franklin would contact a psychic with a message for me?" Deep down I knew the little detective was gone.

Deck made a face. "Not really."

"I didn't think so." I took a sip of beer and ran my gaze over the vegetables arranged in trios along the fence. Squash, corn, and beans were classic combinations from the Southwest Indians that also worked together in my garden. The heirloom tomatoes were planted in threes, supported by sturdy square cages I'd painted bright magenta, periwinkle, and green. The attractive spikes of onions and garlic delineated the curves of the garden edge, warding away pests.

"I wanted to get Ursula to contact him again the other night. After the séance."

He looked at me sideways. "And?"

I shrugged. "It was too late. She was too tired, and the other spirits in the house would have interfered. I don't know which."

"You could ask her again."

"Yeah. I might, if I could do it without Althea finding out. She's remarkably stingy with her psychic."

"I'd think a psychic wouldn't be so easily controlled," Declan said.

"*Hmm.* I don't know that Ursula is really being controlled. I know she likes the pay, but sometimes I've had the feeling she's not being controlled so much as managing Althea. Steve is doing the same thing, it turns out. And heaven knows Althea could use it."

"Steve," Declan said.

"You saw me speaking with him on the set today," I said in a light tone.

But a sour atmosphere settled into the gazebo. Not wanting our evening to be spoiled, I jumped to my feet and began gathering plates and leftovers.

"Let's watch a movie," I suggested.

"Good idea," he said, as willing as I was to change the subject.

He helped me take everything back inside and put things away while I changed into a spaghetti tank and yoga pants. I popped some corn, dosed it with plenty of butter and salt, and we headed up to the loft. Declan sifted through my abbreviated collection of DVDs and selected an old Pink Panther film.

Talk of Althea had derailed me from the question I'd been leading up to, and as we settled onto the futon with Mungo, I ventured, "Do you think you might be able to contact Taite?"

His head whipped around. "What do you mean?"

I held up my palms. "Well, since you obviously have a, er, knack for the whole, you know, medium thing . . ." I trailed off as his jaw set and his eyes blazed.

"I do *not* have a knack, as you put it, for the

medium thing. That was a fluke, a onetime event. I have no idea how to contact the other side. It will never, ever happen again."

"But, Deck—"

"Absolutely not! Why would you even ask me that? Do you have even the slightest notion how weird it was to be *possessed*? And now you want me to voluntarily let some dead guy use me to talk to you?" He was definitely angry, but I could see the fear behind his eyes.

I bit my lower lip. "I'm sorry."

"Good." He settled against the back of the futon and crossed his arms over his chest.

"But you do have the ability, you know. It might help you to explore it."

He clicked on the movie and the theme song swelled. "Talk about boundary issues, Katie. Let it drop."

"Okay."

"Okay, then."

It was a pretty good movie. We made small talk, commented on the acting, crunched through popcorn, laughed at the funny parts.

But the elephant in the room was so big that sometimes it was hard to breathe.

An unseasonably warm wind blew through our part of Georgia the next morning. I'd awoken in a cloud of thoughts about the secrets people keep, and those thoughts stayed with me as I drank my morning coffee on the back patio while Mungo ate maple oatmeal sprinkled with crushed peanuts.

They followed me inside as I got ready for work as quietly as possible. Declan's snores echoed from the bedroom as I showered and dressed in a denim skort and gauzy blouse.

The morning baking went smoothly and quickly, and at around nine Mimsey came into the Honeybee, fanning her face with a newspaper and announcing, "It's going to be a hot one today, girls!"

When I asked if she'd mind helping Lucy yet again, she beamed. "I'd be tickled pink, sugar," she assured me. I gave her a quick hug, admonished Mungo to stay in the office while I was gone, and beelined over to Reynolds Square on foot.

There was one person whose secrets I hadn't thought to explore yet: Simon Knapp himself.

A new guy was working security when I got to the set. I'd never met him before, and his sharp eyes and dour expression did not bode well for my entry this time around. Nonetheless, I waved him over with a big, friendly smile.

"Where's Declan?" I asked when he approached my position on the looky-loo side of the barricade.

His eyebrow cocked as he looked me up and down. "You know Declan?"

"Pretty well, actually," I said, managing not to waggle my eyebrows.

The sternness drained from his face, and he returned my smile. "You must be his girlfriend, Katie."

Relieved, I inclined my head. "Guilty as charged. Ben's niece, too."

"Visiting?"

"Hoping to," I said. "Niklas Egan knows who I am, too." I didn't mention anything about catering, but I didn't need to.

"I'm Tyler." He lifted the heavy rope and I ducked underneath. "Ben asked me to help out for a few hours. Declan had to go to a training session at Five House."

I nodded. Declan hadn't mentioned it, but he'd still been fast asleep when Mungo and I had left for the Honeybee at o'dark thirty.

I said, "So you haven't been working security here the whole time?"

"Filling in," Tyler said. "Just a few times. Ben's over there with the director."

We began walking toward my uncle. "So how well have you gotten to know these people?" I asked.

"Not very. I know about the production coordinator's murder, of course. Hard to believe. He seemed like a decent enough sort."

"I thought so, too," I said.

Ben and Niklas saw me at the same time, and my uncle's face lit up.

"I'll leave you here," my escort said and headed back to patrol the perimeter of the square.

"Katie!" Ben said.

Niklas blinked slowly at me and then turned to Ben. "So we'll start breaking down today and be out of the city sometime tomorrow. Thanks for all your help."

Ben's lips thinned at what could have been sarcasm. It was hard to tell with the director, but I knew my uncle was still smarting from Simon's murder on his watch.

I put my hand on Ben's arm as Niklas strutted away. "Don't mind him. And honestly? I'm going to be really glad when they shut everything down and go away. It'll be nice to be able to come straight down Abercorn to get to work, and there are certain members of that cast I won't miss one little bit."

"Althea Cole?"

"Althea Cole," I confirmed. "Lucy told you about her visit to the Honeybee yesterday?" We hadn't had a chance to talk about it when we'd met after hours.

"God. What a spectacle," he said. "At least Quinn is on our side." He narrowed his eyes. "So what brings you back here? I went through everything I could think of when we moved the tents away from the crime scene area and again whenever I had a spare moment to snoop. Not to mention that Quinn's crime techs were awfully thorough." He looked thoughtful. "Of course, I couldn't get into the private dressing trailers."

"I'm afraid those are probably off-limits," I said. "But can you tell me where Simon worked? He had to have some kind of office or something."

Ben grimaced. "No office for Simon."

"So where did he work?" I asked.

"Nowhere. Everywhere. His phone and computer were his office. He had them with him all the time." His expression brightened. "Peter Quinn confiscated them both. The laptop was a fancy thing, light and small. He carried it with him everywhere. Maybe there's something incriminating on it."

"Maybe," I said. "I'm sure they're checking it out in the crime lab." But I didn't have great hopes. Simon seemed awfully savvy, and I wouldn't have been surprised if that extended to hiding things electronically.

"If he didn't have a workspace, then where did Simon rest?" I asked.

Ben barked a laugh. "Simon? He never rested. Always on the go." He snapped his fingers. "You know, he did go into the prop tent sometimes when he needed a little privacy, like to make phone calls or to talk one-on-one with someone."

"One-on-one? Like with who?"

He shrugged. "Niklas, most often. Althea once that I remember. And his assistant, of course."

"Okay, thanks," I said. "Mind if I take a look?"

"Like I said, the police have already gone through it." He pointed to the one tent I hadn't explored yet. "But be my guest."

That was all the invitation I needed. Skirting around the back of the catering canopy—without even looking inside to see what culinary travesty Robin Bonner had visited upon the remaining *Love in Revolution* cast and crew—I avoided Niklas' attention and slipped inside the property tent.

Unlike the wardrobe tent, this one held mostly

vintage furnishings as well as an impressive array of muskets and bayonets slotted into a wooden cabinet. They had to be worth a good amount of money. Ben's security detail was only partly to keep the paparazzi and curious in their place. Even if most of the filming equipment was removed from the set at night or locked up in one of the RVs, between what was left, the antiques, and the elaborate costumes, there were a lot of valuable items for his teams to guard.

Walking the perimeter of the tent, I peered into crevices and trailed my fingers along items in search of any kind of energy signature. Other than the dusty sense of age that surrounded some of the firearms and a few pieces of furniture, nothing grabbed me. I breathed in the smell of wood polish and straw and soldiered on without any idea what I might be looking for.

I reached a large brown canvas tent collapsed in the corner next to cots and stacks of bedding. Teetering on top of it was a box about two feet high and a foot and a half wide. The front was covered with a hinged lid. The whole thing was pretty light when I lifted it and placed it on a battered table. Sliding the hook on top, I lowered the front to discover a delightful portable desk, much like my own secretary's desk, only suited for camping—or a military campaign. I could easily imagine a scene in which a general penned a missive on that desk, lit only by one of the pseudo-kerosene lanterns nearby. There were other tables and lamps, and another

corner held tack—saddles, bridles, and the fancy
carriage harness I'd seen on the horse when I'd arrived at the movie set for the first time.

Lordy. That seemed like ages ago, but it had
been only a few days. Since then, Simon Knapp
had been killed, I'd learned Franklin Taite was
probably dead, someone had poisoned Owen
Glade with a Honeybee cookie, and my very non-
magical boyfriend had proven that he could channel the spirits of the dead while positing he might
be indirectly related to a leprechaun from the Old
Country.

Whew!

Glancing around, I noticed the props were in a
bit of disarray. This wasn't the original setup, however, since everything had been moved from the
first location near where Simon's body had been
found to this, the other side of Reynolds Square.
Since Niklas had decided to cut short A. Dendum's
stay in Savannah, there probably hadn't been a
need for a lot of neatness for only a few days.

Or maybe the property manager wasn't an or-
ganized kind of guy. Either way, the police—and
probably my uncle—had certainly gone through
everything in here. What on earth did I hope to
find?

I didn't know, but I was still going to try.

The portable secretary's desk had a built-in
drawer. It was stuck and took a bit of wiggling to
get open. Inside there was a sheaf of yellowed but
blank paper, a quill pen, and an inkpot. The image
of the military man hunched over an important

letter flashed through my imagination again. I shook the inkpot and heard the sloshing of liquid. Opening it, I peered inside.

And gagged at the smell. Did real old-fashioned ink actually smell that bad?

Dipping the pen in, I discovered the liquid was clear.

Clear ink? *Invisible* ink? I fingered the papers, wondering. One by one, I lifted them to the light that streamed in from the doorway, but discerned only a modern watermark. It was expensive paper, all right, but aged with something—tea, perhaps—to look like it had been carried through the travails of war. Still, I couldn't get the notion of a secret note written with invisible ink out of my mind.

You read too much Nancy Drew as a girl.

I started to put the paper and inkwell back, then paused with them both still in my hand. Niklas had said they were almost done. Surely they wouldn't need these two obscure props today, right? Feeling like a thief, I capped the inkwell tightly and slipped it and the papers into my pocket to check out later.

Moving on.

I opened the drawers in tables and end tables, checked inside rolled-up rugs, and tested the blades of the bayonets only to approve of how remarkably dull they were. A chair sat to one side, and I could imagine Simon sitting there with his computer open on the folding table next to it, or pacing back and forth in the middle of tent, rapidly speaking into his cell phone. But unless the canvas walls had ears, I wasn't going to learn any secrets about Simon here.

Sitting in the chair, I took one last look around. From that vantage, I spied a piece that looked out of place in its modernity. It was a plain, metal two-drawer filing cabinet. Nothing special, yet there was something about it. The slightest *shimmer* of . . . power shining from the painted steel surface.

Chapter 19

I hurried to the file cabinet and opened the top drawer. Empty. Slipping my hand inside, I felt along the inside of the top of the cabinet. Nothing.

The second drawer was not empty, but the contents were a jumble of small props—old-fashioned pens, papier-mâché musket balls, a set of epaulets, a lady's pair of combs with a matching brush and mirror set, and a sheaf of mismatched paper that turned out to be hard-copy receipts from Atlanta for vintage clothing stores, antiques dealers, tailors, and an army surplus store. Simon had been gathering props for the movie. Some of the receipts were signed by Owen Glade. None of that was surprising.

Again, I ran my hand lightly over the bottom of the drawer above to no avail.

Until one fingertip touched something rough.

I reached farther back and felt paper crackle. Pulling the drawer all the way out, I reached in and pulled away the manila envelope that was taped to the back panel of the cabinet.

Folding onto the floor, I eagerly opened it and pulled out two sets of paper clipped together.

One set was of newspaper clippings from the *Savannah Morning News*. I scanned a column by Steve Dawes about a flurry of food trucks starting up business in town. One of them was the Waffle Baron, Robin Bonner's mobile restaurant that featured specialty waffles twenty-four-seven. Sure enough, the other clippings were ads, first for the Waffle Baron with a Twitter address so fans could find out where the truck was at any given time, and the second for Bonner Catering.

I put those aside and removed the second paper clip from a dozen photos. I didn't recognize most of the people in them, but paused at the one of Van Grayson smiling up from where he sat cross-legged on a carpet, surrounded by the grinning, cherubic faces of his young fans. Another was of Simon himself, standing with an attractive woman in her late forties in front of a sign that read, BOUL-DER CREEK LIBRARY. His arm was around her, and they were both smiling into the camera.

Hard-copy photographs. Pretty rare in this digital age. And meaning . . . what?

Handling the items gingerly, I slid everything back into the envelope to give to Quinn. Who knew if he could do anything with them, but at least I'd teased them out of their hiding place.

Then I paused. If I took the photos, I'd be disturbing evidence. The best thing would be to return them to the file drawer and tell Quinn about them. Then he could come find them in situ.

"Get those lights packed up!" a male voice shouted outside the tent. Niklas had said they were getting ready to break down the set and pack things up, and it sounded like it had already begun.

If the photos and clippings could help Quinn, I couldn't take the chance that they'd be taken away before I could get ahold of him. I'd take them with me.

I was sliding the drawer back into the cabinet when light from the open doorway brightened a scrap of blue velvet at the bottom. Digging through the detritus, I pulled out a bag tied with a cord made of woven gold silk. Certainly Quinn's people had already looked inside. Still, I worked the knot open and poured the contents out onto the canvas floor of the tent.

A small silver goblet laced with embossed ivy leaves shone up at me. Next to it fell a finely carved wooden stick that looked almost like a miniature totem pole, a tarnished brass sheriff's star, and finally, a short, thin dagger in a leather sheath. I removed a fine silk scarf that swirled with all the colors of the rainbow and set it next to the other pieces.

Chalice, wand, pentacle, athame—and a ritual cloth to set them all up on.

This was an altar—portable and innocent-looking among this mishmash of movie props.

With trepidation, I slowly slid the blade of the

dagger out of the sheath. It flashed wickedly, and I knew without touching the blade that it was razor-sharp.

An athame was a ritual blade, not a functional one. Unless, of course, whoever this altar belonged to practiced darker magic than what I was used to.

Whoever.

My mind staggered through the possibilities. Shuddering, I slid the blade carefully back into its leather covering.

That's when I saw the tiny, curved inscription on the metal next to the handle: *SK.*

This was Simon's altar.

Which suddenly made an enormous amount of sense. No wonder Simon had been so good at fixing things! He was a witch or some other kind of sorcerer. And no wonder he'd known Heinrich Dawes, head of the druid clan that had been in Savannah before the time *Love in Revolution* was set.

However, did Simon's magical practice—good, bad, or ugly—account for why I'd become involved in his murder investigation? Because it didn't explain a motive for his murder.

Unless perhaps he was killed simply because he practiced magic?

A shiver ran through me at the thought.

Or perhaps it was because he practiced *dark* magic. Oddly, that made me feel better. The spellbook club believed in the Rule of Three. It informed all our magical workings. If Simon had cast dark magic to fix a problem for someone, it was possible the boomerang effect could have resulted in his death.

His death through human action, though, to be sure. And a death that as a lightwitch, even a white witch, I was still obligated to bring to justice.

Back at the Honeybee, Lucy was on her own.

"Where's Mimsey?" I asked.

My aunt waved her hand in the general direction of Vase Value. "A floral delivery went awry, and the customer came into the shop in person to complain. Her manager called, and Mims headed right over there to put out the fire."

I tied on the first apron that came to hand, a frilly French maid affair. "Has it been busy?"

"Not too bad. We had a run on the goat cheese éclairs, though. They're so popular, I think we should make twice as many tomorrow."

I grinned. "That's the kind of problem I like to have."

She nodded. "Exactly. Did you find out anything?"

I joined her behind the register, talking low so the dozen or so customers ensconced around the bakery wouldn't hear. "Get this, Lucy. Simon was a witch."

Her eyes widened. "Oh!"

"Or at least some kind of sorcerer. Maybe even a druid." I told her the items I'd found hidden in the prop tent. "I can't think of any other reason for them to be there."

"Are you sure they belonged to him?"

A young couple came in the door and headed straight for the register. I waited while she chose a molasses cookie and he selected a coconut bar cookie. Lucy rang them up, and they took their treats with them back out to the street.

When the door closed, I said, "Simon's initials were engraved on the athame."

A decisive nod from my aunt. "Well, that settles it, then. Do you think that's why he was killed?"

"I don't know. Maybe not directly. But it certainly makes it easier to understand why he was so good at fixing things. Plus, Steve told me Simon contacted Heinrich before coming to Savannah, to help find Robin Bonner for Althea. So if there's some kind of good ol' boy druid network, Simon was probably part of it, or at least knew about it."

"Do you think Steve knew Simon practiced magic?" Lucy asked.

"Oh, I don't think so. He said Simon contacted Heinrich, and when I asked how Simon knew to do that, he simply said Heinrich had lots of connections." I paused, remembering Steve's reluctance to tell me about Althea when before he'd always been willing to give me any information he might have. "On the other hand," I said slowly, "he might have known all along. Those druids are a tight-knit lot, and if that's what Simon was, then I could see Steve closing ranks with the others in the Dragoh Society. The Dragohs only have a few members, all in Savannah, but there have to be other groups like them out there—and they'd all be likely to protect one another, right?"

Lucy looked as unhappy as I felt about the idea that Steve would keep secrets like that from me.

We both looked up as the door opened again and Mrs. Standish entered. She wore a zebra-print tunic over wide flowing slacks accented by silver metallic leather flats. Her iron-gray hair curled fetchingly around her earlobes, and her lips shone hot pink rather than her usual raptor red.

Lucy greeted her. "Hello, my dear. Need more éclairs?"

Mrs. Standish's laugh in response held giddy delight as a man who had apparently entered behind her stepped out of her shadow. He removed his straw hat to reveal a smooth, bald head that reached almost to his companion's chin. His build was so slender, his gray trousers and button-down Oxford hung on him like a scarecrow, but his dark eyes were kind and the lines time had carved into his face suggested a man who smiled often.

"Perhaps later, Mrs. Eagel!" she said. "Right now we were hoping for something a bit more substantial. Picnic fare, if you will." Her eyes twinkled.

My aunt and I exchanged amused glances.

"We should be able to come up with something you'll enjoy," Lucy said.

"Wonderful! I knew I could count on you."

I smiled pointedly at the gentleman beside her. "Welcome to the Honeybee."

"This is Mr. Dean!" Mrs. Standish said. Her voice softened. "Skipper." She gazed fondly down at him. "I call him Skipper because he's the caption of his own ship."

For a moment I wondered if she was being met-
aphorical, but then he smiled back at her. "Now,
Edna. It's just a little boat."

Edna? Mrs. Standish had been one of the Honeybee's first customers and had been spreading
the good word about our baked goods ever since,
but I now realized I'd never heard her first name.

"That doesn't matter a whit," she said. "It's delightful." And to Lucy and me, "We're going out
on it this evening for a lovely romantic supper, but
until then I'm going to show Skipper a bit of Savannah. He's new here, you see. Purchased the
house next to mine only last week."

He nodded his agreement, letting her take the
conversational lead. *Wise man.*

She leaned toward us and hissed, "A widower,
don't you know."

Skipper Dean heard, of course, yet didn't seem
in the least nonplussed by Mrs. Standish. I instantly deemed him worthy of her attention. Time
would tell, of course, but I'd never seen her so
happy.

Lucy invented a couple of new picnic-friendly
items for them on the spot: sandwiches made from
our giant biscuits typically referred to as
catheads—because that was how big they were—
layered with slabs of smoky Tasso ham, a thick
slather of sweet mango chutney, and a thin layer
of sour pickled okra. Just watching her assemble
them made me hungry, and Mrs. Standish was
over the moon with delight.

"Oh, you are a genius," she boomed. "A culinary genius. I really must have you cater my next party!"

Lucy shot me a look. I stepped forward. "You have a wonderful time today, you hear?"

"Oh, we plan on it, my dear," she sang and, taking Mr. Dean's arm, floated out of the bakery as if her silver shoes were made of feathers.

"Well," Lucy said with her hands on her hips and one eye still on the door, "at least we know the vanilla éclairs had the desired effect. But I don't understand why everyone seems to want us to cater for them."

I shrugged. "We don't have to. It is flattering, though, to know she likes our food so much she wants to share it with her guests."

The expression on my aunt's face became speculative. "If we could find some good help, it might be a viable way to expand our business. If we want to expand, that is."

"We can talk about it with Ben," I said. "You're right that we'd need some help. A lot of it, really, since we are relying far too much on the kindness of our friends as it is."

She sighed. "It was so nice when Cookie worked for us. I miss her."

"Me too. I hope she comes home soon."

"But she won't come back to work here, will she?"

One side of my face squinched in a kind of facial shrug. "Probably not." Cookie Rios was a witch with a talent for moving forward. She also hated early mornings, and bakery work was unforgiving in that regard.

Changing the subject, I said, "Listen, I want to make Declan a special supper tonight. Any suggestions?"

Lucy waggled her eyebrows. "Special occasion?"

I grimaced. "More like a combination of 'thanks for being such a good sport the last few days' and an apology."

"Apology?"

"I asked him to try to contact Franklin Taite last night."

"Contact . . . You mean you asked him to channel a spirit again?" My aunt sounded almost as outraged as he had.

I looked down. "Yeah." I stubbed the toe of my shoe into the floor. "Pretty stupid, huh?" My head came up. "I try, but I can't seem to let it go."

"I know," she said with sympathy, then briskly, "But I can see why an apology might be in order, and a delectable meal is a good start. Now, let's see. . . ." Her eyes clouded with thought. "Fried chicken?"

"He had chicken and waffles last night from The 5 Spot."

"Ah. Well, it's awful warm out, so why not grill up a couple of nice filet mignons?"

"Hmm. Simple, special and one of his favorite cuts." I closed my eyes, imagining. "Served with spicy red-and-black pepper sauce and creamy potatoes au gratin with chanterelles."

"And Spanish tomatoes with your heirloom tomatoes, peppers, and some nice Vidalia onion."

My eyes popped open. "Yum. Oh, and I want to

end with cheese and poached pears. Maybe some of that butterscotchy Mimolette Althea had at the séance and a nice port wine. I'm sure Bianca can suggest something."

Lucy grinned wide. "A meal like that would make up for anything."

The more I thought about it, the more I was looking forward to it. We'd sit at the patio table Declan had brought me soon after we met, back when I'd barely had any furniture in the carriage house at all, he could grill on the hibachi he'd also given me, and I wouldn't say a single word about magic or ghosts or murder.

Not one.

I was bussing the reading area, where a pack of college kids had just finished an intense study session, when Jaida came in. She wore simple white slacks and a violet silk blouse, which told me it was an office day but not a court day. I raised the dish towel in my hand in welcome. Her response was a short jab of her finger toward the kitchen. Lucy saw and gestured with her chin for me to go ahead and follow. Our friend obviously had something on her mind that she didn't want to talk about in front of customers.

She beat me to the office, and I found her leaning over Mungo and massaging his ears. His eyes were squeezed shut with pleasure, and he didn't bother to open them when I walked in.

I perched on the stool by the tall file cabinet, and Jaida slid onto the swivel desk chair. Mungo grunted, turned around three times, and resettled on his club chair.

"I found some information on your suspects," she said.

My eyebrows shot up. "Do tell."

Leaning back, she crossed her legs. She wore open-toed pumps, and her toenails were painted the same violet as her blouse. "Okay, regarding Niklas Egan, what you heard him tell Detective Quinn appears true. That is, I couldn't find any record of a payoff to his paramour's husband, but Egan went through a very nasty divorce and his ex-wife was not at all shy about blaming his philandering for the breakup."

"That fits with what we already know. Anything about who he was seeing?"

"There was mention of a woman named Chrissa Stuvelle in a gossip rag online after the divorce. Looked like she was heading for a divorce as a result of playing around with Egan, too."

"Online. I guess I could have looked that up."

She waved that away. "We're a team. Anyway, I didn't find evidence in public records that hinted at anything else Simon's unique skills would have been called upon to remedy for Egan. I didn't find anything particularly interesting about the assistant, Owen Glade, either. He's pretty much the dweeb you described."

Jaida hadn't met Owen, since he'd been in the hospital the night of the séance.

"I'm pretty sure I didn't actually call him a dweeb," I protested.

"Maybe not, but that's still what he sounds like. He's from Boulder Creek, a little town in northern California. Only child, graduated in the middle of his class, went to a community college and then onto San Jose for a degree in theater arts. Then he went back home and worked with the local theater. Lived with his mother, a librarian, until hired by A. Dendum Productions. His father is deceased."

Wait a minute. "Boulder Creek? I guess he told me that. But I didn't know his mother was a librarian." I held up my finger and extracted the manila envelope I'd found in the file cabinet from my tote. I shuffled the photos until I found the one of Simon and the woman in front of the Boulder Creek Library and handed it to Jaida.

Her eyebrows shot up. "I wonder if that's her with Simon?"

"Owen told me Simon was working for a production company that was filming in his hometown, and he convinced Simon to mentor him as a production coordinator," I said.

Jaida narrowed her eyes. "Do you think he was involved with Simon's . . . other activities?"

I rubbed the back of my neck. "You know, he doesn't strike me as the kind of guy Simon would trust with sensitive information. He just doesn't come across as that competent. You never know, though, so I came right out and asked him when he paid me for lunch the day after Simon was killed."

Jaida smiled. "And?"

"He didn't seem to know what I was talking

about. Mostly he seemed resentful that his duties were not more glamorous. He was Simon's boy Friday."

"Otherwise known as an assistant. Seems like it would beat living with your mom, though. Glade is twenty-five."

The same age as Robin Bonner. Coincidence? Probably.

"Well, thanks for taking a closer look," I said.

"I saved the best for last, m'dear. Mr. Grayson does indeed have a secret or two."

Chapter 20

"Aha!" I said. "I knew there was something hinky about that guy."

Mungo sat up.

"Indeed," Jaida said, smoothing the fabric of her white slacks. "In his early career, he was arrested for selling drugs. Not on Hollywood Boulevard, either. It was near a high school."

"A children's comedian who sold drugs to teenagers?" I thought of Margie's giddy affection for Grayson. "How was that not a scandal?"

"Ah, but his name was different then. He changed it—*twice*. From Grant Vanders, who went to jail for five months on the drug charge before being let out on parole, to Vance Gray. Six months later he changed his name again to Van Grayson and developed the super-squeaky-clean image as a kiddy comic. First parties, then shows, and finally videos. For a while he made the rounds on a number of kids' shows, too."

"And he doesn't actually like children," I said,

thinking out loud. "Yet that career move gained him enough recognition to get the lead actor role in *Love in Revolution*. He's savvy that way, but he doesn't seem quite comfortable as a star—at least not yet." I was remembering how different his attitude seemed from Althea's. Or maybe he was just a nicer person.

Except he dealt drugs to high school students.

"With his career on the upswing, he certainly wouldn't have wanted his former identity to come to light," Jaida said.

"Do you think Simon knew?" I asked.

"The double name change is clever, and he could have been involved with that, but Grayson could have done that on his own easily enough. However, there was a rather convenient restraining order placed on that tabloid the *Inquisitor* a while back, and the rumor was that it involved a story about Mr. Grayson."

I felt my forehead scrunch. "Wait a sec. You can't stop a story that way, can you? Freedom of the press and all that, even if the *Inquisitor* will print anything they feel like to make sure people will grab their rag in the checkout line. I've heard of people suing after a story runs, but a restraining order?"

Jaida held up her hand. "It wasn't for a story per se. It was on the publisher, and the details were sketchy. I'm betting Simon was involved."

I whistled. "Wow. That would take a lot of juice."

She nodded. "I had to dig pretty far, but I'm still a little surprised Detective Quinn hasn't already discovered this."

"Maybe he has," I pointed out. "If so, he wouldn't feel any obligation to tell me. But he might not have because there's another factor you don't know about yet."

She uncrossed her ankles and leaned forward. "What's that?"

"Simon was some kind of sorcerer—a witch, I suspect, given the altar items he had hidden in the prop tent." I told her how I'd come to find the blue velvet bag and its contents. "But he could have been druidic or something else altogether. The point is, I think he used magic to enhance his ability to get things to go his way—or the way of whomever he was 'fixing' a situation for."

Jaida slapped her leg with her palm. "Well, I'm not surprised at all if Quinn doesn't know about Grayson's past, then. Simon would have cast a cloaking spell."

"Which didn't stop you," I pointed out.

She grinned. "That's because I'm a witch, too."

"You used magic?" I couldn't keep the surprise out of my voice. Jaida had admitted to sometimes using her tarot skills on behalf of her unknowing clients, but that was all.

"Sort of," she said. "As a matter of course, whenever I go looking for information, I do a quick clarifying spell with the Star, High Priestess, and Hermit cards to clear the way. I perform a lot of my own investigation since many of my clients can't afford for me to hire an outside investigator, and I need to be able to quickly weed through the unimportant stuff."

"Lucky for me," I said.

Mungo made a noise of agreement in the back of his throat.

Jaida stood. "Speaking of unimportant stuff, I have a pile of paperwork I've been putting off on my desk. Keep me in the loop, and let me know if you need me to look into anything else, okay?"

I hugged her, breathing in cinnamon and caramel. "Okay. Thanks again. You're the best."

I left a message on Quinn's voice mail that I had information about Van Grayson he might be interested in. As I hung up, I debated whether to tell him that Robin Bonner was Althea Cole's son. Given that Simon had fired Bonner Catering, my cookies had been laced with a prescription emetic, and someone had ended up in the hospital, it was probably best that he know.

Lucy answered the Honeybee phone an hour later, mouthing to me that it was Quinn. She put the phone on hold and turned back to her customer. I slipped the last apple-fennel muffin out of the tin and onto a cooling rack and went back to the office to take the call. Collapsing into the chair, I swiveled to the desk and hit the speaker button.

"Hey, Quinn. Thanks for calling back."

Mungo sat up from his nap to listen.

"Katie, it's been too long since we've spoken. An entire day, if I'm counting correctly." His tone wasn't as sarcastic as his words, however.

"You can tease all you want, Peter, but you did tell me to call if I happened to find anything out.

Well, I found something out about Van Grayson. Did you know he used to be—"

Peter cut in. "I should tell you that I already know that Van Grayson used to be Vance Gray. He probably changed his name because 'Van' is easier for little kids to say—and remember."

"I bet you're right," I said. "But did you know that first he changed his name from Grant Vanders to Vance Gray?"

A long silence then, "That's news to me."

"And as Grant Vanders, he went to jail for five months for selling drugs near a high school."

Quinn swore under his breath, and beside me Mungo cocked his head. "How did you find that out?"

"Well, I know you told me not to do any actual, um, investigation, but you did agree there was a good chance that Simon's 'fixing' could have gotten him killed. So I asked Jaida to do a little digging."

I heard typing. "The officer who is helping me with background investigations didn't get that far. I'll have a talk with her."

"Oh, gosh. I don't want to get anyone in trouble. Jaida said the double name change was pretty buried. She just happened onto it."

"Don't worry. I'm not going to put anything in her file." He sighed. "I swear, Katie, sometimes the way you and your friends find things out is like magic."

My breath caught in my throat before I managed to force a laugh. Unfortunately, the noise that came out sounded more like a camel sneezing than an expression of mirth. Mungo looked at the ceiling, but I ignored him.

"Anyway," I said in a voice that hopefully didn't sound too strangled. "Someone else might have found out, you know? Maybe Simon fixed it so that Grayson wouldn't be revealed as a drug-dealing fraud."

"Right. We'll look into that. Thanks, Katie."

"Um," I said.

"Yes?" He drew the word out.

"It also came to my attention that Robin Bonner of Bonner Catering is Althea Cole's son. She gave him up for adoption when she was sixteen, and Simon helped her track him down here in Savannah and then hired him to cater for the movie."

"*What?*"

"What's that, Lucy?" I called. "Okay, be right there. Quinn, I have to go. Talk to you later!" And I hung up.

Dang it. I didn't have a chance to tell him about the photos. Maybe I can drop them by his office this afternoon.

If dogs could laugh, that was what Mungo did as I hurried out to the kitchen.

The lunch rush was over, tables bussed, and the early-afternoon baking cooling on the counter before going into the display case. Even the espresso counter was gleaming. Eight people were scattered among the tables, most of them regulars who settled in a few afternoons a week with their laptops. Some were telecommuting, a few were students at the Savannah College of Art and Design or Savannah State University, and one unassuming gentleman was an author working on his latest spy novel.

The door opened to admit Mimsey for the second time that day. She was clad entirely in white except for the bright blue bow in her hair. Quickly, she shut the door behind her. "Land sakes, it's hot out there! You'd think I'd be used to it after living my whole life here, but May is simply not supposed to feel like July." Fanning her face, she plopped down on a chair near the register and put her shopping bag on the floor. I suspected her color choice for the day had less to do with magic than with keeping cool, regardless of the old rule about not wearing white before Memorial Day.

"Here you go," Lucy said, a tall, sweating glass of sweet tea already in hand. "Drink this and cool down. Did you walk all the way from your shop?"

"Yes, ma'am, and I do not intend to walk back to my car until the sun goes down."

My aunt laughed. "Well, don't worry. If you want to hang out here for the afternoon, I'll give you a ride."

Mimsey's head bobbed in agreement. "I was hoping you'd say that. I brought a few new books for the library, and while I'm at it, I'll cull what needs to go."

"That's sweet of you," I said.

"Bah. Not sweet. Necessary. Some of those volumes have served their purpose. Must make way for the new!" She pulled out a half-dozen volumes from the bag at her feet and set them on the table before taking a rather unladylike gulp of tea.

Walking over, I picked up the top two. One was a thin volume of poetry by Rainer Maria Rilke and the other was a spy novel by none other than our resident author. After a quick glance his way, I checked out the other titles: *How to Train Your New Puppy*, *Great Expectations*, *Windowsill Gardening*, *The Creative Woman's Guide to Authentic Recovery*, and *Your Stylish Six-Year-Old*.

Picking up the last one, I asked, "Really? This looks one of those guides for stage mothers."

"Don't judge," Mimsey said. "Someone needs this book."

Rolling my eyes affectionately, I returned it to the pile.

"Katie," Lucy said. "Since Mimsey is back to help, why don't you run down to Bianca's and get your wine for dinner tonight? That way you won't have so much to do before Declan comes over."

I hugged her. "Thanks. I was wondering how I could get everything done." I untied my apron. "I'll be back in a jiffy, ladies."

"You don't mind sticking around here, do you?" I asked my familiar. "I know you don't care for the heat."

He curled into a ball and closed his eyes in answer.

I opened my tote to make sure I had my wallet and saw the inkwell and distressed paper I'd found in the prop tent. Removing them, I held the paper up to the light again. There was still no evidence of writing. I remembered writing notes to my best friend in third grade. We'd used toothpicks and lemon juice, let the "ink" dry on the paper, and then held them next to a warm lightbulb to reveal the messages.

Quickly turning the desk lamp on, I touched one of the sheets to the bulb.

The very cool bulb. We didn't have compact fluorescent lamps when I was in the third grade.

Ah, but the arched reading lamp in the Honeybee library featured a full-spectrum incandescent bulb. Grabbing the paper and ink, I returned to the front of the bakery. Mimsey looked surprised, then followed as I went into the reading area and held the papers up one by one to the hot bulb.

The gentleman sitting on the sofa looked up in chagrin as my machinations dimmed his reading light. "Miss, please."

I ducked my head. "Sorry." My shoulders slumped in defeat. There were no messages.

"What on earth are you doing?" Lucy asked, watching with Mimsey nearby.

I gestured them to the kitchen before answering. "I found these in the property tent earlier. The ink seems to be clear, which makes no sense, so I thought it might be, er, invisible ink," I finished, feeling lame as all get out.

Mimsey held out her hand. "Let me see."

I handed her the inkwell, and she opened it. Her head reared back as a foul odor boiled out of the tiny container. Lucy wrinkled her nose. "Oh, put the lid on, Mims. That smells absolutely wretched."

But speculation replaced the disgust on the older witch's face, and she took another deep whiff before screwing the cap back onto the inkwell.

"What is it?" I asked.

She frowned. "I don't know. I feel like I should, though. I've smelled that someplace before." She looked up and saw my urgent expression. "Go on, dear. I'll have your aunt text you if I think of it while you're out."

Mimsey was right: It was land sakes hot out, indeed. Growing up in Ohio, I'd known some hot weather, but my first summer in Savannah had put that to shame. "Hot mayonnaise" weather they called it, a heat laced with thick humidity that never allowed you to feel dry. That was July and August heat, but it had settled down on the city this late May afternoon like a mama hen on her chicks.

I considered walking to Moon Grapes, which, let's face it, was only six blocks away on Factors Walk. I had almost convinced myself when I spotted the quaint wooden sign hanging over the door of the Welsh Wabbit Cheese Shoppe half a block down. It hung at a perpendicular angle to the door, swinging like an old English alehouse might invite some quiet revelers into the snug. I'd stop there first, pick up the Mimolette and any other cheese that happened to catch my fancy for Declan's and my party, then move on to Moon Grapes for the wine.

The image on the old-fashioned placard sharpened into a new-fangled graphic as I approached close enough to see it. I'd driven by dozens of times since the small specialty store had opened and never noticed the details. The sign showed a long-eared hare straddling a low-rider Harley. The jackrabbit wore a pudding-basin helmet, leather jacket complete with diagonal zipper and fringe flying out from his narrow shoulder blades, and boots replete with three sets of buckles up the legs. Despite his regalia, he appeared to be peacefully riding through an English countryside that James Herriot himself would have recognized.

Forget the subtlety of glowing in the heat. I was already sweating "like a whore in church," as I'd overheard someone say in the Honeybee. I headed inside the cheese shop, closed the door, and leaned my back against it as if hordes of Huns were on my tail instead of an overly warm spring day.

What a wimp I've turned into. Imagine how summers here might have been before air-conditioning, in the heavy heat all day. Heck, all night, too. And here I walked a whole block and a half. Go, me.

The place was empty save for the woman behind the L of brightly lit display cases similar to those in the Honeybee and a black-haired girl sitting on a high stool by the double swinging doors leading to whatever was in the rear of the shop. The floor looked as if it was made of renovated barn wood, the walls were painted a deep, rich blue, the ten-foot ceiling shone creamy beige, and the afternoon sun was blocked by rattan shades that drew up from the bottom.

Unlike the Honeybee, this was a stop, shop, and buy sort of shop, a place to sample and purchase your cheese but not linger, much like an old-fashioned butcher or fishmonger. The piles of cheese were artfully arranged behind glass, enticing, inviting, and frankly mouthwatering. It was surprising how different they looked from one another given they all started out with the same basic ingredients.

The woman behind the counter looked up, blinking behind dark-framed glasses. She was in her late forties, but wore her corn-silk hair in pigtails that jutted out from either side of her head like Pippi Longstocking all grown up. Her name tag said "Patsy," and she wore a simple denim sundress that reached past her knees. Her smile felt big enough to encompass eight of me.

I had no choice but to smile in return.

She glided to the counter. "What can we do you for?"

I found myself in front of the plates and plates and *plates* of cheese displayed behind glass. "Oh," I said. "This is going to cost me more than I thought."

Looking up, I saw her nod. "Yeah. It works that way sometimes. But I'm guessing you came in with a mission. At least to start with."

"The other night I ate a delicious cheese. I think it's called Mimolette?"

"Oh, yes," she said, reaching into the case for a cannonball-shaped round. The rind on the outside was pitted and grooved, making it look more like a muskmelon than a chunk of cheese. "French, made from cow's milk, and typically aged three to twenty-four months. This"—she held up the ball—"is twenty-four months old. Incredible."

I could see a slice had been removed, revealing the deep orange color I recognized. "Yes, that's the one Althea served."

"Oh! Are you associated with the movie?" the woman asked, leaning forward.

"Not really. My uncle is working security over there." I scrambled to come up with an explanation. "I guess you know Althea Cole likes to serve your cheese with different wines. I'm friends with Bianca Devereaux over at Moon Grapes."

"Bianca knows her stuff," Patsy said. "It's a pleasure to work with her on pairings."

"You're in touch?" I asked.

"Oh, yes. Since they began filming, Mr. Glade comes in each day at four thirty, selects the cheese for the evening's soiree, and then I call Bianca so she can deliver the appropriate wines for whatever he's selected."

"Makes sense," I said, then paused, remembering.

The bottles of wine, though still unopened, had been on the table above Simon's body before Owen had stumbled onto the scene with his bag of Camembert.

"Um," I said, glancing at the young girl sitting on the stool. Looking beyond her heavy black eyeliner and black lipstick, I saw she was old enough to be a junior or senior in high school. "You know there was someone killed on the set, right?"

Patsy's hand went to her throat and she nodded emphatically. "Terrible. Simply terrible."

"Do you happen to remember when Mr. Glade came in to pick up cheese that day? I believe it was a Camembert."

"Why, at the same time as always," she said.

"Was not," muttered the girl behind her.

"Oh, Iris. Don't be difficult," she said. "Of course it was." She shook her head. "Teenagers. Have to contradict their mothers no matter what."

Iris' head came up, and her eyes met mine. They were deep brown, sparked with intelligence, and there was something else.

She has talent. Magical talent. Latent, but she knows she's different.

She slid off the stool and came up to stand beside her mother. Staring down at a platter of Port Salut in the display case, she said, "He came in early, right after noon that day. And the next day that white-haired chick with the cool eyebrow ring came instead of Mr. Glade."

"Mr. Glade was, shall we say, indisposed that day," I said, avoiding the words "sick as a dog."

Patsy nodded. "That's right, about the woman with the short blond hair, at least. You're wrong about Mr. Glade."

"Ursula Banford," I said. "The one with the eyebrow ring."

"You know her?" Iris asked, looking up at me from under her dark fringe of hair.

I nodded.

"She was nice." She smiled then. It was a sunny,

warm, happy smile, and I smiled back. Then it dropped. "Mr. Glade could have picked up the cheese himself that day, since he was here when we opened."

Patsy shook her head. "Honestly, Iris. I have no idea what you're talking about."

Iris eyed her mother with a puzzled expression, then looked at me. Something passed between us. Iris wasn't lying, but her mother didn't seem to be, either. What was going on?

"Of course you told the police when Mr. Glade came in," I said to Patsy.

"Naturally." She slid a sharp knife out from under the counter and hefted the round of Mimolette. "Now, how much of this beauty would you like?"

I ended up with a varied selection of cheeses, including the Mimolette and a sheep's milk Roquefort that Patsy assured me would be a perfect accompaniment to the pears I planned to poach for dessert that evening. By the time I'd tasted and chosen and she had wrapped up my purchases, Iris had disappeared into the back of the store. It was too bad, as I would have liked to have talked with her more. I bid my new cheese expert friend good-bye with the promise to return often and went back out into the heat.

Iris was waiting for me on the sidewalk.

Chapter 21

"Come on," she urged, gesturing me into a bar two doors down.

"Aren't you a little young to be in here?" I asked as we entered the blissfully air-conditioned dark-paneled room. The place was practically empty.

"Yeah, but they know me," she said. "Can I get a Diet Coke?" she called. "You want anything?"

I smiled and ordered a root beer. We sat at a high table, and as the bartender got our drinks, I noted the multiple piercings, the black nail polish to match her lipstick, the black skinny jeans with rivets all around the pockets, and the plain black T-shirt. I pointed to the elaborate tattoo of a fairy on her upper arm. "Nice."

"You like tats?"

"It's pretty," I said, then wondered if that sounded lame. But she looked pleased.

"I like your necklace," I went on.

"It's an ankh."

"The symbol of eternal life," I said.

She pursed her lips. "You're all right."

I laughed. "Gee, thanks." The bartender brought our soft drinks. "So you remember Owen Glade coming in earlier than your mom does. How come?"

She sucked in half her drink through the straw, brow furrowed. "Stepmom. I don't know. I mean, it's really weird, because she's not usually flaky like that. He even said he was early that day because Althea Cole wanted to have her party earlier than usual."

Bingo. And how else could Iris know that?

"And he did show up the next morning, too," she went on. "Before I left for school. Brought her coffee. It was gross."

"The coffee?" I asked.

"No! That he brought it to her. They went in the back of the shop to drink it and left me out front to wait on customers. I ended up being late to my first class."

"So she knows you saw them together, right?"

"Uh-huh. But she's acting like it never happened. I don't get it."

"I don't either, honey." I put my half-finished soda on the table and fished a bill out of my wallet. Iris reached in her pocket, but I shook my head. "I've got this."

"Thanks."

"And, Iris? Thanks for letting me know about Mr. Glade and your stepmom."

"Why?"

I considered her. "Because something is off, and the police should know."

"Patsy didn't do anything wrong." Iris looked worried.

"I'm sure you're right. We'll get it figured out." I slid off the tall chair. "I'm Katie Lightfoot, by the way. I work over at the Honeybee Bakery. Stop in sometime if you get a chance."

I left her slurping Diet Coke and went back to the blistering sidewalk.

Owen had lied about where he'd been during the murder, but why would he kill Simon? The man had given him a job in what had to be a pretty competitive field when Owen had little experience. Could Owen have been trying to cover for someone else?

My instincts said no. No one was who they seemed to be on that movie set. Owen lied about his alibi, and then he inexplicably came back and brought a woman twice his age a cup of coffee.

What the heck?

I hurried back through the heat to the Honeybee. As I walked, I tried calling Quinn. Sure enough, I got his voice mail.

"Quinn, it's Katie. Please call me back as soon as you can. I found something out about Owen Glade. He wasn't where he said he was when Simon was killed, and I think something hinky is going on."

Lucy looked up in surprise as I walked into the bakery. "That didn't take long."

"I only went as far as the cheese shop." I held up the bag from the Welsh Wabbit absently, glancing around to see who was close enough to eavesdrop. Mimsey must have sensed my agitation because she came hurrying out from the kitchen.

It was fairly crowded in the customer area, though no one was waiting to be helped. Signaling them both to follow me, I dumped the bag of cheese on the counter and went all the way to the back door, where we could still see the register but wouldn't be overheard.

Slumping against the wall, I said, "Owen lied about his alibi. He was at the Welsh Wabbit much earlier than he said the day Simon was killed. I don't know why the owner couldn't remember that when Quinn asked her—or when I asked her—but her stepdaughter was there and assured me Owen came in much earlier."

The two other women stared at me. "Slow down, Katie," my aunt admonished. "Now, are you sure?"

My head bobbed emphatically. "The girl, Iris, even said it was because Althea Cole wanted to have her wine and cheese get-together earlier than usual. Now, how would she know that?"

They looked at each other. "But why would the owner lie to Detective Quinn?" Lucy asked with a wrinkled brow. "I've met her, and she seems really nice."

"I thought so, too. She just seems . . . mistaken. Vague, if you will. Maybe she's absentminded. Though why she wouldn't just say she couldn't remember when Quinn asked her, I don't know." I grimaced. "Iris said Owen came in the next day and brought her mother coffee, though. I can't imagine she'd be attracted to him, but do you think she might actually lie for him?"

Mimsey's lips parted, and she drew in a sudden breath. "Oh, my stars. Katie, come with me."

She bustled into the office, and I followed behind her. Lucy looked after us regretfully, but moved back out to the front with the customers. By the time I joined the older witch, Mungo was standing with his front paws on the arm of his club chair, his bright eyes intent on Mimsey.

My own eyes went wide when I saw the inkwell in her hand. She held it in front of her face, cover open, and sniffed at it delicately. Looking at the ceiling in thought for a moment, she nodded once and snapped the top shut. Turning, she placed the inkwell in the back of the supply cupboard.

"Whatever you do, Katie, don't let that get near anything that you're cooking."

I thought of the oatmeal cookies. "Why? Do you know what it is?"

"Well, as you determined, it's not invisible ink. But it's not innocuous, either."

"It sure doesn't smell innocuous," I agreed.

"It wasn't until you told me about the cheese shop owner that I was able to put it together."

"Put together what?" I tried not to sound impatient.

"That is a fermentation of essence of forget-me-not and some kind of soap plant—it could be yucca or even bracken, but my bet is that it's something commonly called soap lily. *Chlorogalum pomeridianum*. It grows wild in California. And after it brewed with the forget-me-nots for a while, the fermentation was stopped by the addition of salt. Very old-school. I haven't run across such a thing for a very long time."

I frowned. "Brewed? Mimsey, are you saying . . . ?"

Her chin dipped in affirmation. "It's a potion. Specifically, it's a potion to erase memory."

Stunned, I asked, "But why?"

"Well, for one thing, don't you think it would be handy for a fixer to be able to erase a memory here and there?" Mimsey pressed her lips together. "Though it's certainly not without risk."

"And what if it got into the wrong hands?" Like Owen's. I thought of the coffee Iris swore he'd brought Patsy at the Welsh Wabbit. The coffee she didn't seem to remember drinking.

"Exactly," Mimsey said.

Next, I tried calling Ben, but he didn't pick up, either. Sheesh. Couldn't anyone answer their phone anymore? But, of course, he was working, so it shouldn't have surprised me. I tapped out a text, hit send, then tried Declan.

Deck, bless his heart, answered on the second ring. "Hi, Katie." He sounded distracted.

Or upset. I couldn't tell.

"Are you done with your meeting?" I asked.

"Yeah. I'm back at the set. What's up?"

I took a deep breath. First things first. "Well, I was hoping you'd let me make you a nice supper tonight to make up for last night."

"Supper last night was fine."

Yep, he was mad. Time for an apology. "You know what I mean. Asking you to try to contact Franklin Taite."

Silence.

"I never should have done that. I'm sorry, and I want to make it up to you with a nice steak."

"Well," he said, and I could tell he was coming around. "I guess I could be talked into that. Steak, you say?"

"Filet mignon."

"Mmm. Grilled?"

"Of course."

"I'll cook," he said.

I laughed. "The meat, yes. Everything else I'll take care of. Now, is Ben around? I tried to call him, but he didn't answer."

"Nope," Declan said.

Confused, I asked, "Well, where is he? I found out something about Owen Glade that I want to tell him."

"That's who he's with."

Alarm trilled through me.

Declan continued. "They finished the final scene earlier than the director thought they would. They're packing up now. The spectators are pretty much gone, but I stuck around to help the crew."

"And Ben?"

"Glade asked him to help take some of Althea's stuff from her dressing trailer to the house where they're staying. She's packing for the drive to Dahlonega tonight. Hang on a sec."

I heard him tell someone he'd be right back; then the background noise faded. When he returned, his voice was lower. "Now, what's this about Glade?"

"He lied about his alibi. He wasn't at the cheese shop when Simon was murdered."

"How did you find that out?" he asked.

"I'll tell you when I get there. Don't go anywhere."

"Katie—"

"I'll pick you up in ten minutes." I hung up and turned to see Lucy in the doorway of the office. "Luce," I began.

"Go," she said. "We've got things under control here."

"Will you try calling Detective Quinn again?" I asked, grabbing my tote and motioning for Mungo to jump in.

"Of course, dear."

"Tell him what I found out at the Welsh Wabbit and that I'm going over to the rental house to talk to Owen."

Her eyes widened. "Oh, I don't think that's a good idea at all, Katie."

"Don't worry. I'm taking Deck, and Ben's already there."

She still looked worried. "Well, okay. I'll try Peter again."

"Thank, Lucy." I bent and kissed her on the cheek. "I'll be back as soon as I can."

I hurried out to my car, waving at a startled Mimsey on the way. As the door closed behind us,

I heard her ask my aunt, "Now where's she going?"

Declan stood waiting on the corner of Abercorn and Congress. I pulled to the side of the street without parking. A car behind me honked, then zoomed around the Bug. I twisted to put my tote bag in the backseat as he opened the passenger door and lifted Mungo onto his lap. He was still buckling his seat belt as I checked my mirrors and took off.

As I drove, I related my conversation with Patsy and Iris at the cheese shop.

"I don't get it. Why would Owen Glade kill Simon?" he asked.

"Good question." Still, Owen hadn't seemed to feel a bit of sorrow or regret about Simon's passing. He'd only complained about how Simon bossed him around. "And we still don't know that he did," I said. "Only that Owen lied about when he was at the Welsh Wabbit. He could have been someplace else he didn't want anyone to know about, or he could be covering for someone."

Like Althea.

"Or he could have killed Simon, left, and then come back after the body was discovered with a bag full of Camembert as his alibi."

My boyfriend made a noise of disbelief.

I barreled on, telling him about the altar items I'd found that indicated Simon was a witch of some kind. In my peripheral vision I saw Declan's eyes cut toward me in question. But when I turned my head, he was gazing placidly out the windshield as if I'd been talking about the weather. Mr. Poker Face.

However, when I told him about the memory-erasing potion, he couldn't help but roll his eyes. "You've got to be kidding. A magic potion?"

"Hey," I said. "You did say you wanted to know more about this aspect of my life. And if Mimsey says it's a magic potion, I believe her. It certainly smells bad enough."

"Hmm. Eye of newt probably does."

Steve wouldn't question one iota of what I've told you, I thought but managed to stop myself from actually saying it out loud. Instead I said, "We'll have a chance to ask Owen directly in a few minutes."

"It's hard to seriously imagine Owen Glade as a murderer," Declan said. "Still, wouldn't it be better to wait for Detective Quinn before questioning the guy?"

"Of course," I said, exasperated. "I called and left a message on Quinn's voice mail, and Lucy said she'd call, too. He may already be on his way. But Ben could be in danger." My uncle was as capable as they come, but I couldn't help worrying a little. Besides, if we did get there before Quinn, I'd have a chance to drop a few hints about the potion in the inkwell to see if Owen reacted.

A van was parked in front of our destination. A. DENDUM PRODUCTIONS was emblazoned on the magnetic sign adhered to the side. I found a spot half a block away and pulled to the curb. Declan set Mungo on the sidewalk and unfolded his frame from the Bug. I came around to join them.

"Stick close," I said to my familiar, but didn't put his lead on. Together the three of us approached the three-layer-cake house. The wrought-iron gate creaked open at Declan's touch, and we climbed the four steps leading up to the porch. I pushed the doorbell and waited.

And waited. Declan reached around me and knocked firmly on the thick wooden door.

There was no response.

"Maybe they've already left," he said, and turned to go.

I dug my phone out of the pocket of my skirt and dialed. Declan paused on the front step. "Who are you calling?"

"Ben."

My call went to voice mail. "Hey there. It's Katie again. Call me."

Declan had backed down the steps and now stood with his neck craned back, looking up at one of the middle windows. "Call him back," he said, returning up the steps two at a time.

My brow knitted. "Why?"

"Just call him."

As I dialed my uncle's cell again, Declan leaned forward and put his ear to the door.

"Listen," he hissed.

I let the hand holding the phone drop and pressed my face next to his. It took me a moment, but then I heard it, too.

The sound of crickets.

My uncle's ringtone.

I ended the call, and they stopped. Declan and I exchanged a wide-eyed look, then reached for the door handle at the same time. I wrapped my fingers around it first, but it didn't matter. The door was locked.

"Ben!" Declan yelled, and pounded on the door with his fist.

I shook the handle, as if that would make it miraculously unlock. "Back door," I said, and we took off at a jog around the house, Mungo leading the way.

The small front yard, so close to the front sidewalk, belied the surprisingly large area in back. Formal gardens surrounded a small patch of lawn in the middle, filled with neat rows of annuals studded with towering animal topiaries—eagle, puma, dolphin, and snake. A stone girl poured water in perpetuity from her earthenware jug in the fountain in one corner, and the muscular branches of an ancient wisteria hugged the pergola, which shaded a small seating area near the back entrance.

Which was also locked.

Declan moved immediately to the windows and began checking them. Following his lead, I started doing the same thing, working my way to the other corner of the house.

No luck.

At the corner, I continued around, but the two windows there were too high for me to reach. Then my gaze dropped and I saw the slanting door built into the ground.

Declan joined me. "The place is locked up tight."

I pointed to the wooden door. "Basement?"

He shook his head. "Unlikely. You won't find very many basements in this part of town. The water table is too high." He bent and fingered the rusted metal ring on one side. "Only one way to find out." Grasping it firmly, he planted his feet and pulled.

Chapter 22

For a few seconds I was sure that door was locked, too, but then a horrible sound erupted as the wooden door screeched free from its swollen frame. Declan staggered back, pulling it open all the way. He pulled a hooked chain out of the opening and latched it to another ring set into the ground that I hadn't noticed, effectively propping the door open.

We peered inside, blinking as our eyes adjusted to the dim light. The strong musty smell of mold and dust drifted up, and I blinked. My dog hovered on the edge, then without warning bounded down the steps, his black fur mingling so quickly with the darkness that it looked like he'd disappeared completely.

"Mungo!" I whispered, which after the loud squeal of the door opening was almost comical. "Come back here."

A low *yip!* sounded from below. Leaning farther in, I could see light reflected off his eyes and then the flicker of tiny white teeth.

"Stay here," Declan said, and started down the stairs.

"No way," I said, taking my phone out of my pocket. Using the light from the screen to navigate, I followed.

We found ourselves in a small space, really a hole in the ground. The dirt walls dripped moisture, and green mildew streaked the back wall, which was made of brick. The smell was worse at the source, and I wrinkled my nose. It was like some primordial dungeon. Paradoxically, when I moved, a cloud of dust rose from my feet. I sneezed.

"I think this is where they used to store coal, back in the day." Declan pointed to the back wall. "That's where it would have been accessed to stoke the furnace, which would have heated the whole house. They bricked it off once they updated their heating system." He put his arm around my shoulders. "So much for getting in this way. Let's go wait for Detective Quinn out front."

"And call 911 if he's not here already," I said, turning toward the stairs.

"Oh, I don't think that's necessary," Declan said.

But something had caught my eye. I pointed. "Up there." It was an opening in the sealed wall where the mortar had failed and the bricks were crumbling. "I could fit through there."

"Are you sure?"

I gave him a look. "Pretty sure. But where would I end up?"

"The old boiler room, I imagine. It would likely be connected to the kitchen."

"Give me a boost," I said, bending my left leg at the knee.

"Katie," he protested.

"Uncle Ben is in this house with at least two, if not three, murder suspects and no one will answer the door," I said. "Boost me up first. Then check out front for Quinn and call 911 if you have to. I'll get to the back door and unlock it."

"Oh, all right," he grumbled, and linked his fingers under my foot.

I gripped the edge of the opening and straightened my leg. Brick and mortar broke off under my hands as I launched up and forward, my momentum sending me arse over teakettle through the narrow opening. There was a ripping noise as my gauzy blouse snagged, and I thumped to the stone floor on the other side.

Ow.

I sat up after a few moments, gasping to catch my breath.

"Katie! Are you okay?" Declan demanded from the other side.

"Shh. I'm fine," I called in a low voice as I looked around. The light from my phone was lost in the daylight that streamed in from a small window set high into the wall near the ten-foot ceiling. I put it in my pocket.

Declan had been right. A huge metal stove was tucked into a brick alcove. A chimney led straight up, and rusted metal ducts led out of the room.

The door hung open on its hinges, and a rustling sound inside alerted me that I likely had rodent companions.

As well as some spiritual ones. I could almost feel the resident ghosts swirling around me in surprise.

"There's a door," I softly called to the opening I'd just tumbled through. "I'll try to see what's on the other side. Take Mungo and go find Quinn."

More grumbling, but I heard the sound of his steps on the wooden stairs that led back outside. I turned back to the door opposite the furnace, hoping there was indeed a kitchen on the other side.

It was at the top of two wide wooden slats that served as steps. They were framed by a wobbly railing, and the bottom one was broken. Gingerly, I put my foot at the outside edge of the one above it, testing it carefully before putting my full weight on it. I reached for the round doorknob and turned it.

And turned it. It spun like a stripped screw. Sighing, I laid my forehead against the flimsy door. It was up to Declan now.

The sound of a woman moaning reached my ears.

Ursula?

I rattled the doorknob again. *Screw it.* I braced my hands on the rickety railing, lifted my foot, and kicked.

It took three tries, but each time, the frame splintered a little more. On the third kick, the door flew open. I rushed through and found myself in a glorified mudroom. It held gardening tools and expensive ski equipment, no doubt belonging to the absent owners of the house. Another door beckoned, and I trotted to it. The woman's moan sounded again from the other side, louder this time.

The knob turned easily, but it was hard to open nonetheless. Something on the other side was blocking it. Suddenly, the impediment shifted, and I pushed the door open a foot, which was enough to squeeze through. I found myself in a glamorous kitchen full of marble countertops and shining appliances. Other than the mudroom in between, Declan had been right about where I'd end up.

Ursula lay at my feet, eyes closed but conscious enough to moan. Ben sat on the Italian tile floor with his back to her, and I realized he must have pulled her out of my way, even though his hands were tied behind his back. I dashed to him, quickly pulling the gag from his mouth and letting it fall around his neck.

"Katie, be careful," he choked out, licking his lips. A trickle of blood traced his hairline. "Owen has Althea upstairs. He's furious about something, and throwing around all sorts of accusations."

"Where are the others?" I asked, working at the knots that bound his wrists.

"Knife," he said.

I rose obediently to retrieve a knife from the wooden block on the counter and came back to saw at the nylon cord.

"Grayson and Egan left already," Ben said, his voice raw. "Owen knew that and tricked me into coming here. He thinks I took something of his."

"He hit you?" I asked, eyeing the blood on his face.

My uncle nodded. "Surprised me but didn't knock me out. Stunned me long enough to tie me up, though. Ursula tried to fight him, too. I think he hit her harder. He seems afraid of her."

The blade snicked through the last cord, and Ben's hands were free. Bringing them together in front of himself, he rubbed feeling back into them while I turned my attention to Ursula's bonds.

"Katie!" Declan called from outside.

I swore under my breath and handed Ben the knife. "Deck's waiting for me by the back door."

"Go," he said, taking over with the knife at the psychic's bound wrists. "But be *careful*."

I ran out of the kitchen, through to the dining room where we'd had the séance, and out to the front hallway. Declan bellowed again, and I back-tracked to another hallway from the kitchen that led to the rear of the house. Flinging the back door open, I ushered him inside, Mungo at his heels, while placing a finger over my lips in a be-quiet gesture.

"What's going on?" he asked in a low tone.

"Owen attacked Ben and Ursula, tied them up."

"My God."

"Did you call 911?" I asked.

He nodded. "Right before you let me in."

"Good. Come on." I led him back to the kitchen,

where Ben was bent over Ursula with a glass of water, trying to get her to drink. She was sitting upright but still seemed disoriented.

"Can you get her up?" I asked.

Ben reached for her, but Declan gently pushed him aside. "I've got her." He lifted the groggy woman unsteadily to her feet, bent to one knee as she collapsed over one shoulder, and rose with her draped around his shoulders in a traditional fireman's carry.

As impressed as I was, there was no time to waste on kudos. "Let's go," I said, turning toward the hallway that led to the back door.

Owen Glade blocked our way.

His hair stuck out in tufts on his head, and one arm of his round glasses was bent so the lenses sat crookedly on his nose. His lower lip was beginning to swell, and a small cut on his cheek oozed blood. Despite his disheveled appearance, he had a tight hold on Althea's hair at the nape of her neck, pulling down so her head was at an awkward angle. Her face was pale, and her eyes were wide with terror.

Which might have been because in his other hand Owen gripped a rather nasty-looking gun.

"Put the psychic down," he grated.

Declan didn't move.

Owen shook Althea by the hair, and she whimpered. "Put her down!"

Slowly, Declan bent so Ursula's feet touched the floor; then he lowered her the rest of the way to the hard tile floor.

I kneeled beside her, and Mungo joined me.

"Leave her alone!" Owen demanded.

I stood again, but not before I saw the spark of full consciousness in her eyes. And from the brief look she gave me, Ursula was one angry medium.

"Owen," I said with my palms toward him in a gesture of surrender. "There's no reason to hurt anyone."

He snorted. "That's what you think, baker."

Baker? Seriously?

"The police are on their way," Declan said.

"You called the police?" Owen's face flushed with outrage.

I stepped forward. "Of course we did. You don't think you can get away with all this nonsense, do you?"

"Katie," came Ben's warning voice from my left.

"You have no idea. And you." He pointed at my uncle. "You shut up unless you're going to tell me where you put it."

From the corner of my eye, I saw Ben shake his head. "I wish I knew what you were talking about."

"I know it was you," Owen grated. "Snooping around all time. You found it."

Ben tried again. "What are you—"

"Shut up!"

"He doesn't have it," I said. "I do." I knew he meant the inkwell.

Owen's gaze lasered to me. "You? Ha."

Althea moaned. "Let me go."

He shook her head so hard I was afraid he'd

fracture a vertebra. "You be quiet. You could have killed us all with that stuff you put in the cookies. I've never spent a worse night in my life than I did at that hospital."

"What's he talking about?" Declan asked.

"Althea poisoned the Honeybee cookies," I said.

"Why?"

"I'll tell you later," I said.

"Will. You. Stop. Talking!" Owen said.

Althea kicked at her captor. "He killed Simon."

He yanked back on her hair.

"Stop it," I yelled. "We already know you killed Simon, Owen. Everybody knows. Your potion didn't work. Your alibi is bogus."

He stilled. The blood drained from his face. "You know about . . ."

"Forget-me-nots fermented with soap plant," I said. "I found the inkwell. I took it, not Ben."

"Where is it? Do you have it with you?"

I ignored the question. "But the potion wasn't yours." I was guessing now. I heard Ursula move behind me, heard her deep breath. I continued. "It was Simon's potion."

"*Simon*." Hatred dripped from the name.

"Did he do something to you, Owen? Because we'd all understand how you'd hate him if he did. He wasn't a nice man." I was really reaching now, working on nothing more than instinct.

Owen's eyes filled with tears. I thought of the picture of Simon and the woman in front of the library.

"Or maybe he hurt someone you loved?"

"No!" he screamed. "I hurt her. I borrowed some of the potion to give to Becca Ford, only Mama took it by accident." He was crying now. "It was only supposed to make Becca forget that she didn't like me so I'd have a fresh chance with her. But Mama took it, and there was no *focus* to it."

No focus . . . Oh, my goddess. My hand covered my mouth. "Oh, honey. How much of her memory did it wipe out?"

"Me! It wiped out me, my childhood," he choked out. The gun was pointing at the floor now, but his grip on Althea seemed as strong as ever. "She knew she was my mother, but she didn't *know* me anymore."

I heard Declan's intake of breath as I took a step toward Owen. "And you blamed Simon."

Owen wiped his eyes with the back of his gun hand, dislodging his glasses even further.

"Simon blamed himself. At least at first. That's why he gave me that stupid assistant job. Trying to make it up to me. She remembered him, though, even though they'd only dated for a month or so. He still goes to see her . . . went to see her . . ." He trailed off. "He told me that day, that day that I . . ."

"Hit him with the wine bottle," I finished for him. "And then stabbed him."

My uncle made a hissing sound.

Owen's eyes blazed. "Simon told me he'd done all he could. That he was going to have to find another assistant for his next job, that he couldn't keep carrying me forever. But he wasn't going to stop seeing my mother."

I took another step, and the gun came up. For a long moment all I could think was that the barrel looked impossibly big, like a black hole in space. Then my familiar lunged at Owen's leg, snarling and snapping.

"Mungo," I screamed. Declan grabbed me around the waist and swung me behind him. Owen kicked out, but Mungo was too fast for him, especially since he wouldn't let go of Althea.

Ursula grabbed my hand, and I pulled her to her feet. As power zinged between us, I recognized her trio of personal guides and felt dozens of the resident spirits coalescing in the room at her command. The scent of gardenia wafted through the air. I let go of her and touched Declan's arm. Suddenly his back arched.

"Let go of that woman," he roared in an Irish accent I knew only too well.

Startled, Owen stopped dodging Mungo, who sank his teeth into his leg. Owen howled. Mungo let go and ran back to me. Althea twisted in his grasp, pulling on her own hair until she could claw at his face.

Owen pushed her away, and she ran from the room. He raised the gun toward us again. Declan's muscles bunched under my hand as Owen's finger squeezed down on the trigger.

"No!" I shouted.

Time slowed. The room grew brighter. Colors throbbed. Magic coursed through my core, down

my arm and fingers, and met an equal force in . . .
Declan?

It *was* Declan. Or Connell. *Both* of them.

The gun roared to life. I saw the bullet leave the
barrel. Without thinking, I focused all of the power
flowing between us and *pushed* at the missile
winging toward my boyfriend's heart. Lightning
flashed in the kitchen, blinding me for a second.

The bullet veered off course and hit the wall behind us.

Owen's eyes widened. "You! You're like Simon!"
He turned and ran.

Ben spared me a wondering look and started
after him.

"Let him go," Ursula said. "The police are outside. He won't get far. Katie?" She gestured at me.
"You're . . . glowing?"

The last of the light faded from my skin. "I'm
fine," I said as if personal incandescence was an
everyday thing. In truth I felt like a live wire, still
sparking with electricity.

I shook Declan. "Connell, you give him back.
Now."

He sighed, twinkled those eyes at me again,
and was gone. I'd never been so glad to see my
man gazing down at me, even if his confusion
soon turned into a scowl.

A gunshot blasted out front. Shouts echoed
from the hallway, and moments later Detective
Quinn and several uniformed police ran into the
kitchen. "Ben! You okay?"

My uncle nodded. "Thanks to Katie here. And a few other friends."

Quinn turned back to where two officers were handcuffing Owen in the dining room.

"Is anyone hurt?" I asked.

"No. Little fool wasn't trying to shoot anyone. He wanted us to shoot him."

"Katie Lightfoot," Owen called. "Please visit me. Bring it with you."

"What's he talking about?" Quinn asked with a frown.

I shrugged. "No idea." But I knew he wanted the potion. If the police wouldn't put him out of his misery, then forgetting would be the next best thing.

Chapter 23

Declan leaned back in the iron patio chair and made a show of rubbing his stomach. "That was amazing."

I took a sip of the Cabernet Sauvignon Bianca had recommended. "Remember there's still one more course." Inside, pears were cooling in a wine-pinked cinnamon-and-cardamom syrup, and the deep golden Mimolette was coming to room temperature.

He groaned, then grinned. "I supposed I can manage a few more bites."

It had been nearly five o'clock by the time Detective Quinn completed his interviews and we'd filled in Lucy, Mimsey, and Jaida at the Honeybee. Althea had insisted on accompanying Ursula to the hospital despite the psychic's protests that she hadn't suffered a concussion. The paramedic gave Ben, whom Owen hadn't hit as hard, permission to go home as long as he took it easy. My aunt and uncle had headed to their town house for a well-deserved, low-key evening alone.

Despite the adrenaline rush of nearly losing our lives a few hours earlier, or perhaps because of it, Declan and I had decided we still wanted our steak supper. He'd gone to the market to pick up the ingredients, and I'd dropped by Moon Grapes to update Bianca and get some wine.

Now we sat in the early gloaming of the late-spring evening with the remains of perfectly seared filet mignons, creamy potato au gratin, and a mélange of grilled tomatoes, peppers, and sweet onions on the table between us. Mungo lay at his full length on the grass off the edge of the tiny patio with his eyes squeezed shut in post-feed-bag bliss. A soft snore rose from his throat as the first of the lightning bugs blinked on by the gazebo.

"Did Peter tell you they found the empty bottle of Côtes du Rhône in the recycle bin at the house?" I asked.

Declan nodded. "Nice luck, that. They found Glade's thumbprint upside down on the neck."

I pictured the bespectacled Owen using the wine bottle like a club on Simon's head, then shuddered as I remembered what he'd done next.

"He'd apparently tried to wipe the rest clean," Declan went on. "Not even Bianca's prints were on it. Just that thumbprint and some prints from Althea and Ursula."

"Right," I said, thinking back. "That must have been the wine Althea was drinking at the séance. Ugh." I wrinkled my nose. I'd heard Ursula tell Quinn that she'd cleaned up afterward. If she'd thrown the empty away instead of recycling it, that piece of evidence against Owen would have been picked up with the garbage the next morning.

Silence descended between us as we each ruminated over the events surrounding *Love in Revolution* and Simon's death. My contribution had been the envelope with the newspaper clippings and photos. It was a small thing, but at least the photo of Simon and Owen's mother would confirm their connection. However, Owen's confession in front of five witnesses would be the strongest element of the case against him.

I glanced up to see Declan regarding me with unsmiling speculation.

"What?" I asked.

"You glowed," he said.

I licked my lips, unsure of how to respond.

"Like a lightbulb. Did you know that?"

"Um, yeah."

"It's happened before, then."

"Yeah."

"When?"

"Just a couple of times," I protested.

"So other people already know this about you?"

"Some." I shrugged it off.

"Steve?"

I looked at Mungo, still sleeping heavily, and didn't answer.

After a few moments, Declan said, "You saved my life."

My eyes came up to meet his. "*We* deflected Owen's bullet. You and me."

"And Connell," he added.

"And Connell," I agreed, examining his face. "You seem okay with that. Or if not okay, at least better than when your long-lost leprechaun uncle first showed up at the séance."

He ignored my leprechaun reference, tapping his fingers on the glass tabletop and staring at nothing.

I waited.

"It was kind of cool in a way," he finally ventured. "The way we connected, you and me? Doing that thing we did. It was like harnessing raw power out of thin air."

I began to smile, but Declan held up his hand. "Don't get me wrong. I still think it's pretty weird. Unsettling. Okay—terrifying. And the business about being a medium? I don't know how to even start figuring out what that means."

"That has me stumped, too," I said.

He didn't seem to hear me, thumping the front legs of the chair on the stamped concrete of the patio as he leaned forward. "And why now? When I'm thirty-three? Doesn't ability like that usually show up when you're a kid?" He shook his head and repeated, "Why now?"

"I've been thinking about that." I hesitated, then plunged ahead. "It might be my fault."

Declan frowned; then his face cleared as he worked it out. "You mean because you're a catalyst?"

I bit my lower lip. "It's possible. But even if being around me somehow triggered your ability as a medium, or at least your connection to Connell, it was something you already had within yourself."

"Latent talent, you mean."

"Uh-huh. Are you okay with it now that it's surfaced?" I asked the question casually, but my heart was pounding. The future of our relationship might depend on his answer.

"Are you okay with being a lightwitch?" he asked.

I opened my mouth, then closed it, considering. Then, "I guess I have to be."

Taking a deep breath, he said, "Then I guess I have to be okay with this ability, or curse or whatever it is that I have." He reached over and took my hand in his. Our fingers intertwined. I felt his strong pulse and the physical power in his gentle grasp. "I'm really glad about one thing that came out of all this craziness," he said.

"What's that?"

"I know you better than ever. I thought I did before, but I didn't. Not really. Not when it came to the magic stuff."

I smiled.

"But now that's different. And, Katie?"

"Yeah?"

"I love you."

Standing, I leaned over and put my arms around his neck. He pulled me onto his lap. It was a while before we got to dessert.

Later, in the dark of my bedroom, Declan's voice drifted through the cooling night air. "Katie? Are you awake?"

I inhaled the fragrance of the night-blooming nicotiana growing under the open window. "Yes."

"About the whole talking to dead people thing . . ."

"Dead person," I said. "Singular, and possibly not even a person."

"Yeah, whatever. You really do have to let go of the notion Connell is a leprechaun. Anyway, do you think we could kind of keep it under wraps?"

"The spellbook club already knows. So does Ben."

"Will the ladies tell anyone?"

"Nah. They aren't much on gossip, but I'll ask them not to mention it to anyone if you don't want them to."

"And I know I don't have to worry about Ben," he said. "He'd know what kind of crap I'd get from the guys at the firehouse if they caught wind of any of this."

I thought of my altar tucked away in the loft. That was my choice because I was a rather private person, but even I could guess at Declan's buddies' reaction to his newfound gift.

"I get it," I said. "Don't worry."

"Thanks."

A few minutes later I said, "Declan?"

His response was a soft snore.

"I love you, too," I whispered anyway.

I parked in the alley behind the Honeybee at five a.m. and unlocked the door. Mungo trotted out to his bed in the still-dark reading area and settled in. I stowed my tote bag in the office, grabbed a black-and-red-striped apron, and flipped on the lights in the kitchen. On went the oven and in went the sourdough loaves that had been rising all night. As I consulted the white board on the wall where Lucy and I kept track of the daily specials, a rap sounded on the glass of the front door.

Thoughts racing through the possible reasons anyone besides Lucy or I would be at the bakery so early, I quickly checked that the back door was locked. Even in the hours before daylight, I'd never felt unsafe in the bakery, but it was better to be safe than sorry. I grabbed the phone off the cradle before making my way to the entrance. My steps faltered when I saw who stood on the sidewalk peering in at me.

I stopped in front of the door. "Althea?"

"Please, Katie. Can I come in?" Her voice was barely audible through the thick glass, but I could detect the pleading tone.

My hand reached into my apron pocket for the key to the dead bolt, but there it paused.

"Is everything okay?" I asked through the glass.

"Oh, for heaven's sake. Will you please just let me in? I'm here to apologize." No longer pleading, but she had me hooked. I opened the door.

Althea entered, briskly rubbing her bare arms. The night had cooled considerably after the high temperatures of the day before. I keyed the lock behind her and turned.

"Apologize?" I asked.

"Yes. God, is there any coffee?"

I pressed my lips together. "I'll make some." Returning the phone to its cradle on the way, I moved behind the espresso counter.

As I set up the drip coffeemaker with a rich Kona blend, Althea wandered around the bakery, trailing her fingers along the tops of the tables, adjusting a vase of anemones on one and briefly standing in front of the empty display case with her hands on her hips before moving into the reading area. I watched every move, glad the glass shelves were still empty. Whatever her stated reason for showing up at the Honeybee at o'dark thirty, I couldn't afford to trust her.

She flipped on the lamp by the couch. "Oh!" she exclaimed. "Your little dog surprised me."

"He likes the books." I took two steaming mugs and joined her. Roused, Mungo moved to sit under the coffee table near my favorite seat on the couch. "And the people who read them."

She reached down and patted him awkwardly on the head, her allergies apparently forgotten. My familiar grinned up at her, and I felt my shoulders relax. If Althea meant harm, I trusted that Mungo would let me know."

"Cream or sugar?" I asked.

"Black's fine." She took her mug and folded into one of the brocade chairs.

"And fewer calories," I said as I took a seat, then wanted to kick myself.

This morning she didn't look like the Althea I'd

come to expect. She wore a light cotton sweater, jeans, and tan boat shoes. Her hair was pulled back from her face in a high ponytail, exposing a face devoid of makeup. Her age showed in the tiny lines around her eyes, but at the same time she looked oddly younger.

"You're here early," I ventured.

She took a sip of coffee and nodded. "I've been at the hospital with Ursula all night."

"All night?" Alarm threaded my words.

"For observation," Althea said. "The doctor suggested it, and I begged her to do as he asked."

Begged? Althea?

"It looks like she'll be fine," Althea said. "When she fell asleep, I went to the Hyatt and showered, but I couldn't sleep." Her gaze moved to the side; then she blinked and seemed to force herself to look at me. "One of the reasons I couldn't sleep is because I needed to tell you how sorry I am." She paused, her internal struggle evident in the slight twist of her lips.

Setting my mug on the coffee table next to a couple of books we should have put away the night before, I prompted, "Sorry for . . . ?"

She took a deep breath. "For being so mean to you. For trying to make your bakery look bad. And for putting that stuff on your cookies."

I tipped my head to the side, searching for the right words. "Why do you have that 'stuff' anyway?"

Her nostrils flared, and I mentally braced myself. But when she spoke, her words were slow and measured. "I have an eating disorder. I'm going to get help for it. That and some of my other problems." Her eyes flared with dark humor. "There's nothing to make you decide to save yourself from yourself like having some nutcase almost kill you." She took a deep, restorative swallow of coffee. "Ursula said she'll help me."

"Good for her. And good for you," I said. "But why would you want to make anyone sick with our cookies?"

She barked a laugh. "Boy, you aren't going to make this easy for me, are you?"

"I—"

"No." She held her palm up to me. "It's okay. I have a feeling I'm going to be asked a lot more when I'm in treatment." Her hand dropped to her lap. She looked down at Mungo, seeming to speak to him when she said, "There were two reasons I did it, I'm ashamed to say. And they were both for Robin Bonner."

"Your . . ."

"Friend," she finished.

A lie on the surface. Then again, maybe they were friends as well as mother and son. Who was I to say? And Steve's admonition that Althea might be trying to protect her son from the notoriety that would no doubt come simply from *being* her son still rang true.

"See, I wanted Robin to be successful in his new venture as a caterer," she said, finally looking up at me. "He's a good cook, but he was used to running a food truck for the late-night crowd. That worked well because he's such a night owl. Not a morning person at all. And it seems he has a few problems with self-discipline."

"Which is why he showed up late three days in a row."

"I tried to tell Simon—well, it doesn't matter. Once Simon had his mind made up, that was it. But he didn't have to fire my . . . friend so publicly!" Even now her distress showed, despite the Botox. She took a sip of coffee, grasping the mug in both hands. "Anyway, I wanted Owen to hire Robin back, so I tried to make sure no one would want to eat any of your food. Plus—" She stopped herself.

"Plus what?" I asked.

She put her drink on the table and stood, moving to stand in front of the largest bookshelf with her back to me. Mungo popped to his feet, watching her. Dawn was beginning to creep through the blinds on the windows.

"You picked those particular cookies for a reason, didn't you?" I asked.

Her head bobbed, which made her ponytail swing back and forth. "I knew Ursula would eat at least one of them."

The psychic had been right. She'd been the target, not Owen.

"Owen only ate half a cookie," I said, hearing my voice rise. "If Ursula—or anyone else—had eaten much more than that, she might still be horribly ill. Or worse."

"I know," Althea whispered and turned to face

Mungo and me. "And so does Detective Quinn. I confessed."

"Good." I hoped he would charge her with reckless endangerment at the very least. "Why Ursula?" I asked. I was pretty sure I knew the answer, though. Althea had poisoned the cookies before she even knew about our planned séance with Simon; then she protested having the séance, and finally ruined it in the end.

She came back to the chair and sank into the cushions. "See, I hadn't seen Robin for a very long time."

I bit my tongue and waited.

"I found I didn't really know him that well. But he's my . . . friend. So if he killed Simon because he'd fired him and embarrassed him, then I wanted to protect him. I believe in Ursula's powers, you see. Really believe. She's passed on advice from my own spirit guides." She looked sheepish. "I don't always follow that advice, but at least I can get it with her help."

"So you protected one friend by poisoning another," I said.

Althea reddened. "I'm not proud of my actions. I have some issues. I guess you know that." She sighed. "Heck, anyone who reads *People* or watches the news knows that. But like I said, I'm getting help. And Ursula forgives me."

Mungo jumped up and put his paws on her knee. Apparently, he forgave her, too.

"Will you?" she asked, her voice timid. "Forgive me?"

Thoughts of Aunt Lucy and the Rule of Three crowded into my mind. I nodded. "Of course. And I wish you the best of luck in the future, Althea. I admire what you've decided to do."

She stood, blinking back tears. "Thanks, Katie. For all that." She shrugged her shoulders, not in dismissal but as if she were letting go of a great weight. It made me happy to feel like I might have contributed to that. I rose, and she moved toward me. She hesitated. I held out my arms, and she moved into the hug, awkward at first and then giving a good squeeze in return before backing off.

The rising sun cut through the window, illuminating the hope on her face with golden light. Looking down, she picked up one of those books that shouldn't have been sitting on the coffee table. "This caught my eye. Do you think I could buy it from you?" Then she seemed to think better of her words and dropped it back. "Never mind. That's silly. I can find my own copy."

I picked up the book and held it out to her. "No, that's what the books in the Honeybee are for. Everyone can just take what they want, or bring what they want."

"Oh!" She smiled. "Thank you!"

I led her to the door, unlocked it, and sent along my best wishes to Ursula as she left.

Rarely had I seen anyone so happy to get a free book. How lucky that Mimsey had *just happened* to bring in that title only days before.

The Creative Woman's Guide to Authentic Recovery.

Chapter 24

The friendly bell over the entrance to the Honeybee chimed, and I completely ignored it. Once again Lucy was brewing coffee drinks, Ben held reign at the register, chatting up customers, and I could concentrate on developing a new recipe for sweet brioche pizza. Finally, things were back to normal.

"Well, look what the cat dragged in!" Lucy exclaimed, cutting through my internal debate over whether to include toasted coconut as a topping. "Katie! Come out here."

I wiped my hands on my orange-and-purple paisley apron and walked around the corner of the refrigerator. When I saw why Lucy had summoned me, I stopped cold.

"Cookie!"

She grinned, and I rushed out to throw my arms around her.

"When did you get in?" I demanded. "Why didn't you let us know you were coming? We would have had a welcome-home party. Oh, well, we still can. Come on." I pulled her toward the empty furniture in the reading area. "I want to hear all about your time in Europe."

"Katie, wait!" She pulled back, laughing. The lilt of her Haitian accent was evident in those two words, and I realized how much I'd missed it.

I stopped. "You want something to eat?"

Still laughing, she shook her head. "No. I want you to meet Oscar." She pronounced it Oh-scar.

I looked up to where she was pointing. A man stood by the front door. His dark shock of thick hair curled down to his bright hazel eyes, and his full lips curved into a blazing white smile. He was, simply put, gorgeous. I smiled a welcome at him and said in an undertone, "Oscar, huh?"

She nodded. "I met him in Paris. He's from the Dominican Republic. We have a great deal in common."

"What happened to Brandon?" I asked.

"He didn't want to leave France," she said. "And I did." She flipped her hand in dismissal, and something flashed.

I grabbed her hand. "Is that an *engagement* ring?"

Eyes sparkling, she shook her head. "Oscar and I are married."

I didn't know whose mouth dropped open wider: mine, Lucy's, or Ben's.

In celebration of Ben's return to the Honeybee, I'd taken Saturday afternoon off to tend to the neglected weeds in my garden. My uncle had been happy to cover for me, especially since he wanted to play his usual round of Sunday golf the next day.

Cookie had offered to be on call if we needed her over the weekend, as well. I didn't know if they'd call her in today, but I knew I'd have a hard time not getting her to at least stop by the Honeybee on Sunday—to answer the gazillion questions I had about her new husband, if nothing else.

Iris, Patsy's Goth stepdaughter, had taken me up on my invitation to stop by the Honeybee, and while there had filled out a job application. She was about to graduate from high school and had already been accepted at the Savannah College of Art and Design. Lucy and Ben had both taken to her, and heaven knew we needed some regular help. Iris was slated to start part-time at the bakery in two weeks.

A toad hopped out from under the sprawling leaves of the watermelon vine and stared at me with bulging yellow eyes. "Well, hello," I said, and continued to pull weeds from around the tender base of the plant. So far I'd made it through about a third of the vegetable patch and still had the herb garden to weed as well. At the rate I was going, I'd finish the task about the same time Declan got off work at the firehouse on Monday.

The toad was good luck, however, a sign of cleansing and renewal in magical circles and simply a harbinger of good ecology in the scientific world. "Bring your friends," I encouraged him, and moved on to tie up some indeterminate tomato vines.

Mungo sprawled on his back in the morning sunshine, napping after a big breakfast of bacon and eggs with toast and his favorite orange marmalade. The hot weather had faded away to unseasonable coolness, surely a temporary shift, which I welcomed nonetheless.

In my peripheral vision, my familiar rolled onto his stomach and turned his attention to the front of the house. Moments later I sensed rather than heard the gate open. Looking up from where I crouched on my knees, I saw Steve come into the yard.

Pushing myself to my feet, I brushed dirt from my knees and hands. "Hi." It had been months since he'd stopped by the carriage house out of the blue. That, plus his recent declaration of affection, put me on my guard. I waited, rooted among my vegetables.

"Hey," he said easily and strolled over to Mungo. My dog rose to his feet and allowed a scritch under the chin, but he'd never greeted Steve with the same enthusiasm he showed Declan. "Doing a little garden maintenance, huh?"

"Yup."

"Take a break?"

"Okay." I stripped off my gloves. We settled into mismatched chairs in the gazebo, and I offered him some lemonade from the sweating pitcher I'd brought out for the work.

"There's only one glass," he said.

"I wasn't expecting company. But I haven't had any yet, so this is clean." I filled it with lemonade and handed it to him.

"You don't seem that happy to see me."

My fingers drummed on the table as I debated about what to say. "Steve," I began.

He held up his hand. "Listen, I get it. In fact, that's why I'm here. I think I kind of scared you the other day. When I said I was still hoping?"

"Not scared. Just . . . Steve, you can't wait for me. I'm not going to change my mind."

"I know. I needed to clarify what I meant. I'm not expecting you to dump Declan or change your mind. I know you guys are solid—maybe even more so now that he can channel spirits from the other side."

A grimace sneaked onto my face before I could stop it.

Steve smiled. "He's not too happy about that, I imagine."

"Would you be?"

His eyes widened. "Seriously? Of course I would. Imagine how useful it could be."

"How practical of you."

"Yeah. Well, anyway, he's not your run-of-the-mill firefighter anymore. I can see how that would bring you even closer together."

"Declan was never run-of-the-mill," I said quietly.

Steve shook his head. "I'm botching this. I'm sorry. All I wanted to say was that you don't have to worry about me waiting for you, because I'm not. I mean, if I meet someone, I won't hesitate. It's just that I haven't yet."

I smiled.

"And honestly, it's hard to imagine who would interest me more than you do."

My smile dropped.

He stood. "But someone will. I'm sure of it." He stepped out of the gazebo and I heard him mutter, "And soon, I hope." He turned. "Just wanted to clarify. Thanks for the lemonade."

I stood and followed him out into the yard. "You didn't drink any—"

"That's all." He was walking rapidly toward the gate now. "See you around."

"Steve!"

He paused and waited with a pained expression for me to catch up.

"Did you know Simon Knapp was a sorcerer of some kind?" I asked.

He blinked. "What?"

"Did you? Was he a druid, by any chance? Is that how he knew Heinrich?"

He frowned.

I waited.

"I'm sure I don't have any idea what you're talking about," he said. "I have to go."

"But—"

Mungo gave me a wry look as Steve barreled through to the front yard and the latch snicked closed behind him.

"Well, that was interesting," I said. "Do you think he was lying about Simon?"

Yip!

I heard the gate open again and looked up hopefully.

But it wasn't Steve returning. Instead, Ursula rounded the corner of the house, grinning ear to ear when she saw me. "Steve said you were back here. Hope you don't mind me showing up like this. Your aunt gave me your address."

I waved her in. "How's your head?"

"Hard as stone, apparently."

"How are you at weeding?"

"Lousy."

I laughed. "How about drinking a glass of lemonade, then?" I indicated the pitcher still sitting on the table in the gazebo.

"Much better." She laughed.

"Hang on. I'll get another glass." I went into the kitchen through the open French doors.

When I returned, she was standing with her hands on her hips, examining the garden. "Katie, this is stunning. I've never seen a vegetable garden landscaped like this. Simply beautiful."

"It's a potager garden," I said, pleased. "I've added a few of my own design elements, but all plants are attractive, don't you think? And arranging them like this pleases me aesthetically as well as taking advantage of beneficial companion planting." I bent and snapped a spent flower head off a marigold that was tucked in next to a cherry tomato plant.

"There's something else." She paused, her eyes narrowing in thought. Or perhaps she was listening to one of her spirit guides, because suddenly she laughed. "You're a garden witch as well as a kitchen witch!"

"Um, yeah. It usually works that way," I said, covertly checking the Coopersmiths to see if my neighbor was anywhere about. I heard Margie call to the twins through the open window. Relieved, I turned back to Ursula. "It's not something I advertise."

"Why not?"

"Hmm. Well, I'm certainly not ashamed of it. But not everyone understands. And since Lucy and I practice at the bakery, I don't want customers to think we're doing anything weird to the food. All we do is harness the magical aspects that are already in the seasonings we use, even the food itself."

She nodded her understanding and turned her attention to the gazebo, where I was pouring the lemonade. She stroked the bare wood, which was beginning to turn gray from the weather. "And this? It feels well guarded."

"It is." I didn't offer more, feeling strangely vulnerable. Ursula might be psychic, but she wasn't a witch. It wasn't that I didn't trust her—I simply felt private about my Craft.

Ursula pursed her lips, then nodded once. "Okay."

I handed her a sweating glass, and she took a sip. "Mmm. Mint, too. Nice." She folded her lanky frame onto the grass next to Mungo. "I'm here because I got a message for you that I promised to pass on."

Three dragonflies winged past, heading for the tiny stream in the corner of the yard. A shiver ran like a mouse down my spine, and I sat down beside her. "Oh?"

"It's from Franklin."

I bit my lower lip. "He came to you again?"

She nodded. "Yep. He said for me to tell you he's sorry."

"About what specifically?" Though I could think of a few things, truth be told.

"That he didn't tell you more about what it means to be a . . . lightwitch?"

I nodded. "Go on."

"I've never heard of a lightwitch," Ursula said. "Anyway, he said you already know what you need to do if you pay attention."

Great. More of the same. "Did he say how he died?"

"Nope. But he said he's going to remedy his failure to properly mentor you before he passed."

"How is he going to do that?"

"He's sending someone."

"He's . . . Who? When?"

She threw her hands up in the air. "Don't know. That's all he said."

My shoulders slumped.

She drained her glass and got to her feet. "Listen, I have to meet Althea to drive back up to Dahlonega."

I stood as well, and Ursula threw her arms around me, surprising me with the force of her hug. "Don't worry, okay? I don't know what a lightwitch is, but I can tell that Franklin is a good soul and he has good intentions. So do you, Katie." Together we walked to the gate, Mungo padding through the grass behind us. She opened it and put her hand on my shoulder. "Really. Everything will be fine."

I watched her stride out to her rental car and returned her good-bye wave as she drove off.

Mungo leaned against my leg, and I bent to pick him up. Snuggling him under my chin, I muttered, "The problem is that her idea of fine and mine might not be exactly the same thing."

My familiar's soft pink tongue swiped at my cheek, and I had to smile.

"You're right. Even with all the crazy stuff, life is awfully good, isn't it?"

Yip!

Recipes

Detective Quinn's Favorite
Lemon Sour Cream Cake

Makes one 8" x 8" coffee cake

2 cups all-purpose flour
1½ cups sugar
5 teaspoons freshly grated lemon peel (be sure to avoid
    the white pith of the lemon, which is bitter)
1 teaspoon cinnamon
3 Tablespoons fresh lemon juice
½ cup vegetable oil
1 cup sour cream
1 large egg
1 teaspoon vanilla extract
1 teaspoon baking soda
1 teaspoon baking powder
confectioners' sugar (optional)

Preheat oven to 325 degrees. Butter and flour an 8" x 8" glass baking dish.

Stir together flour, sugar, lemon peel, and cinnamon in a large bowl.

Add the oil and lemon juice, mixing until evenly moist and small clumps form. Set aside one cup for the crumble topping, leaving the rest in the bowl.

In another bowl thoroughly blend the sour cream, egg, vanilla, baking soda, and baking powder.

Add sour cream mixture to flour mixture all at once and beat with an electric mixer until the batter is smooth.

Spread the batter in the prepared pan, and sprinkle the reserved crumble topping evenly over the top.

Bake 40 minutes or until a toothpick comes out clean. Transfer the pan to a rack to cool.

Sprinkle with confectioners' sugar, cut into squares, and serve. Can be made one day ahead.

Fast and Easy Gluten-Free Peanut Butter Cookies

Makes 12–24 cookies, depending on size

1 cup sugar
1 cup chunky peanut butter
1 large egg

Preheat oven to 350 degrees. Mix the three ingredients thoroughly together and roll into small balls.

Put on a cookie sheet and flatten with a fork.

Sprinkle with a dash of kosher or sea salt and bake 10–15 minutes (depending on size) until slightly browned.

Allow to rest on cookie sheet for a few minutes before transferring to a rack. Cookies will crisp a bit as they cool.

Honeybee Carrot 'n' Apple Cake or Muffins

Makes one 10" x 14" sheet cake

1 cup vegetable oil
1 cup sugar
¼ cup molasses
4 eggs, well beaten
3 cups grated carrots
1 cup applesauce (chunky or smooth)
1 cup unbleached flour
1 cup whole wheat flour
2 teaspoons soda
½ teaspoon salt
2 teaspoons ground allspice
2 teaspoons ground cinnamon
1½ teaspoons vanilla extract
1½ teaspoons orange extract

Preheat oven to 325 degrees. Butter and sugar a 10" x 14" pan.

Cream oil, sugar, and molasses.

Add eggs, carrots, applesauce, and vanilla and orange extracts. Mix well.

Mix dry ingredients together in a separate bowl.

Add flour mixture to carrot mixture a small amount at a time, blending well. Batter will be quite thick.

Spread in the prepared pan and bake for an

hour or until a toothpick inserted in the center comes out clean. Cool before frosting.

This recipe will also make approximately 24 muffins. Start checking for doneness after 40 minutes in the oven.

Cream Cheese Frosting

8 ounces cream cheese
¼ cup butter
1 teaspoon vanilla extract
1¼ cups confectioners' sugar

Beat all ingredients together until smooth.
Spread on the cake.

ABOUT THE AUTHOR

Bailey Cates believes magic is all around us if we only look for it. She's held a variety of positions, ranging from driver's license examiner to soapmaker, which fulfills her mother's warning that she'd never have a "regular" job if she insisted on studying philosophy, English, and history in college. She traveled the world as a localization program manager but now sticks closer to home, where she writes two mystery series, tends to a dozen garden beds, bakes up a storm, and plays the occasional round of golf. Bailey resides in Colorado with her guy and an orange cat that looks an awful lot like the one in her Magical Bakery Mysteries.

CONNECT ONLINE

baileycates.com

Searching for the perfect mystery?

Looking for a place to get the latest clues
and connect with fellow fans?

"Like" The Crime Scene on Facebook!

- Participate in author chats
- Enter book giveaways
- Learn about the latest releases
- Get book recommendations
  and more!

facebook.com/TheCrimeSceneBooks

Obsidian

P.O. 00003737323 20190701

M884G101